The Man Curse

RAQIYAH MAYS

BROADWAY NIGHT OUT
15030 Ventura Blvd.
Suite 11, #531
Sherman Oaks, CA 91403

ISBN paperback 978-0-578-74405-6

This is not a romance novel.
This is not about the Bible.
This is not for prudes.

This book is for those who have ever wanted lasting love
and felt like they might not find it...

Most likely you are still paying the price for these childhood experiences. The absence of strong, positive role models almost always leaves scars, and as an adult, you will have to struggle to resolve the experiences of a painful past.

—Derek S. Hopson and Darlene Powell Hopson,
Friends, Lovers, and Soul Mates

1

I USED TO THINK THE MAN CURSE BEGAN with my mother in Trenton, New Jersey. She had been seven or eight years old; she remembered feigning sleep, her eyes squeezed tightly closed. And a man, his face a disfigured blur, pushed open the door to her bedroom. He pulled back the covers and rubbed his dry, ashy hands over her calves, knees, thighs, and eventually settled on her...

"Wait," Meredith cried, cutting off my story in midsentence. With the concern of a best friend, she asked, "Your mother told you this?"

"Yeah," I replied. Like it was normal. Like most mothers would talk to their kids about sexual assault. Meredith had been my best friend since middle school. But I'd never told this story to her. I'd never shared what I'd written about it. Not till I realized I might be cursed, too.

"I'm sorry. I shouldn't be cutting you off," she said, pulling out a cigarette and flicking her lighter. "Okay. Go ahead..."

I reopened my notebook.

My mother says the next few minutes or hours are missing in her mind. The room suddenly smelled of tuna and peppermint toothpaste. His pocket change jingled as he slipped on a pair of pants. She felt him leaning over, his face centimeters away, hot breath melting her ear as he said, "Remember. I *will* kill you *and* your mother. Don't say shit." When she heard the door close and sensed an empty room, she opened her eyes and never saw that man—outside of daydreams, nightmares, and reminders—again.

"So…" Meredith jumped in, massaging her temples, disturbed, as if her ears had been raped. "She just blurted this story out while you were watching *60 Minutes*?"

"Yeah," I said, shrugging my shoulders. "They were doing this report on child predators. I remember she was making some muffins for dinner. And this all just came out."

"And you were how old?"

"Thirteen, I think. I can't really remember."

"Yeah, because hearing that was traumatic. What the fuck?"

I remember thinking the same thing when I heard the story. I had stared in disbelief. Eyes stretched wide in horror. Silence saturated the room and the sound of my loud swallowing was like a vibrational echo that bounced from one living room corner to another.

"Wh-what… ?" I'd blurted out, stammering. I'd mainly mastered the stuttering that had haunted me since kindergarten. But in moments of discomfort, the difficulty always returned. "Wh-what happened?"

She told her story, detail by nasty detail. She wondered whether he'd done the same to Aunt Connie, who was sleeping in the next room. Her voice quivered, elevating to a suspenseful crescendo as she reached the end of the assault scene.

"I don't remember his name," she'd said. "I remember his voice… and the sound of those keys jingling."

"Girl…" Meredith shook her head, angrily stabbing a cigarette into the ashtray. "I'm sorry. You were way too young to hear something like that. Thirteen is a teenager. I mean, that's what a grown-up tells a therapist, not her damn kid. You might as well have been raped, too."

Meredith Benjamin had always been my protector. The one who always had my back. If I needed to escape a fight with Mom,

Meredith was there, either on the phone or, lately, speeding around the corner in her beat-up brown hand-me-down family van. Rusty fender and all, wheels squeaking to a halt, about to fall off as they reached my driveway. She played both best friend and psychologist, using the degree she'd gotten from Johns Hopkins to practice her listening and feedback skills on me.

"Where was your grandmother during all of this?" she asked. "Does she know?"

Not at all. Grandma Fey was rarely around when Mom was a young child. She was often in New York, working several jobs, whatever she could find, saving the necessary funds to bring two daughters to live with her. She'd leave my mother wherever she had a friend or fellow church member. But usually they'd spend summers with Ms. Adelle, Grandma's girlfriend from childhood days in South Carolina.

Bethany Adelle had a quaint home, where Mom and Connie each got their own bedroom with an adjoining bathroom. While Bethany worked her usual twelve-hour-plus, overnight nursing shift, Mom and Connie were allowed to stay up late and leave food on their plates. They could sit on the front porch and play with the neighborhood kids after the sun descended and streetlights illuminated. There were no curfews, rules, or lost TV privileges. All was carefree; that is, until *he* moved in.

His voice was deep, like Barry White's, a baritone bass. My mother recalled romantic vocal cords, actions disguised with tender hugs and talks on laps quickly morphing into hideous form— flirtatious comments, "accidental" touching, and a traumatic after-midnight visit.

Even decades later, Grandma Fey knew nothing about this attack. And Mom didn't know whether the same was done to Aunt Connie. Yet whenever talk of a sexual assault would arise—via a news report, TV topic, or magazine article—my mother would turn to me and divulge her story once again, and I'd squirm inside behind a face frozen in confusion.

"And now," Meredith asked, "because of that ass Dexter, you think you're cursed, too?"

"I don't know. Sometimes," I said, staring down the empty road.

"But if I am, I'm breaking this damn thing. And at the moment, Dexter is my personal curse."

2

A WOMAN KNOWS when a lie is lingering. It's the small things that jab at the intuition, causing knots of anxiety that twist the stomach.

Like when your lover's phone rings and your insides cramp, your sixth sense grumbling at hearing irregular vocal inflections. He takes the call in the next room. Your ears jump to attention, like a dog on alert, clearly able to hear through whispers full of vague answers in a feigned upbeat tone. Like the singsongy lilt that makes a baritone into a tenor. When Dexter does this, before I casually interrupt by walking into the room and speaking loudly, he sounds like he did when we first started dating a year ago.

May 15, 1996. My senior year, a week before graduation, I'd moved off campus from Morgan State to live in a one-bedroom on the second floor of a multifamily apartment building. Didn't know what I wanted to do with my English degree. Couldn't figure out how to turn my writing into profit, although I freelanced as a copy editor for a professor on campus.

To help pay the $300 monthly rent, I worked a second job at a men's clothing store in the local mall. My four-day-a-week, semi-part-time, minimum-wage job made me just enough for rent, clothes, hair, partying, and weed. The icing was that I was in the perfect place to meet men, those with disposable incomes looking to buy a suit. I ran into all types of gentlemen—officers, lawyers, doctors, marketing executives—mainly bachelors who'd come shopping alone, looking for a woman's-style feedback. And I was happy to offer my advice, having them stand in front of a mirror and lift their arms, allowing me to measure their length and neck size, mixing and matching ties to collared shirts and pin-striped suits.

But the moment Dexter walked in, my world slowed to a halt. Literally, things moved in screen-grab motion as his magnificent muscular body strode with confidence toward me, smiling.

"Hi, pretty lady." His accent told me that he had to be from the South. "You work here?"

Dexter was a short man, standing an inch under my stilettos at five-five. He had a tiny bald caramel head and a gold hoop in his left nostril. His oversize fatigue jacket and black Timberland boots with the tongues hanging out added to the thuggish sex appeal that a girl from the suburbs loved.

"You need some help?" I asked, looking him up and down. "Would you like to see a suit?"

"Yeah, a black one," he said. "I'm going to church with my mother." My heart melted.

"Okay, well, lemme see what we have," I answered. "You live around here?"

"Just moved to town. Finished with the army and don't want to sign up again. So here I am."

I could feel his eyes checking me out as we walked through the section. Turning, I saw the store manager, Paul, smile at me as I started to sort through the rack of black suits, finding one perfect for his small frame.

In the months I'd been working at J. Riggings, the staff had come to love my outgoing, sociable spirit. Management was impressed by my numbers: I made huge sales, with men often buying two suits at a time. It was my first job in retail, and I enjoyed it. Besides my least favorite part—standing for four to six hours—I loved meeting any man who needed my assistance.

"Lemme measure you," I said, stretching the blue tape wide. "Is this church visit a special occasion?"

"Well, yeah, considering I haven't been in years. But when you've been in the military, you need God in your life."

I tried to hold my impressed smile while maneuvering the tape measure, slowly rubbing my hand across his biceps as I checked his arm length. Then I placed the measure inside his leg, stretching it from under his crotch to the floor. When I stood up, our eyes met and time stopped again. Slow and light, I thought I'd fallen in love right there.

"Let's have you try on a few things I picked out."

"I'm sure whatever you choose is perfect," he said, following me to the dressing room. "Your husband must be a fly dresser."

"Oh, I'm not married."

"Boyfriend?"

"Nope."

"Why?"

"I haven't found the right one yet," I replied, sick of the tired lines men and women used to explain being single. The predictability was such a turnoff. I didn't bother hanging Dexter's suits. Instead I lazily dropped them on the small stool in his stall.

"Can I get your number?"

I snatched off one of the price tags and wrote it on the back.

"I work Monday, Wednesday, Friday, and weekends. But you can catch me in the early afternoons or evenings after nine."

He called promptly at noon the next day. Later that afternoon he came over, and after a couple of hours of flirty foreplay, we were on the sofa, him on top of me, pulling my panties down, diving into a steady stroking flow. He was as thick and solid as a smooth, green banana. I was as wet and juicy as a ripe, fuzzy peach. It was the best sex I'd ever had.

"I don't normally do this," I said afterward, embarrassed, feeling like a whore. "Move this fast, I mean…"

"I know," he said, stroking my hair. "You like to have a boyfriend."

"How can you tell?"

"I just can. You probably keep a boyfriend."

"Maybe." A coy smile curled onto my face. "Maybe I like being in a relationship."

"You like stability. And that's how I know you're not a ho or something. You just want a steady man to be with. So lemme be your boyfriend."

I should have realized that was a little too fast. "Why do you want to be my boyfriend?" I asked, laughing. "You don't even know me."

"Because I know we're supposed to be together. And when you know, you know," he said, sitting up and grabbing his pants. "In the military, we rely on instinct to survive. And my instincts are always right."

♁

We were inseparable after that. And a year later, all I could do was regret every minute of it. I couldn't wait to get back to Maryland and break up with him.

"I told you I didn't like his ass. Told you I thought he was crazy." Meredith sucked her teeth as she stared into the rearview mirror, putting lipstick on. "I always know the crazy ones. But you know what? I do the same thing. Whenever you've told me about my crazies, I never listened."

"Well, Dexter was worse than any of your exes," I said. "I wish I had an older brother to beat his ass. But maybe it's just me. Maybe this is what I attract."

I was about to go on when my Aunt Connie knocked on the window. Meredith rolled it down.

"One. You took too long to go to the store," she spit. "Two. You're being rude. This is your family reunion, Meena. Cousins here you haven't seen in years. And three. Your mother is looking for you. She needs your help inside. Did you even get the garbage bags?" I nodded, but Aunt Connie did a sudden about-face back into the house. Short and brisk, direct, and far from sweet, she had the ability to get her point across with few words and lots of attitude.

I apologized to Meredith. "Sorry. Just come inside and get a plate. Meet the coven of so-called cursed bitches."

3

As we walked into the house, the elder women sat around the kitchen table. Food was piled on plates, stacked next to plastic cups.

Meredith and I entered the kitchen just in time to hear the tail end of my cousin Gina's latest man-gone-wrong scenario. In her midfifties, single, she had flown in from California with an everlasting pessimistic attitude that seemed so contrary to the sunshine everyone bragged about on the West Coast.

"Whaaaat?" someone blurted out. "I can't believe he did that."

"That's what they do," said Gina. "Dogs. All of them."

"It's part of the curse," Mom commented with a shrug, brushing crumbs off the kitchen counter. "I'm alone today because women in this family are destined to have problems when it comes to men."

Mom had never spoken these words before, at least not directly to me. I'd grown up hearing about the curse when eavesdropping on adult conversations during rare family occasions. Usually, it would take just one cousin discussing her man drama before words such as "curse" and phrases such as "issues with men" began morphing women of the Mitchell clan into bitter hens—fussing and clucking about roosters kicking dirt on them. After that issue passed, the conversation turned biblical, with a battle of verses and chapters validating the theory of a family generational curse.

"'The Lord is slow to anger and abounding in steadfast love, forgiving iniquity and transgression, but he will by no means clear the guilty, visiting the iniquity of the fathers on the children, to the third and the fourth generation.' Numbers 14:18."

"Yeah, but what about 'You shall not bow down to them or serve them, for I the Lord your God am a jealous God, visiting the iniquity of the fathers on the children to the third and the fourth generation of those who hate me.'"

"Amen," the room would sing. "Exodus 20:5."

"Well, don't forget Galatians 3:13. 'Christ redeemed us from the curse of the law by becoming a curse for us—for it is written, "Cursed is everyone who is hanged on a tree."' That's us. 'Cause we black and we was slaves and we hung from trees."

"Well, what about Anna Belle?"

Silence stiffened the room. I breathed a deep sigh and looked at Meredith.

"Who's Anna Belle?" she whispered in my ear loud enough for everyone to hear. But few looked up. Others acted as if they weren't moved by the question.

"'She of the Mitchell clan will be without he.' That's what the curse says, right? I don't know if I believe that," my mother said, sucking her teeth. She dug in her bag and pulled out a tissue. "I mean, yes, there may be a curse. But to blame Anna Belle? 'Cause she cheated? I don't know. I'm sure plenty people cheat and go on to be in happy relationships."

At age eighteen, Anna Belle Mitchell, my great-great-grandmother, had an affair with the pastor of the church. His wife, upon finding them in bed together, took a strand of Anna Belle's hair left on the sheets and placed a curse on it. That doomed Anna never to find healthy, lasting love with a man, banishing her from jumping the broom. "She of the Mitchell clan will be without he" is what the pastor's wife apparently said seconds before her death. This legacy of broken relationships would be passed down through the family of Mitchell females forever.

"That's scary," Aunt Connie said, like she always did. "That's why I don't want a man. Too much drama."

"I don't believe that crap," Mom answered. "I believe in God. And God answers prayers."

"I believe in God, too. God punished. Anna Belle sinned. And now we're paying for it."

"Shut up, Connie."

"Why I gotta shut up? It's the truth."

"No, it's your truth."

"Yours, too. When's the last time you had a man?"

"I don't need a man, I got God."

"Don't you want to get married?"

"Yes, Connie."

"Well, don't you need a man for that?"

"Why are you asking questions you know the answer to? You sound stupid as usual."

"You know what? I'm sick of you church people acting like God is all you need," Connie said as she got up, grabbing her purse. "Y'all get on my nerves with that. When you know you want a man, but you spend all day in church praying on some man, when you need to be out getting a man. But you can't get one, because you're cursed. All of you. I'm so sick of talking about it."

She tripped over the foot of a chair, grabbed her car keys, and rumbled off.

When Mom and Aunt Connie spoke, they typically argued about everything. Mom would talk down to her, and Aunt Connie would get pissed, hang up, or walk out. They were polar opposites. Mom was a 700-credit-score, size six valedictorian who'd gotten a full ride to NYU. She'd recently accepted a new position as VP of human resources at Quest Diagnostics. Aunt Connie was size twenty. Deep in debt, she'd barely graduated high school and spent most days off complaining about her hourly pay as a nightclub bouncer. Her favorite pastime was curling up in bed with a bag of cookies, watching *The Price Is Right*. Aunt Connie ending a conversation with an angry, sudden exit was a familiar scene from past family occasions. So was the way this man-curse argument usually ended. Besides the snarky remarks, such as "There she goes again," the episode would close in a silence filled with throbbing tension.

I suddenly remembered the first time I'd felt this type of man-curse discomfort. I had to have been about ten, at a family reunion. I remember the weird feeling, like a woozy butterfly fluttering in my stomach before dropping dead, a heavy lump in the gut. I quickly ran upstairs to my room. Filled with plush stuffed animals, my space was permeated with the color pink, like a woman's scent that lingers after she's left the room. Shelves atop my window seat showcased a lopsided Barbie leaning against Ken inside their white classic convertible. Nancy Drew and dusty Ramona novels by Beverly Cleary were nestled between two glass jars filled with pennies. An old Cabbage Patch Kid wearing brown pigtails and a plaid red dress smiled, holding a birth certificate that read "Katherine Fagin." And a *Ghostbusters* movie poster hung next to a blown-up *Return of the Jedi* photo featuring Luke Skywalker and Princess Leah.

I plopped down by the window, watching two squirrels chase each other around an oak tree trunk, scurrying a path up to its top leafy branches. Holding up my left hand, I jutted out the ring finger and twisted a trash-bag tie below my wedding knuckle. I didn't believe in that curse. It couldn't be real, because I was getting married. I'd already picked out my dress in an old *Ebony* Fashion Fair magazine I found at the library. And I'd planned the ceremony: it would be on a sandy beach, and we'd be barefoot, with waves crashing to the sounds of a sweet flute blowing whimsical bridal tunes, floating above the sea. I was different than my relatives. And one day I'd show them all. One day I'd save the ladies in my family from depressive doubt and expected loneliness. I'd be married and break the man curse. It became one of my biggest goals in life.

"Meena, go put out some new trash bags in the backyard," Mom snapped, bringing me back to the present. "And tie up the bags that are full. The flies are hovering. It looks nasty." I motioned to Meredith to follow me outside.

♋━━᠗

In the backyard, the Mitchell family reunion was on display. A biannual event, it brought together cousins I loved, along with aunts and uncles I had to flip through the mental Rolodex to recollect. My Aunt Deon had volunteered to host this year's event at her Jersey home, a four-bedroom ranch on a suburban, country-like street without sidewalks. The acre-long backyard sprawled like a state park.

A wide-lensed glimpse at family reminded me that breaking the curse would be a hefty task. Heavy on estrogen, light on testosterone, the predominantly female crowd of cousins highlighted missing male elements in my family's misguided man-map. Spotted with holes and confusing paths, the way to Mr. Right was a marathon walk of tripping over trials and falling in error. It was understandable. I'd never had a consistent adult male figure to guide me with wisdom. I didn't grow up with examples of unconditional fatherly love. I hadn't gotten any testosterone-laden advice on boys and ways to manage their moves. I'd never had a grandfather. There were no older brothers to scare guys I dated into treating me like a porcelain doll. My mother had never known her father. Aunt Connie knew where her sperm donor was but had never met him. And my grandmother rarely, if ever, talked to us about her relationships to either of their dads.

Under a tent the elders of the family sat in a circle next to my grandmother, her brothers, and her sisters. Aunt Bernice and Aunt Gayle wore large, colorful hats and flowery dresses. Their handbags were oversize Gucci classics. They held their heads high when walking, sitting as the proud heads of the sixty-and-over table. The lone elderly men of the group, Uncle Johnny and Uncle Clay, sat holding their canes as they talked about "the man," the movement, and the problems with black people.

"They still trying to kill all us off." Uncle Johnny snorted. "Always shooting us."

"Or locking us up," Uncle Clay answered. "It's slavery. The prison system is slavery."

More family members had trickled in since Meredith and I had gone to the store. From Philadelphia came my favorite boy cousins, Bernard and Bishop—the superstar athlete twins. They threw a football back and forth next to their mother, Cece, and her sister, Gladys. The family from Brooklyn featured my cousins Trey, Dedra, Deja, and their mother, Denise. I always knew when they arrived because they spoke in a volume that boomed above everyone else. My cousin Tommy, from the Bronx, came tripping toward me. A year older than I was, he was always drunk or high. He arrived with a tipsy wobble, dropped his paper bag, and a bubbly yellow substance began oozing out.

"What up, cuz!" he yelled, pulling out a can of Old English from the damp bag. As he reached over to hug me, I held my breath so I wouldn't get asphyxiated from the bar fumes. "You want a sip?"

His twelve-year-old sister, Sereena, blasted music from her headphones. I could hear Lil' Kim, "I used to be scared of the dick / Now I throw lips to the shit / Handle it like a real bitch." She combed her hair and popped gum, rapping lyrics out loud for the entire yard to hear. They'd arrived with their mother, Aunt Nancy, who was bound to begin boozing as soon as the clock passed noon. Her rough, raspy voice evoked thoughts of those who'd lived a concrete life, in jungles crowded with drugs, liquor stores, and welfare checks. She'd married into the family after meeting my Uncle Lewis. Relatives blamed Vietnam for his death. A valedictorian and decorated army vet, upon returning from the war he found himself unable to be hired in the country he'd loyally protected.

Lewis drank day and night, until his organs drowned in brown, toxic fluid.

I felt a tap on my shoulder, turned around, and saw my cousin Winnie smiling. Named after the wife of the South African president Nelson Mandela, Winnie did not look like much of an activist. She wore a long, stringy weave down to her butt, with streaks of blond running through the strands. She stood at five foot five, with handles and chunks, and her thick arms were tattooed with artistic displays of hearts wrapped in the names of her boyfriend and children. At eighteen, Winnie had already given birth to twin girls. As she stood in front of me, hands on hips, round and plump, it was hard to imagine she'd skipped the ninth grade to become student government president and valedictorian of her high school. I looked down at Winnie's shirt to see a huge stomach bulge.

"Please tell me you gained weight," I said. "Tell me that's not what I think it is."

"If you returned calls, then you'd have known about this weeks ago," she said, rubbing her belly. "But it's a boy! I'm so happy. I'm done with having little girls."

I kept staring at her tummy, reaching out to touch it before yanking my hand back.

"I hear pregnancy is contagious, so I'm good," I said, turning up my lip. "I'd die if I had a baby right now. How many months are you?"

"Five," she said, smiling. "And I know you got career plans, but when you have a baby, you'll want another right away. I love being a mom. Ooh, and look who I brought."

She stepped to the side and pointed at Philip. He'd been Winnie's boyfriend since the eighth grade. For some reason, he always had specks of dry paint on his shoes and pants from work he'd done as a contract painter. His baby face made him look like a teenager instead of a twenty-one-year-old man.

"Daddy finally let him move in with us."

"Whaaat?!" I said. "They're cool with that?"

"Yeah, until the baby is born and we can afford to get our own place."

"Where does he sleep?"

"Where do you think?" she said, sucking her teeth. "In my room, duh!"

Winnie's parents had always been more liberal than anyone I'd ever known or understood. Her father, Uncle Neddy, was my mother's first cousin. But he seemed to be from a different family, born in another universe. His lackadaisical rules and laid-back demeanor were the polar opposite of my mother's uptight parental discipline.

Winnie's mommy-to-be bulge cuddled up against her man made me think about Dexter. We were happy like that in the beginning, caught up in the newness of early-relationship euphoria. Caught up in a cloud of foggy sight that makes it hard to see past fake representatives. The ones who present their best selves, hiding their flaws, faking it just to pull you in and trap you, before their real selves appear when the relationship is tested. Dexter tricked me. And to break this curse, I had to get rid of him and make sure I'd never be fooled again.

4

THE ARGUMENTS BETWEEN DEXTER AND ME had grown so intense, our love affair was as steady as a raft floating amid the seas in an always-brewing storm. It didn't help that I'd let him invite himself to come live with me, raising a puppy together, playing make-believe mommy and daddy. I felt as if I had no room to breathe. No place to escape. But he had no place to go. It was a codependent addiction of resentment, distrust, and lust.

The day before I left Baltimore for the family reunion, we continued to play out our dysfunctional norm.

"Whose dress is this?" I asked casually. It hung in the back of his closet as he stuffed plastic bags that were headed for my apartment. Short, green, dotted with sunflowers like yellow spots in a grassy field, it slid off one side of the hanger, in need of a body to fill it.

"I dunno," Dexter answered, dumb and stupid. He was milling around the room, grabbing his garden of fake plants and stuffing them into a second garbage bag.

I hated those answers. The kind that knocked inside the belly, alerting me to a piece of lying shit coming from his ass.

"You don't know? How do you not know about a dress in your closet?"

"Maybe it's my brother's girlfriend's."

"Why would her dress be in your room in your closet?" I was in full investigative mode by now. The more he lied, the more I pried. "I thought you liked to keep your door locked."

"Yeah… um. I don't know," he said nervously. "I don't know whose this is. You want it?"

"No, I don't want this ugly, cheap-looking dress," I yelled. "What the fuck, Dex? Did you have some girl here?"

"No…"

"Dex. Did you have some girl here?"

"No."

I wasn't moving until he answered with truth. My face was perfectly blank except the seething red anger in my pupils.

"Is it that ex of yours?"

"I mean, maybe. Maybe she left it. I don't care about that bitch anymore."

"Bitches leave things behind so they can come back." I let the sentence linger in the air like a haunting poltergeist. Then I grabbed his car keys off the bed. "Take me to her house."

"For what?"

"So I can see you tell her that you two are done."

"What?"

"Take. Me. To. Her. House." I was slow, deliberate. "That's unless you're lying."

"No! Meena. What the fuck? Why don't you just believe me?"

"Because you're lying. And if you are, you're not moving in with me. Fuck you."

"So where am I supposed to go? My brother moved in with his girl. We didn't re-sign the lease. I have nowhere to go."

"Oh, well." I shrugged my shoulders, a tiny smirk on my face. Dexter grabbed the keys from my hand and headed out the door as I followed in tow. Starting the car, pulling out of the lot, he turned up the radio, blasting a Funkmaster Flex mix tape. I turned down the volume.

"Why are you touching my radio, Meena?"

"Because you're a liar."

"I'm taking you to her house."

"So. You still lied about that dress. Why did you lie?" He was quiet.

"Why did you lie?" More silence.

So I screamed, "Why did you lie? I *hate* liars!"

Next thing I knew, Dexter had hit the accelerator. We were speeding down an empty side street. Trees, vinyl siding, everything in a blur.

"Fuck this, yo!" he hollered. "I'ma fuckin' die! You see this, Meena? You driving me to kill myself! *Fuck!*"

I screamed. Yet that only helped his foot add weight to the accelerator.

"Dexter! Slow down! *Please?*"

He swerved and let the car do a 360-degree doughnut, landing on the opposite side of the road. Tears streamed down my face, my cheeks drenched. He began to drive normally, simmering down. Pulling into an empty warehouse lot, he leaned over and kissed me in a way that led to foggy-windows sex in the backseat.

A week later, fresh from the family reunion, Dexter promptly picked me up from the train station in his shiny green Hyundai. The backseat was filled with balloons, a bouquet of roses, and an oversize teddy bear. He stepped out of the car, hip-hop blasting, smile wide, and planted a kiss on me as he picked my body up off the ground.

"I missed you," he said, laughing. "What's up, babe? You smell so good. I miss that smell."

We whizzed off to the park, soundtracked to the bass of Jay Z vibrating through the streets. Chrome rims sparkled amid the gorgeous summertime sun. Reflections of Dex's herringbone necklace glistened with every cheesy grin he gave with those glistening white teeth. Back at the apartment, he'd cleaned each room to pristine perfection. Dusted. Mopped. Vacuumed. The place smelled

Pine Sol fresh. Laundry washed, folded, and packed away. There was no way I could break up with him that day.

The next morning he dropped me at work and headed to his job, selling insurance door-to-door, persuading families to invest in their futures. The moment break time hit, he came searching for me. Popping up at the mall. Randomly surveying racks at my store, looking for something new to buy. Lurking.

"Why is he always here?" my store manager, Paul, asked with a furrowed brow. "Does he work?"

"Yeah, but when he gets off, he comes here."

"Well, why? You're at work and him being here is a distraction. I mean, don't you think so?"

"Well, I can still do my job. Do you want me to tell him to leave?"

"I understand he's buying things. But it's just strange how he's always here. It's like he's watching you."

"He just loves me, Paul. But I appreciate your concern. Thank you."

"Just looking out for you, kiddo. Stay focused. And take your break now. I need you ready for the lunchtime rush."

I grabbed my purse and motioned for Dexter to follow me. He grabbed my hand as we headed out of the store.

"So what do you want to eat today, pretty lady?"

"Sushi, I guess."

"Cool, I had a taste for spring rolls and a little fish," he said, grabbing my skirt. "Maybe we can head to the car for a quickie and—"

"Dexter," I said, cutting him off, "you gotta stop coming to my store so much. My manager talked to me about it today."

"Why? I buy stuff, I'm not hurting anybody. It's not like there's anybody in there. They need to be happy they have a regular customer." He tried to grab my waist. I nudged back. My look hadn't changed. "What did he say?"

"He just wondered why you were always at the store. He said it seems like you're watching me."

"So, maybe I am. You're beautiful. And so what, it's none of his fucking business. I'll tell him."

"You'll tell him what?" I said, alarmed. "And get me fired?"

"You don't need that bullshit job. I got you, Meena."

"Maybe I like that bullshit job. If it wasn't for that bullshit job, I wouldn't have met you."

At this point we were screaming in the mall, standing in front of the food court. I swerved my neck as he circled around me.

This was our thing. Zero to one hundred in a second. One minute lovey-dovey, the next enraged.

"I'm not hungry anymore," I said, turning on my heel. "I'm going back to work."

"Cool, I'm going to talk to Paul."

"No, you're not. You're leaving."

"Why don't you want me to talk to him, Meena?" he said, walking past me, accusing me. "You fucking him?"

I was used to his jealousy by now. "What? No, he's married."

"So, that doesn't mean anything. I remember what happened with your Jamaican fling that summer."

I ran in front of him and put my hand on his chest. "If you talk to Paul, I will break up with you. Leave, Dex."

Suddenly his eyes were teary. "You would do that? Why? I love you."

"Because you're making a scene in the mall. We're arguing. This is where I work. You're embarrassing me, Dexter. Please leave."

Then he began whining. "But I need you in my life. I love you."

"I know," I said, walking close to kiss him on the lips. "Pick me up at six p.m., outside the mall. Don't come inside, okay?"

"Okay," he said, holding in his tears like a toddler. "I'm sorry."

"I know."

"I love you."

"It's obvious."

Dexter was always saying how much he loved me. The problem is that love is not enough to make a relationship work. Even once we moved in together, making candlelit dinners and having loud sex every night, our situation continued to implode.

5

YOU KNOW THAT MOMENT when you blow up a man's phone. Send multiple pages. Text messages. Calling so many times, hoping the back-to-back ringing beats him between the ears so hard that he can't help picking up and replying.

I could hear the exasperation in Dexter's voice. "Meena, I told you I had a meeting."

"Well, where are you?"

"I told you," he said, sucking his teeth. "I had to go to the office."

"But it's Sunday," I whined. "Why are you at the office on a Sunday?"

"Meena, I can't do this right now. I have to call you back."

"But wait…"

"What?"

"Just…" I sighed, and elongated an exaggerated pause as I strained to hear something in the background. "Hello?" he asked, tense and impatient. "Call me when you're leaving."

"I might be a while."

"You didn't say that earlier. I thought we were having dinner."

"Meena, I will call you back."

I threw the phone down, screaming, "Asshole!"

Brooding on the couch, face turned up, I stared at Grandma Fey's picture on the mantel. All the yelling Dexter and I did reminded me of Grandma telling one of her stories at the reunion.

The life of the almost-retired side of the party, she talked at an escalated volume, cracking up at her own jokes. With a tendency to recount the details of a family fight involving knives, cussing, and screaming, Grandma Fey and her happy giggles brought contagious laughs and discomfort.

"I watched Mama pull a knife on my daddy. Yeah, Daddy hit her while she was cookin'. And Mama grabbed a butcher knife, put it to his neck, and said, 'If you hit me again, I'll kill you.' Mama didn't take no crap." Grandma laughed loud and boisterously, swaying back and forth. Her bright purple dress swept the ground with each move. A gold tooth glistened as she opened her mouth extra wide. "Uh-huh," she'd add with a nod, before taking a finger to scratch the dry scalp flaking under her curly tight wig.

Grandma Fey's mother, or Ma Betty, as we called her, had died like her daddy, Great-Great-Grandpa Marcus. Like her father, Ma Betty passed with no memory of who she was and what she'd been born on earth to do. The Alzheimer's was so severe that she was placed in a nursing home where visits from family members became as uncommon as married black women. She died alone, under covers stained by infected bedsores oozing puss. Her death caused a rift in the family between those who'd regularly visited and ones who hadn't.

As usual, the family curse had touched her. Decades before Ma Betty became sick, she was an upbeat go-getter, proud voter, skilled baker, and soul food chef. Traumatized by disappointment and heartbreak, Betty decided to spend the rest of her days without a man. Ironically, her three younger sisters followed this same path, remaining single till their deaths.

When random family reunion time came and they all got together, the matriarch Mitchell ladies would find themselves on familiar relationship ground.

"Want a man, but don't need one. Probably won't get one," I remembered hearing Ma Betty say during one of our holiday family visits to her home in Brooklyn. "Hand me that towel," she'd instructed my mother, who was in the kitchen, watching her drizzle lemon glaze frosting over a moist, bundt-shaped pound cake. "Mitchell women are cursed. Gon' be all alone, forever."

Sitting at the kitchen table next to me, sipping a tall cup of Pepsi while watching an old Western, Grandma Fey yelled without taking her eyes off the TV, "Don't put those things in Deena's head."

"Well, it's true," Ma Betty snorted. "*I* know."

"It is not," Grandma spit back. "I been married."

It was the first time I'd ever heard that Grandma Fey had married. As I found out, she was eighteen when she'd met a charming, light-complexioned man with curly black hair—Bill Boone. They dated two weeks before jumping the broom. Six months later, she was home pregnant when a woman knocked at the door.

"Hi, does Billy Boone live here?" A short, plump woman waited for an answer. She wore a large sunhat with a daffodil pinned to the side.

"Yes, Bill lives here," Grandma Fey said. "May I help you?"

"Who are you?" the little lady asked, putting her suitcase on the steps. "Do you live here?"

"I'm his wife, who are you?"

"His wife."

Grandma says she almost passed out when those words came from that woman's mouth. But still, Southern hospitality was upheld as she invited her inside for tea. Over sips of Earl Grey, Grandma found out that Bill had disappeared from his *other* home in Raleigh, North Carolina, leaving behind a pregnant, penniless wife. This lady, Peggy, had eventually found out where Bill lived by tracking a postmarked envelope he'd sent containing five dollars and a handwritten letter with three words: "For your troubles."

Fey and Peggy cried together, sharing dates, experiences, similar occurrences, anguishing over their pain. And when the meeting was over, Fey prepared for the confrontation.

"I'ma kill his ass," she said, as Peggy smiled and replied, "I understand."

Hours later…

"Motherfucker, where you been?" she asked as her drunken mate faked a smooth swagger through the front door, before tripping over the edge of the living room rug. He held himself up by digging his nails into the plastic coating on the arm of the couch.

"I been out, I told you," he slurred. "Why you worrying?"

"'Cause I smell your breath. And you said you'd be home by ten. It's three a.m."

"Damn, you always questioning me, woman. I don't question you when you out at your church events all day long. Let me be."

SMACK.

The slap across his face caused sideways slobber to fly across the room, splattering against the window. Stunned, he pushed himself up off the chair to receive a beating of words.

"What kind of man leaves his pregnant wife home without a call? You ain't shit. I knew I shouldn't have married you," she screamed, right hand steady on her hip. "And you got the nerve to bring my church into this? You need Jesus."

"Bitch," Bill replied slowly, stumbling up straight. "I don't care who the hell you are, the mother of my child, my wife, whatever, don't you touch me." He balled up his fist and punched her so hard that she fell into the living room shelf. Family photos in their frames tumbled to the floor. Blood-soaked tears streamed down her face as a gash oozed from her forehead.

"See what you done made me do?" he said. "Damn!"

"I hate you," she screamed back, one hand rubbing her pregnant belly. "I hope you go to hell for what you did to me and your other wife."

Bill paused, shaken, before saying, "I don't know what you talking about."

"Yes, you do. Peggy? Your *other* wife?" His mouth opened slightly. "Yeah, the one from Raleigh. She came to visit today. You left her pregnant and had the nerve to send her five dollars 'for her troubles,'" she said, holding a porcelain angel that had slipped off the shelf. "You remember that, don't you?"

"I don't need this," he said, waving his hand in the air. Stumbling toward the front door, Bill stopped before leaving, staring through the screen in shock at a woman walking quickly up the sidewalk, grabbing a boy's hand. The four-year-old tried to keep up as his tiny legs dragged behind. His mother clenched his fingers and the straps of a large black purse, holding it tightly to the side of an oversize pregnant stomach.

Turning to help Fey stand, he caressed her arm, easing her up off the shelf, lifting his woman high. And with the angel figurine, she bashed him on the side of the head.

"Owww!"

Grandma Fey always laughed when she told this part of the story. "Owwww," she'd say in a high-pitched voice, mocking Bill's pussylike whimper. Continuing the saga, she told the parts where he cussed and held his throbbing head. And then the final moment, when he stared at Fey's bloated belly, turned without a word, and left. Decades later, my mother, who was a fetus at the time of the fight, had yet to meet her dad. And the story, as it always did, left an awkward moment of silence, which Grandma Fey broke by looking up and yelling at me. "Meena, don't you bring no crazy boys home. Get you a nice one," she said, pointing at me. "Smart. But don't let him hit you. Or I'ma beat him."

I'd never had that problem, I thought, sitting alone on my couch, staring through the blinds. The sun dipped behind clouds casting shadows across the horizon that opened up to torrential rain showers. I picked up the phone to dial, pausing to look at the numbers, before throwing the cordless back on the couch. Glancing out the window for signs of a green Hyundai, I grabbed the phone again and dialed Dexter's number. Once. Twice. Voice mail a third time. The anxiety strangled my stomach, tightening muscles into gassy contortions. I decided, as I tossed the phone down a fourth time, I was ready to do something about this situation.

6

During moments of idle time, when the store was slow, when seconds felt like hours, I could see Dexter's cute face. His smooth, caramel skin and shiny bald head bopping down the hallway. Those lips I loved to kiss, whimpering and shaking as he rubbed them up and down my body. His licking and sticking his tongue down my neck, onto my nipples, inside my belly button, and around my clit. I throbbed at the thought of him ripping through my underwear, pushing inside, stabbing me there. I was addicted. A week seemed to be our peace record. Accord and love and calm till the seven-day mark hit.

We had actually gone over the limit by the next Sunday, when he announced, "I'm going to get gas." We were lounging on the couch, preparing to watch basketball. "And I'ma pick up some chips."

I didn't want him to go, and he didn't need to. "We have Doritos in the cabinet," I said, pulling him back down to the seat. "Why do you have to go get gas now? The game is about to come on."

"Because I probably won't have time in the morning before work." That triggered a memory, and I asked, puzzled, "Didn't you just get gas yesterday?"

"No."

"I didn't see the tank half-full?"

"Maybe, but that was yesterday."

This was getting weird. "Well, where have you been driving? This isn't a big town."

"Why the hell are you asking so many questions?"

"Why do you have a problem with that?"

"Because I feel like you're accusing me of something."

A light began flashing inside my mind. "Well, why do you feel like that?" I stood up, looking down at him. "Is it guilt?"

"I'll be right back, Meena."

"How are you gonna leave in the middle of me talking to you?"

"Why do you always want to beef? Damn, I'm getting sick of that shit."

"I'm going with you."

"No, you're not, Meena. You take too long to get ready."

Now we were getting to tired old excuses. "Whatever. I'm going."

"No, you're not."

"How come? What are you hiding?"

"I'm not getting into this. I'll be back." He walked out the door and drove off.

The liar vibe made my intuitive sixth-sense antenna shake. I ran into the bedroom to check his pants pockets, thinking I might find a phone number scribbled across a tiny piece of paper. At the same time I was praying my thoughts of his deception and cheating were simply ludicrous mind tricks of an abandoned girl gone cuckoo from lusty love. I almost believed it was all in my head when I heard a buzz across the room and turned to see his pager vibrating on the bed.

My heart palpitated as I walked slowly over to it. Butterflies fluttered in my stomach as I sat down, picked up the black pager, and looked at the digits lighting up the screen.

I didn't recognize the number. Holding the pager in hand, I wondered whether I should return the call. Wondered whether he'd walk in the door and catch me in the act of snooping. I looked out the front window. No sign of Dexter. So I grabbed the cordless and dialed. "Hello," a female voice answered. I could hear a basketball game playing in the background. "Hello?"

I hung up. My stomach did cartwheels. A tiny ping made me breathe harder and harder, my heart pound faster. I waited five minutes, still staring out the window. Praying. Breathing. Saying to myself, *Lord, if there's anything I need to know about this man, please let me know.*

I picked up the phone and called back the last number dialed. "Hello," said a female voice. I could hear the echo of a commercial jingle, mimicking the channel on my TV.

"Yeah, did someone call from this number for Dexter?"

"Yeah, who's this?"

"This is his girlfriend. Who's this?" Dial tone.

I sat still in shock as Dexter's key fought to open the front door. "Babe, we gotta get this lock changed," he said in the hallway. "It's broke as hell. Can you please unlock the door for me? I don't have time for this today."

I walked to the door and promptly bolted the second lock. "Uh, Meena, can you take the chain off, please?"

"Are you cheating on me?" I asked, opening the door slightly and speaking through the tiny space the chain allowed. "Tell the truth."

"Oh, my God. Again, Meena? No."

"Tell the truth, Dexter. Are you cheating on me?"

"Where is this coming from?"

"Who is 932-4452?"

"I don't know."

His voice didn't sound innocent in the slightest. "Who the fuck is the bitch answering that number?"

"You called it?"

"Maybe."

He had the nerve to cop an attitude. "Did I give you permission to return calls to my pager? Why are you so fuckin' nosy?"

"And you're a lying bitch. Who the fuck is the chick answering that number?"

"Meena, open the door. Your mind is playing tricks on you again. Come on, I gotta pee."

"Pee at that bitch's house."

"Let me the fuck in or I will break this door down."

"And I will call the police on your black ass."

With one heavy push, Dexter banged into the door. The force tore the chain off the wall, making it fly across the living room. Exposed to his anger, I threw the pager at him. He ducked to the side too late. Wincing in pain, he firmed his lips and walked toward me.

"Get the fuck away from me," I said, putting my hands on his chest. "Get up off me."

"Why did you throw that pager at me? Look at my head." A tiny knot had risen on the left side of his temple.

He moved to grab my arm, but I pushed him away, picked his car keys up off the floor, and made a stabbing motion toward him that scratched his arms.

"What the fuck! Meena!" he screamed, throwing a right hook at the wall, leaving mangled plaster and an imploded hole.

Turning to run toward me like a linebacker, Dex grabbed both my arms, pinning them behind my back as I fell to the floor.

"Get off me!" I screamed, struggling as he raised his fist. "Get off me!"

I looked up at him from the floor. His face was a mixture of anger and confusion.

"Go ahead. Hit me!" I screamed. "Hit me! Do it, motherfucker. Do it!"

His fist behind him, ready to pelt me with tight punches, stayed raised in the air as a tear came out the corner of his eye. I kicked and pushed myself free of his hold.

"Fuckin' bitch," I said, eyes glazed with rage. "Can't even hit me. Pussy-ass motherfucker."

I could see myself saying these things. Standing outside my body, observing the scene, being my own audience. And as much as I knew that what I was saying was wrong—a horrible, dysfunctional display of love—I couldn't stop. It was like something wired in me; I was like a robot activated by words to move into action, displaying hate, violence, and pain. I didn't know where *that* crap came from. But it was like an awakening of lava that had been festering and simmering, hidden inside an unknown deep volcano.

Dexter sat on the floor, legs bent, hands covering his face.

"You cheating on me, Dexter?" I asked, still fuming. "Tell the truth!"

"No."

"Tell the truth."

"No."

"Tell the fucking truth," I screamed, tears running out my eyes. "If you love me, don't lie to me."

"Okay, okay, yes! Okay? Yes," he said, sweating. "But it was just once. And I don't know how she got my phone number because I never gave it to her."

The curse was alive and well. "I hate you."

I got up, ran into the hallway, and outside into the street. Picking up one of the red bricks the landlord used to decorate the front yard, I ran to Dexter's car and threw it at his windshield. The rectangular hunk of stone shattered the glass and managed to bounce back at my hand and then to the ground. A large circular crack dented the windshield as Dexter ran out of the house.

"What the fuck did you do?" he cried. "Why the fuck did you do that?"

"I hate you," I yelled back, as the neighbors across the street looked on, laughing. "You're a bitch."

Dexter got into his car and sped away down the street, screeching and kicking up dust every inch of the way.

I walked back into the apartment and looked at my finger. The right middle one was swollen black and blue, puffed up twice its size. The pain throbbed and swelled. But I couldn't feel it completely, seething anger numbing my senses. Enraged, I looked around for Dexter's belongings, promptly packing up and pushing his things into the hallway—clothes, shoes, jewelry, his ten fake green plants he'd posted up around the house for his plastic green-thumb hobby. I pushed the cabinet and sofa in front of the door, just to block him from getting inside. Out of breath, I crawled into the bed, crying, a plastic bag of ice nursing my throbbing finger. I woke an hour later to shouting.

"Let me in, Meena! Why is my shit in the hallway! What the fuck?"

I didn't answer.

"Meena, I know you hear me." Dexter's voice was deep, loud, and angry, his Southern twang more pronounced than usual. "Let me in."

He paused.

"Let me in, Meena!" he screamed at the top of his lungs. "You want me to keep the building up tonight? I will."

No answer.

"Oh, you playing the ignore-a-nigga game. Cool. Watch this one call the police on your ass."

I sat in bed crying for the next thirty minutes, until I heard a tap at the door.

"Who is it?" I asked.

"The police. I need you to open the door, ma'am."

I looked through the peephole to see two burly white men in uniform, standing beside Dexter, who looked depressed with bloodshot eyes and a red and blue knot on his forehead.

I unlocked the door.

"Ma'am, has this man been living with you?"

"Yes."

"How long?"

"I dunno, a couple months."

"The law says that if he's been living here for sixty days or more, he's a legal resident and can't be thrown out. You'll have to let him in."

"But this is my apartment. My name is on the lease. I let him live with me!"

"Ma'am, you'll have to let him in, that's the law."

I looked at Dexter and rolled my eyes before turning and walking back into the bedroom to call Meredith.

"Hello?"

No answer.

"What's wrong, girl?"

"Please come get me. *Please…*"

"Girl… what happened?"

"I'm moving out. Dexter cheated on me. Cops said I can't…" I sniffled and coughed, unable to finish my words. "Just come get me!"

"It's seven o'clock. I won't be there till at least ten. Can you go somewhere till I get there?"

"Yeah, I'll just… I dunno. I'll just go to the mall or something. I dunno. Just please come."

"I got you. Just get out that house," Meredith said. "Promise me you'll leave and won't say anything to him?"

I looked at the cops standing there, hands on holsters, eyeing the apartment. "She broke my necklace, my pager, she's out of control, Officers…"—he glanced at their badges—"…Bennett and Douglass. She's out of control, guys. Crazy."

A long-simmering boil soured my stomach. I imagined myself leaping over the suitcases, using the forward momentum to punch him in his stupid face. But instead I grabbed my keys and pocketbook and walked out the door. "I promise, Meredith," I said into the phone. "I'm leaving now. If I stay here they'll arrest me. So please hurry up. I'll be around somewhere. Call me when you're close."

I hung up the phone and walked down the block. An hour went by before my phone rang. Dexter's name lit up the caller ID and I stuffed the phone in my bag. I sat at a random bus stop. Staring at the cars whizzing by. Suddenly thirsty and hungry, I walked in a daze into a diner, sat in an empty booth, and ordered a hot chocolate, banana split, and a glass of water. Sipping slowly, I stared at the words on a newspaper, ink smudged with my tear-drops, till Meredith rang the phone. A short ten minutes later, she was outside the diner, picking me up and taking us back to the apartment.

I walked into the house. Grabbed a suitcase and began dumping clothes inside. Dexter was wearing boxers, in bed, on the phone with his mother. Nodding his head and giggling. After packing my backpack, I grabbed the leash off the front door and the dog's traveling bag.

"No, she stays here," Dexter said, following me into the hallway.

"You can't take her. I bought her."

"You bought her for me!"

"Well, you can't take her."

"You fucking bitch! I hate you. You—"

Meredith tugged at my arm. "Come on, girl. The dog ain't worth it."

I sucked my teeth, seeing Dexter in my bed, with my dog, on *my* phone, talking to his mother.

"Yeah, Mom, she's leaving," I heard him say. "She's crazy. She destroyed my car."

"Did you tell her how you attacked me?" I yelled, hoping she'd hear me. "Did you tell her you cheated on me? Did you tell her you raised your hand to hit me?"

"Come on, Meena," Meredith urged, tugging at my bicep. "He's a bitch."

"He's on my phone! In *my* apartment. On *my* motherfucking bed. And *I'm* leaving? I hate him!"

I was almost out the door with Meredith, before I did an about-face. I marched back into the bedroom and yanked the cord from the wall, tearing the clear plastic connector off the phone cord. *Fuck him.* "Asshole!" I screamed before finally leaving out the front door and driving off.

7

THE NEXT MORNING WAS A REMINDER of how much I hated not having my own space. A place to be alone, breathe, and scream if need be.

I'd grown accustomed to it in college. But now? Being back home? Pure misery. I hated the sound of my mother's early-morning voice talking to herself. She mumbled about everything—worries and mostly things crumpled up in her head. Things that she wished were said differently in the past. She talked to herself so much, it was loud at times, angry or comical, ending in laughter or a huff and puff. She sounded like an actor practicing a script. It drove me nuts. Insane. Hearing her talk at eight in the morning, to no one, when I'd gone to bed at three after a night of smoking and drinking. When I wanted to sleep in, the breeze from my cracked window blew a slight opening to my bedroom, and I could hear her crashing through cake dishes downstairs, mumbling to her only friend: herself. It made me want a straitjacket.

This particular morning, the one-person conversation was about Aunt Connie and their latest argument. Apparently Mom had tried to call her. Connie replied with a dial tone. The light sleeper in me was awoken by Mom's mumbling around the kitchen.

"Stupid. She's so stupid," I heard her say. "Acting like a damn baby. Always."

I could hear the slam of the kitchen cabinet. She crashed through pots, looking for something to cook with. Maybe a tin for blueberry muffins.

"She's just not smart. Dumb. She's been this way since she was a kid. She's still the same. Then she's gonna hang up on me?"

I tossed and turned with each grumbling word.

"Oh my God!" I breathed under the pillow, until I finally sat up in bed. "I mean, really?" I said to myself. "What the fuck. This is some bullshit!"

I stretched for the cell phone and checked my voice mail. There were ten.

Message 1: "Hey, babe, it's me." Dexter's voice was sad and raspy. "I miss you. So does Baby. She's the best dog ever. Please call me."

Delete.

Message 2: "Heeeeey, pretty lady. Hope you got my last message," Dexter said, this time sounding shiny and happy. "It's a beautiful day. We're in Virginia. Baby and I are at the beach. She's chasing seagulls. We wish you were here!"

Delete.

Message 3: "Yo... Why are you not calling me back? Something wrong with your phone? You on your period? What the fuck? Hit me back. You said you love me. Show it."

Messages 4, 5, 6, 7, 8, 9: Hang-ups.

Message 10: "Hey, girl!" It was Meredith, always the early riser. "Where you at? Hiding from your mom? Yo, I got that good sticky stuff. Straight from Brooklyn. What you doin' tonight? Call me back... beeeyatch!"

I tripped out of bed and slowly sleepwalked down the stairs to make coffee. Mom was still slamming pots around. I breezed past her and grabbed the teakettle. The silence between us was typical. Almost uncomfortably normal. Although I hated mornings and despised talking until I had caffeine, with Mom it was a tiptoe-ing-on-eggshells relationship that had trained me to speak only when spoken to. I often didn't know what to say to her or how to word it for fear of being snapped at.

It had been like this since childhood. As I'd sit home watching HBO, she'd spend late weekend nights out with coworkers, hanging at hotel bars, sipping on Zinfandel. At the time, she was an independent lady with a $40,000 salaried job and health benefits. During the day, she worked as an assistant at a financial management firm, where she answered phones, scheduled meetings, and filed documents. Despite the generous administrative assistant pay for the '80s, she disliked her job's tedious duties, resenting the lack of mobility and raise after three years of loyalty. This, combined with hating her single relationship status, loathing the Valentine's Day advertising weeks in advance, made for an unending depression. She wanted to be in love, hated being alone, and blamed the opposite sex for her misery.

This all made living with my mother difficult. It was like being forced, daily, to play a stressful guessing game of what taboo topic to avoid.

"Jerk!" I remembered my mother slamming the phone down against the kitchen wall mount, opening the cabinet, and reaching for the flour in a sudden urge to make biscuits. "Talkin' about *I* need to get a life. And why am *I* sending mixed signals. And why can't *I* wait for him to call me back," she murmured while taking the milk out of the refrigerator. She emptied a scoop of flour into a bowl, added the other dry ingredients, and poured in the wet ones. A piece of eggshell slipped into the bowl. "Shit!" she said. "They're all dogs!"

I'd usually be sitting in the next room, trying to watch television, when she'd go off on a cranky tirade. I always thought that if I used the TV to phase out her voice, she would forget I was there and not direct her anger toward me.

"Meena, come here!" she yelled.

"Yes!" I answered, without taking my eyes off the screen. "I said, come *here*."

As I walked to the kitchen, my heart began a gradually more rapid beat.

"Clean up that sink," she spit. "A kitchen full of dishes is nasty."

I quickly turned on the faucet, wet the sponge, put a few drops of detergent on it, and picked up the cup to scrub. One time, not realizing how hard the water was running, when I rinsed off the cup, sudsy water sprayed to the left where my mother was standing. Her back hand moved as fast as a flyswatter.

SMACK!

The side slap knocked me off balance as I grabbed my right cheek and stared at her, teary-eyed, wondering why I'd been hit.

"Turn that water down, stupid! Why you got it running so high? You wet my damn blouse!" She looked at me with a familiar grimace. "Gimme a paper towel!" I grabbed a towel and passed it to her. She snatched it away and smacked me with the opposite hand. "Don't look at me like that!"

I wasn't sure how I was looking, especially when I tried so hard not to make eye contact or stand in the way of her notoriously fast hands. But she was a mother. She had this gift of seeing things from the back of her head. Perhaps past my fear, she sensed seething resentment. Maybe she could feel my urge to run away, knowing I had nowhere to go. Maybe she could read my mind, and see the constant countdown of days, months, and years till I was old enough to go far away to college, and be free from her stifling hold over my emotions and my life. Free from the daily bubbling in my stomach that gave way to gas whenever her car pulled into the driveway. Free from being out of breath from rushing around before she got home at six o'clock.

Each evening at five forty-five was the same. I would run through the apartment, quickly cleaning any evidence of after-school playtime. The pleated skirt and ruffled top I'd thrown on the floor after changing into my play clothes would be scooped up and stashed in my bedroom closet. The Pathmark peanut butter jar and sticky knife covered in jelly would be unstuck from the kitchen

counter, washed, and put in its proper place. Schoolbooks, shredded paper edges, and pencils rolling across the living room table
would be moved and replaced with the fake potted plant that normally occupied my homework spot. Dishes were washed, dried,
and neatly stacked by plate and cup size into wooden cabinets.
And when I knew I had cleaned every corner, at 5:59, when the
engine of her 1985 Ford Escort came rumbling into the driveway,
I would wait, tense, my stomach somersaulting with anticipation.

I never knew what mood Mom might be in after work. Was
it good? Would she walk into the house with a smile and say,
"Helll*oooo*? I'm h*ooo*me. Nobody to say hello to me?"

Or was it dark? Would she open the front door, suck her teeth,
and after a long, sad exhale, drop her bags, and observe every
stick of furniture as if she were a home health inspector? Moving
through the house, she was like an uncontrollable locomotive,
steaming from the top, blowing her loud whistle to make things
move.

"Why is this mail on the chair? Put my mail on the table. And
what's that piece of tissue on the floor? Meena, come pick this up!
Why's that TV so loud? Are you deaf? And what's this plate doing
in the sink? I told you to clean out the sink before I get home. This
place looks like a pigsty!"

I'd curse myself under my breath: "Stupid!" Mad that I'd gotten
that cup of apple juice just before Mom pulled into the driveway.
But I always remained silent. Sitting like a mannequin, motionless,
expressionless, eyes glued to the same spot on the TV screen as I
watched my favorite show, *Double Dare*, on Nickelodeon. Kids ran
wildly, smiling and laughing as they were dared to do crazy stunts
for dream prizes. I always wished I could be there, with them, away
from New Jersey.

"Meena, turn off that crap," she'd say. "Put the news on."

I'd hear Mom's long, tired sighing from the kitchen that was
always followed by "I hate my job." Then she'd add, "I gotta get a
new one."

The loathing was contagious, because I couldn't stand being home. Especially in the mornings when she'd wake up cranky, grab a leather belt, and beat my butt into a welted rouge, as she cussed at me for not getting up with the alarm clock. Other mornings she'd corner me in the bathroom and pound me with her fists, eyes glazed in a tired rage prompted by a minor infraction, like not reminding her to buy more toothpaste after using the last bit. Or for major fuck-ups, like admitting I'd lost the house keys… again. From day to evening, I'd stress to please. Racing to get to school on time, speeding home to fix the house up, aiming to do right and be a good daughter, only to miserably fail and be harshly reminded of my stupidity. I was tired, mentally sore, emotionally worn down to the balls of my feet from tiptoeing room to room, finding a safe space away from the hurricane gust of emotions spewing around 222 Lincoln Street.

As a result, after I moved back home, I stayed in my messy room. Dresser drawers open with T-shirts hanging from the sides. Pants scrunched up inside out, thrown across the middle of the floor. Clean clothes piled high inside a laundry basket next to the bed. A mountain of assorted clothes, camouflaging a chair. One wall was spotted with pictures representing memorable moments of my past. A set of black-and-white photo booth pics showed the trip Meredith and I took last summer to Great Adventure. My first-grade class picture had me smiling toothless in the back row. In another, Dexter and I stood on the beach, kissing for the camera. Not sure why I hadn't taken that one down yet. And one from my eighth-grade graduation of me in a cap and gown. Down at the bottom in the corner was a tattered photo my mother had given me years ago, of me and my father, smiling as I sat on his knee.

When it came to memories of him, recollections grayed the brain like thin clouds of vanishing smoke. My mother would mention him briefly, here and there making passing mentions of her relationship with him and his with me. But it was all in tidbits. Everything else I was forced to make up.

I had one vivid memory, of sitting in my father's burgundy Cadillac. I remember the white leather seats sticking to my tiny thighs. I wore a yellow dress with sunflowers and bows that ruffled in the warm Brooklyn breeze. The car engulfed me as I sat in the front seat, stretching my neck to see out the window. I was four or five, smiling as we passed stray dogs, peeing and sniffing grimy green garbage bags on street corners.

"Daddy, can I have a dog?" I asked as he steered with his left hand. His right fingers stroked his scruffy goatee. "I wanna doggie."

"Sure, baby, I'll get you a dog one day."

"Okaaay!" I sang happily, smiling, swaying from side to side, doing a little dance as I thought about playing with my puppy. But that day never came. Daddy didn't get me a thing once his relationship with my mother ended. All he ever gave me were fleeting, insecure memories that made me question his love. Although I did inherit his last name—Butler—his looks, a slight overbite, and all five feet six inches of his height. I had his brown hair, which when under stress tended to fall out at the top of the scalp. I even developed the dry caramel skin that peeled and itched in the summer sun. And a back full of clogged pores and spotted with acne scars.

The stories Mom shared about my father, outside of his physical flaws, always began with "You look so much like him." She'd stare at me in awe and then speak in the past tense: "He loved you so much. He loved him some Meena."

She told me we had a wonderful relationship. I was Danny Butler's little girl, wrapping my arms around his leg as he dragged me from room to room, cooing and giggling. The same couldn't be said of his relationship with Mom, though. Their tumultuous romance turned dark, somewhere in the street, with fists and fights. There's one episode she shared that stands out, because I was asleep in the backseat when it took place.

"Who's that?" my father asked, waiting for an answer. He leaned on the Caddy with arms crossed. Toothpick in mouth, checkered applejack hat to the left, blue collared shirt opened to the chest, and black corduroy bell-bottoms sweeping the ground. He'd stopped to pick Mom up from NYU's campus and take her to work. But she was always late, running with perspiration. The excuse this day: her missing book.

"Stupid," Danny huffed. "How do you lose one of those big-ass million-page novels?"

"I told you not to call me stupid."

"Why, Deena?" he asked as he gunned the gas and sped off, screeching down the block. "Would you rather me use one of those big words you learned in your big college books?"

"No, I'd just rather you pick one up and get some common sense," she replied, buckling her seat belt. My mother's sarcasm was legendary. Quick with the comeback, sometimes funny, often insulting, her mouth was her most powerful weapon and biggest downfall.

SMACK!

The sound came from my father's right hand smashing into Mom's exposed cheek. He somehow still managed to expertly drive with his left hand, maneuvering the steering wheel down the street.

Violence wasn't a surprising occurrence between Danny and Deena. Although they'd been together three years, their relationship had moved as fast as a NASCAR race. Celebrating their six-month anniversary, they announced she was pregnant and moved in together. Over the following months, his tantrums escalated into pushes, grabs, and nighttime slaps. By day, he spent hours on the downtown streets of Brooklyn, sitting at a six-foot table, selling bronzed jewelry and mahogany figurines to black power people looking for African scenery. While away from him, my mother would map out an escape route inside her head, calculating. But at the end of each day, she always stayed. Even as beatings grew more painful and frequent. Her love, entangled and twisted, was rooted in a codependent pity for a man she felt needed her, because he didn't have the stable funds to rent an apartment alone.

"What now?!" he screamed with an indignant look of self-justification as he made a left onto Gates Avenue. My mother grabbed her throbbing left eye, exploding into a purple mass of swollen skin. "What now?!" he repeated, waiting for an answer, looking for a reason to strike again. "Smart-ass motherfucker."

Mom cowered in the seat, tears flowing, her sight blurry. When the Caddy screeched to a stop at a red light, she jumped out, pulled off her black platform shoes, and limped down the block. Her Afro crooked, mascara running, she never looked back.

Cars blew horns as rubbernecking drivers stretched to see why some barefoot woman was walking down the block in November. My father watched, too, a tiny smirk on his face. He crept along behind her sad stride as she turned onto a quiet, tree-lined block and picked up the pace. Danny expertly parallel parked, pocketed the keys, hopped out, and jogged to catch up.

"Deena, come on. Meena's in the car. You know I'm sorry," he yelled after her. "You know I love you!"

"Fuck you, Danny!"

"I love you and Meena," he said, out of breath. "You two are the family I never had. But you think you can say whatever to me, and my mama don't even talk to me like that."

"I'm not your mother. And don't bring Meena into this," she said, arms crossed, neck swerving. "Will you love her the way you love me? Look at my fuckin' eye!"

He walked up and tried to caress her face. She dodged his hand with a swift back bend and body curve that made her lose her balance. She stumbled to catch her footing.

"Come on, Deena! What the fuck? See, that's your problem, stubborn as shit."

"You the one with the problem, Danny. Always wanna hit somebody."

"You know what?" He paused to crack his knuckles, bending each finger slowly. Each bone rattled and unlocked itself into what my mother foresaw as an Ike Turner warm-up. Deena took tiny steps back.

"I gotta go to work," Danny said, as he turned around to check on his car. "And so do you. You wanna stay out in this cold-ass street looking crazy, you go ahead. I'll drop Meena with your mom."

"Go then, bitch!" she screamed with disgust. "I hate you."

My father stopped in his tracks. His right hand slowly curled into a fist, as he stared at the Caddy for a long, contemplative moment. My mother tiptoed backward, pursing her lips. She jumped for no reason as he headed to the car without a word, hopped in, and pulled away.

The next day, when he left for his daily hustle, Mom moved back into Grandma Fey's tiny Bed-Stuy home on Putnam Avenue. She dodged Danny's calls for three weeks. Until one day, the doorbell rang.

"Hey, Deena."

My father, flashing a broad, toothy smile, stood on the front step with a long-stemmed bouquet of ruby-red roses.

"Hey," she replied, stomach fluttering.

"You know I miss you and Meena. I'm so sorry, I love you so much. But I understand why you left. And I know. I know. I'm just sorry." His tear ducts filled as he rambled along. "Can I just see Meena? Please? I miss my baby so much."

My mother said she remembered taking an eternity to answer that question, staring at his pitiful face. He'd never looked uglier. "Okay," she said, taking a deep breath. "But you got five minutes, 'cause she's asleep and I'm in the middle of a study group, so you can't stay long."

"That's cool," he said, nodding his head in agreement, smiling. "That's okay."

He stepped inside with a sweet and apologetic grin on his face. The vibe changed when he saw Mom's classmate sitting on the living room couch.

"Danny, this is Marcus. He's in my Black Studies class with me and we're—"

"Where's Meena?" My father's cold eyes were frozen on Marcus.

"Upstairs in the bedroom," Mom answered, voice shaking.

"Lemme walk you up."

When they reached the hallway outside my room, all that my mother remembered were the sudden sharp pains running through her face. They throbbed in patches, over her right cheek, at the tip of her nose, up to the middle of her forehead, piercing between her eyeballs as fists landed on her, punches on a human body bag.

She was laid out across the wooden floor, trying desperately to cover her face. But my father kept hitting her, body shots to the stomach, slaps to the head.

"Stop!" She huffed and puffed, gagging on blood trickling down her throat. "Stop!"

The beating ended when Marcus ran upstairs, grabbed my father from behind, and threw him against the wall. His skinny five-six was like a limp chicken pinned down under Marcus's six-two, 250-pound frame.

"Get off me, man! Get off me!" Danny screamed. "This ain't got shit to do with you."

My cries echoed from the bedroom.

"You don't hit women!" Marcus said, pushing him farther along the floor. "What's wrong with you, man?"

"Fuck you," Danny said, struggling. "Get the fuck off me!"

"I'll let your pussy ass go when you leave." Marcus tightened his grip, pulling Danny's arm behind his back. Mom got up and ran into the bathroom. A bright red imprint of busted lip blood smeared the door handle.

"It's cool, man. It's cool," Danny said, out of breath. "I'm leaving." Marcus loosened his grip, letting my father up off the ground. "Watch out for that bitch," he said, pointing toward the bathroom door. "She sneaky. I ain't fuckin' with her no more."

And he turned and left. It would be years before I saw him again.

8

DURING THE TIME I was living with Dexter, I often missed the safety and closeness of being in a familiar, feel-good place. The plush rose carpet with purple swirl flower designs. The window seat that played home to stuffed animals I'd collected my entire life. The soft, fluffy pink comforter atop my canopy bed, matching light and airy curtains flowing from rods. I didn't realize how much I'd missed it all. I loved being able to walk downstairs and eat as I pleased. No empty OJ cartons to greet me. No fruit basket with just one grape left. I hated when Dex did that. Eat a whole bushel of red grapes and leave me two, like he was being thoughtful. No man to cook for. None of his loud radio static blasting through the rooms, filling the space with noise, clogging thoughts in my head. At home, it was just me, my bed, my closet. Me happily alone.

For the first week after I came back from Baltimore, everything was perfect. I'd sleep till noon and wake up to an empty house. Walk downstairs. Watch *The Young and the Restless* while cooking a huge Southern brunch of grits, eggs, potatoes, and biscuits. All were on my to-do list. At the end of the day, my mother would walk into the house with a smile on her face, asking about my day. I'd update her on the latest episode of *The Bold and the Beautiful*. We'd laugh. And it felt good, like a sisterly bond, rooted in her genuine happiness of my being home from school. But after a week, once she began to grow accustomed to my familiar presence, it was like I'd somehow soaked up all of the warm, welcoming energy, and made it turn to mildewy, stinking resentment.

"Meena, you could've cleaned these damn dishes up," she snapped, throwing her purse on the counter. "You been home all day, you don't have to live like a slob."

I let out a slow exhale, trying to ignore her, feigning being focused on the TV, video bouncing across the screen with a long-haired girl gyrating to the beat. But it became hard to pay attention when my mother began speaking under her breath. Whispering and cussing in audible tones that made memories flashback, like deja vu, to childhood.

"Damn slob. Can't clean up. All you gotta do is wash the damn dishes, clean up your own shit." She sucked her teeth. "Meena! Come get your damn books from off this table. This is not your desk!"

I jumped as my mother hastily turned back to the kitchen sink. I slowly slid my Knicks cap off, remembering why I hated being home. Why growing up, I couldn't wait to go to college and be away from the constraints of my mother and her venomous hold upon my heart and soul, which always seemed dampened by the wear and tear of criticism crashing my self-esteem. I wished she'd go to therapy. I wished she'd talk to someone about the miscarriage she'd had six months ago that doctors attributed to stress.

Jumping up, I bounced off the couch, hopped in the shower, and got ready for Meredith's arrival. After I threw on my clothes and combed my hair into a tiny ponytail, the sound of her car horn made me fly downstairs. Strolling to the kitchen, feigning casual boredom, I realized my heart was beating through my chest. I'd never gotten over the childhood fear of asking my mother for permission to go somewhere. I'd never let go of the fear of her interrogations that preceded giving the okay to leave the house.

"Did you clean your room? You didn't leave smears on the glass, did you?" she'd ask in this accusatory tone. "Did you finish your homework? Clean up these dishes first. Fold that laundry first. You clean that bathroom?"

And if I didn't do those things, if I ever copped an attitude, rolled my eyes, cleaned up sloppily, interrupted her on the phone, or horribly timed an ask when she was in a bad mood—it prompted her to cancel the plans I'd dreamed of having outside the home with friends.

But I wasn't in high school anymore. I was twenty-four. Grown. Living at home. Yes. But still grown.

"Mom, I'm going to the mall with Meredith."

She didn't say anything for a long minute, standing at the sink, washing dishes, giving no acknowledgment. No turn of the head. Acting as if she didn't hear me. This was normal.

"Mom…" I repeated, moving closer but instinctively staying far enough away from her right hook. "I'm going to."

"I heard you," she snapped, falling back into a long, brooding silence broken by Meredith's blowing horn. "Which mall?"

"Bluehill."

"With who?"

"Meredith."

"Bring some milk home. I need to make a lemon pound cake for your grandmother tomorrow."

"Okay," I said, turning to jog/walk through the front door, a huge smile on my face as my heart slowed to a relaxed beat. Occasions like this made me remember the anxiety of the old days. When I absolutely couldn't go as I pleased. Curfews as a teen were legendarily tight in my mother's home, requiring me to be inside by two a.m. On some nights I'd be out of breath, sweat trickling down my forehead, Meredith driving twenty miles above the speed limit, tires screeching up the block as she rushed me home to make curfew.

Thank God for Meredith. Her knack for listening and laughter made me forget about it all. As soon as I got into her car, she pulled out of the driveway, gunning the motor all the way to a park around the corner. Under a tree in a shady spot, she pulled out a cigar and passed it to me. Taking out a small dime bag of weed, she began breaking it up inside a Dunkin' Donuts napkin. I watched the preparations with a smile. A little nervous, a bit excited. I'd started smoking during freshman year of college. And not only did I like the way weed made me feel, but smoking was a bonding activity. At school, everyone would gather in someone's room to puff blunts, filling the air with a smoky, pungent odor of sticky Jamaican ganja. Wu-Tang Clan blasted from the speakers.

Since then, Meredith had mastered the art of rolling a blunt. Taking her fingernail and cutting a line down the middle of the cigar, she emptied its brown grassy contents, then licked the empty leaf moist. Pulling out stems and separating clumped-up pieces of cannabis into tiny shredded morsels, like a chef using finger-tips to sprinkle cheese on a salad, she delicately dropped flakes of weed into the open brown carcass. The final step: she picked it up, licked one edge, and rolled it into what looked like a small, fat *taquito*. Quickly drying her masterpiece with a lighter, she lit a side and inhaled. Holding the smoke in for ten seconds, puffing up her cheeks, she exhaled a sphere-like cloud that engulfed me. She pulled two more times, then gave me the honor.

"Puff, puff, pass," she said, before letting out a hoarse laugh that ended in a dry, smoke-induced cough. "Damn, that's some good shit." Weed. From the earth. Natural and free. I'd never heard of anyone dying from smoking marijuana. No heart attacks, hives, blister breakouts, or any side effect in fine print. One hundred per-cent safe. I put it in my mouth and inhaled into a two-second hold before blowing it all away.

"Noooo," Meredith said, laughing. "You gotta hold it in longer."

"Why?" I asked, like a green kindergartener. "It hurts my throat."

"'Cause you need to feel it."

I pulled again. This time trying my hardest not to exhale for ten seconds. By eleven, I began to choke, dying from self-induced smoke inhalation. Meredith cracked up, damn near falling out the window.

"That was good," she said, cheesing hard. "Now try to hold it in a little longer."

"What am I, your guinea pig today?"

"No, just my entertainment."

"Fuck you. I am not here to entertain your bored suburban ass," I said, picking up the lighter. "Bitch."

I pulled again, this time counting the hold in my head, keeping the smoke in for twelve seconds. When I exhaled this third time, I didn't cackle, instead blowing the smoke out smooth, like a seasoned cannabis pro.

"Nice," Meredith purred. "My little piggy."

"Shut up."

For the next fifteen minutes, we smoked weed until it dissolved into a tiny black butt. Meredith burned her fingertips trying to get the last of it, squeezing her lips tight to get the most from the roach. She looked like a crackhead.

"Um," I mumbled, eyes closed, grinning. "Are you a weed head?"

"Um," she answered, "yeah," before we busted out laughing.

"Me too." I opened my eyes to dig in my purse for a piece of gum. "Yup, head and weed. I like it."

"Well, I like weed before head."

"Well, I like head *while* smoking weed."

"Ooh, you right, that sounds the bomb!"

"*Yuuup*," I said, sucking on the gum's frosted spearmint flavor before chewing it into a burst of freshness. "So good."

I glanced over at Meredith, her eyes red, shut to tiny slits. She nodded her head harder than ever to the radio. Blasting Hot 97, with Puff Daddy and Faith singing "I'll Be Missing You."

"I'm so sick of this song," she said. "I mean, I miss Biggie. But damn, every hour? This song depresses me. Messing up my high."

She popped in Missy Elliott's latest CD, *Supa Dupa Fly.*

Weed became my weekends, with a hip-hop soundtrack. Getting in Meredith's car, driving to the park, smoking, and rapping while high. It was the greatest pastime ever.

On Monday, I returned to Merrill Lynch's creative services department. It had been my summer internship since sophomore year. I'd only applied because my professors kept stressing how I needed an internship for my résumé. So I submitted my application, interviewed with a recruiter who was visiting my college campus, and was offered a paid summer internship proofreading company brochures. They loved me so much that I was able to freelance whenever I wanted. Dressed in a pair of thin navy blue pants, black pumps, and a silk white shirt I'd bought from The Limited, I reported for duty to learn the ins and outs of working in a corporate publishing department—from copy editing to art design, management, and production. I lunched with gossipy, nosy white people, wanting to know my background. Like whether my mother was married, whether I had siblings, and where my family was from. I smiled, politely answering with one-word answers. "No."

"Yes."

"South Carolina." I did this in the spirit of my mother echoing sternly, "What happens in this family, stays in this family."

So although I didn't share much, I did get to know my coworkers through company functions, socializing, mingling. I loved my job. But I quickly learned that I never wanted to work anywhere I was required to dress up every day. It was expensive and I hated sweating out my blouses during the summer New Jersey Transit commute to South Jersey. I'd wait on the platform—sun beaming, humidity melting—hoping to pile into a crowded train car where the air conditioner worked. The tomboy in me craved jeans, sneakers, and cheap T-shirts. Yet, despite the dress code, the checks were good for someone in their twenties. And I knew having a company like Merrill Lynch on my résumé would impress employers and take me to a respected level.

Now that I was out of school, I switched from working in Merrill Lynch's editorial department to shadowing designers in the art department, where I met Emmanuel. He was a manager and one of the only black men on the job; we naturally gravitated toward each other. With his fine chocolate skin, a tiny gap between his two bottom front teeth, muscles bulging through his suit shirt, and his fresh Jamaican accent, he seemed to move nicely among the powers that be.

"Is that your family?" I asked, glancing at a picture of him standing between a redhead and a little boy with a wild, fuzzy Afro.

"Yeah, that's my wife, Susan, and my son, Weston."

"Do you want more kids?"

"Well, she's actually pregnant now," he said, nodding his head. "How many months?"

"Six."

"Well, congrats, Daddy." I smiled, shaking his hand. "That must be exciting."

"Not really," he said, and he started stroking the back of my palm. "You know, I'm a man."

Nervous yet turned on by the sudden aggression, I suddenly became conscious of his finger working its magic. I slowly moved my hand. "So what does that mean?"

"It means that I have my needs."

"Uh-oh." I laughed. "Sounds like a problem."

"Yeah, well, you're a pretty girl, you don't need to worry about that."

"Worry about what?"

"You know, causing a man problems. I'm sure you know how to handle us."

"And I'm sure you know how to handle a woman." I grinned. "I know what they like."

"I know what *you* like." I felt a wet throbbing in my vagina, as I crossed my legs and looked him over—his eyes, his pecs, the seat of his pants, then back to his eyes again. It had been weeks since I'd had sex. Dexter was gone. Wet dreams were on replay.

A tiny smirk creeped onto Emmanuel's face. I bit the side of my lip and blinked slowly, careful to maintain eye contact. That's all a woman needs to show a man she's interested. Steady eye contact and a smile.

"Ooh, you need to stop," I said, pointing to the computer screen. "Don't you have work to do?"

"I do need to get on it," he said. "You wanna help?"

"Maybe," I said, getting up to walk away.

"Where you going?"

"Lunch," I answered, slightly twisting my hips, knowing he was watching. "I suddenly have a taste for a hot dog."

9

I KNEW BETTER THAN TO GET INVOLVED with a married man. My fear of bad karma haunted me with visions of my future husband cheating on me. Lurking beneath the confidence I exuded in responding to Emmanuel's flirty advances was a woman conflicted between the vulnerability of being fresh out of a relationship with Dexter, raw with the angry pain of love gone wrong, and the hunger for testosterone-filled attention, the yearning to feel the sweetness of a man strung out after sipping the juice oozing from between my legs. And the fact that he was twenty years older than I was made the thought of this particular conquest even more exciting.

Over the next few weeks, the flirting episodes between Emmanuel and me became more intense and frequent. He'd see me at the Xerox machine and make an excuse to brush past, or hand over a stack of papers that needed to be copied. He'd try to take lunch the same hour as I did, and verbally flirt with me the entire meal—how he loved my lips, eyes, body, the way I chewed, and the pinkie I lifted when I drank from a glass. He'd talk to me about smoking weed, and I'd hang around after work so he could drive me to the train station while we puffed a joint together.

Yet after months of foreplay, as summer green turned to autumn gold, I wasn't taking the next step. I'd seen the future path of situations like this. Because my mother had already walked that road with a man named Larry.

The truth is that the times I liked being around my mother were when she had a man. Those were the moments I recall her being happiest. I remember when she brought Larry home. He was a tall, skinny, milk chocolate–complexioned brother. Tiny freckles spotted his nose and a gruff goatee blanketed his chin. He was the only tall man I'd ever known not to play basketball or even like it. Hating the height-inspired stereotype, he chose instead to play with cars. Tinkering in classic rides like 1960s Mustangs and Corvettes, Larry drove a vintage ride with a classic rock music system. I usually knew when he arrived, because I'd hear the loud giggles coming from the back of his throat It sounded like a laugh clogged in a mucusy sinus infection.

Despite sounding of sickness, his humor was contagious, and the jokes made my mother crack up. The anticipation of his coming filled her with delight, lifting the heaviness of life and stuffing it away into a secret baggage claim. She'd fly through the house, humming sweet melodies. And float into the kitchen to whip up a light buttercream frosted cake. Pulling out pots, pans, and special plates, Mom would prepare an elaborately soulful feast of Larry's favorites: golden fried whiting, spicy collard greens, creamy macaroni and cheese, and moist yellow corn bread. She'd slip on heels, squeeze into a fitted dress, curl her hair, retouch her makeup, and head to the door to let Larry in.

"Honey, I'm home!" he'd always say as he walked in with an overstretched grin.

"Hey, Meena!" he shouted, seating himself at the head of the dining room table. A hot plate waited next to a cold beer. "How you doing?"

At first I didn't reply, instead staring at my fork, cheese clinging to my teeth.

"Somebody's talking to you, Meena!" my mother snapped.

"Fine," I answered, cutting my eyes at Larry. "I'm done. I'm going to do my homework."

"It should have already been done," she hissed. "Get on my nerves..."

At the time, I didn't understand the resentment boiling my blood, bouncing from Mom to Larry. I was annoyed by her jaunts in Wonderland, coordinated with his visits. I wondered why she wasn't as happy with me as she was in his presence. She never laughed out loud, eyes closed, head cocked back when we were alone. She never whipped up a holiday-size meal for me. And as relieved as I felt that the abuse and neglect stopped upon Larry's arrivals, I hated the truth. How she would morph into a smiling Stepford wife and then switch back to her evil alter ego the moment he pulled out of the driveway. I understood enough to dare not take my mad Meena world out on Mom. So I found ways to project it onto Larry, mostly through oneword sentences and silence.

It took months until I began warming up to him. Things changed the day he arrived with select company.

"She just jumped inside my car," he said, holding the screen door open. "I don't know her name." Walking outside, I saw a small black and brown dog, peeing on the sidewalk. It looked like a tiny version of a rottweiler, but its tail and ears weren't clipped.

"She must like me," he said, looking at my mother from the side. "I got out to get gas and she just jumped in."

"Yeah, right," Mom said, rolling her eyes with a slight smile.
"It's the truth!"

My mother had always been firmly against having a pet, thinking I wasn't responsible enough. She complained of paws scraping her shiny wooden floors. And pee soaking into the living room rug.

"This dog is not my responsibility, Meena," she said with a furrowed brow. "You have to get up early in the morning to walk her. Do it again after school and before you go to bed. Feed her, wash her, keep her in your room, and in the basement or outside when you're not home. I don't want my house smellin' like dog."

"I can keep her?" I screamed, smiling, chasing the puppy as it scurried into the house. "I'ma name her Lady!"

"And keep it out of my kitchen!" Mom yelled after me.

I scooped up Lady, ran to my bedroom, and caressed her on my bed. I'd wanted a dog since I was three, but never imagined having one while living under my mother's neat-freak roof. I sat back, watching Lady acquaint herself with the room, realizing that I actually liked Larry. He was like God to Mom: when he spoke, clouds scattered, opening the way for sunlight to shine a loving glow upon our hearts, transforming my mother from wicked witch to benevolent peacemaker. I hoped they'd get married. I dreamed of having a real daddy.

Until I overheard a phone call one night.

"When are you coming by? You said you were coming this weekend."

My mother's deep, husky voice was raspy, dragging, lethargically trying to recover from botched heart surgery by Dr. Love. The sound of concerned emotion in high-pitched vocal cords awakened me. So I snuck to her bedroom door and stood stiff as a mannequin to listen. "Larry, will you listen for a minute? I need you to fix my car. I… I…" Her voice drifted into a sob. "What? I don't care what she needs. Acting like you have a wife. You said you were separated."

My mind raced with questions, disbelieving what I'd just heard. Married? Larry? Since when? Had Mom known when they first started? She couldn't have. They seemed like the epitome of perfection. So happy and loving, never arguing. Larry would come home to dinner. She'd sit on his lap, stroking the goatee rooted with gray hairs curling from his chin. He'd crack a corny joke and she'd damn near fall on the floor laughing. I was both confused and sad, wanting to gain answers to my questions while giving hugs to show comfort.

But I didn't want to get slapped for eavesdropping. So I stood in place, stiff by the door, slightly crouched over, sore in my right leg from standing still enough not to make the floor creak.

"You're not going to divorce her, so stop lying. I am so tired of this shit. The lies, the bullshit… I knew what? Uh-uh, don't try and make it like… You know what? Fuck you, Larry! Fuck. You." And she slammed down the phone.

I didn't move. Stuck in shock, too scared to breathe, muscles in my body aching for a stretch. I wanted to hug her. Then I was surprised by a sound I'd never heard before. I could hear the bed squeak as she sat on the side sniffling, trying to muffle depressed moans with a tissue. When the phone rang, I ran back to bed, synchronizing and camouflaging my footsteps with each ringtone.

This breakup went on for about a month, until one Sunday, I walked in the house and saw Larry sitting at the dinner table. Smiling, he and Mom lovingly gazed at each other, like two honeymooners. After dinner, as they washed dishes together, I saw him smack her butt, grab a belt buckle hole, and pull her close to kiss.

I ran upstairs to my bedroom, angry, bothered by questions racing through my brain. The first person I called was Meredith.

"He's back."

"Whaaat?" She stretched out the word, enunciating the *t*. "Did he apologize?"

"Not to me."

"Did your mother say anything about him coming over?" Silence.

"And then they just started making out?"

"*Yes*." This time I enunciated, stressing the *s*, full of surprise.

"That is gross," Meredith said. "I'm sorry, girl…"

I didn't reply. Tears bubbled up, coating my pupils. Confusion glossed my eyes. Betrayal and bewilderment glazed my heart. How dare he act as if everything was okay? While he played house with his part-time wife, leaving broken promises on Lincoln Street. Like the one where he promised to take Lady and me to the park, leaving us to silently cry, staring out the bedroom window, waiting for his car to pull up. Like the lie he told Mom. Stealing her heart. Masking his matrimony. Taking advantage of a young single woman and her child. Larry was the Devil shaped with four legs and a horn between his eyes. He was one of those dog men I'd heard about in family discussions—high on promises, low on reliability, prone to letdowns, and scarce truth. Leading women to a shit-filled destiny: fallen, broken, begging in a dusty cloud of disappointment. His trickery was painful treachery.

That night, after changing into a nightshirt and dozing off, I was suddenly awakened by the faint sound of a woman in pain. I'd always been a light sleeper, often waking to the faraway chirps of birds in trees from the neighbor's lawn. The whimper came in steady intervals, making me sit up still, careful not to move, hoping to make out the sound. I looked at the clock, which read 2:00 a.m., and listened. Every thirty seconds, slight gasps of breath creeping up the steps, under the door, down my spine, curling into chilly goose bumps.

Tiptoeing out my room, I felt the blue, body-length Mickey Mouse T-shirt I was wearing sweep the floor. I tried to squeeze through the crack of my bedroom door without fully opening it, causing the bolts to squeak.

Someone might be hurting Mom. The thought petrified me. Maybe she left the TV on.

I tried to force myself into positive thinking as violent screenshots from horror films like *Friday the Thirteenth* and *Psycho* bounced blots of bloody scenes across my brain.

I stood at the top of the stairs, listening for the moan again, on alert for that sound of illness and pain. Standing on my tiptoes, thinking it might make my footsteps lighter and quieter, I crept halfway down into chilly darkness. Refusing to turn the hallway light on, I strained to see through the living room blackness, managing to make out something that looked like two bodies. As my eyes focused, clearing up the postsleep daze, I knew exactly what I was seeing. The sight made me bite the right side of my mouth and fold up my lips in shock.

There in the darkness of two in the morning, on the floor, next to the sofa, lying faceup on the beige rug, was my mother. She sat twitching and wincing, with nasty farts coming from her ass. She moaned intensely, wiggling, as she opened her legs wide for Larry, who was facedown, slurping out her vagina.

I didn't know what to do but sit on the steps and cry. Pulling at the soft rug comforting my shivers, quietly I wept, sniffing up snot rolling from my nostrils. I used the backs of my hands to wipe the tears, blurring the graphic triple-X scene. I don't know why I didn't run back to my room and lock the door. I just sat there, twelve years old, watching, bawling, and sniffing. My crying became noticeably louder, until I heard my mother call my name.

"Meena," she said through the dark, sitting up, arms crossed over her breasts, looking in my direction. "Meena, come here."

Larry scrambled for his jeans, nasally giggling and grinning as he accidentally placed his foot in the wrong pant leg. He threw my mother her bra.

"Meena," she said.

I could've sworn she was laughing at me, too, a tiny smirk on her face, perhaps straining to find humor in the discomfort and embarrassment.

"Meena…"

But I ran. Crying out loud, rushing up the stairs and into my room. No one followed. No one came to comfort me. No one talked about what I'd seen. And even when I overslept the next morning, I expected my mother to be up screaming at me like she usually did. But when I peeked out my bedroom, her door was shut. Not even the sound of the morning radio blared as usual. Hoping she wouldn't catch me before leaving, I dressed as fast as I could, wolfed down a couple of slices of jelly toast, grabbed my book bag, tiptoed around the spot where I'd seen Mom and Larry doing *it*, and ran out the house to catch the 7:20 bus to school.

Outside, a satisfying cool fall breeze relaxed my hot body as I ran down the block. Happy I'd made it on time. Relieved Mom wasn't able to catch my sleeping late. Haunted by visions I wasn't ready to speak on. I was embarrassed to have seen it, ashamed for not stopping myself from watching. Swearing to tell no one; perhaps Mom and I made the same promise, because to this day, she has never talked to me about that night.

That memory continued to haunt me even as I flirted with Emmanuel. But I wasn't Mom. I was better. Smarter. Careful to keep a wall around my heart, have fun, and not fall victim to stupidity. The curse on my family had showed up in a way I refused to repeat.

10

MEN ALWAYS WANT what they can't have. Women are the same. But for guys, withholding sex becomes like a fun tunnel-vision game of hide-and-go-seek-to-conquer-the-pussy. Emmanuel was on a mission to win me. He was funny. Sweet. Paid for lunch daily. But the intent look in his eye never changed.

"You need to come see my house."

"Why? You want me to have dinner with your wife?"

"No, she works," he said. "I want you to see where I live."

"Why?"

"You know why."

"I don't know…"

"Yes, you do. We're both adults here. You know the situation." I looked at him, impressed and turned on by the aggression.

"I'll get some ganja, straight from Jamaica. None of that yard shit. We'll pass by my spot, smoke, and I'll give you a ride home."

"I don't want anybody from work seeing me leave with you."

"Well, we can do it after the company holiday party next Friday," he said. "There'll be so many people that nobody will notice us leaving together."

"Maybe," I said with a smirk on my face. Our eyes met, and I felt the return of the inner leg throb. It felt as if the walls were vibrating, pulsating. I could feel stickiness in my panties. I wanted

Emmanuel now. When I crossed my legs, my shoe brushed his foot. He smiled back, looking down at my chest.

"Hello, Meena."

"Hey, Emmanuel."

Caught off guard, I jumped when my tender flirty moment was interrupted by Regina and Joan. Regina was my supervisor and head of Merrill Lynch's publishing department. Joan was her second in command.

"Oh, uh." I coughed a little, after nearly choking on the ice I was sucking. "Hey."

"Is Emmanuel teaching you a lot about the art department?" Regina asked.

Joan added, "He's one of the best."

"Oh, yeah. QuarkXPress and Photoshop. I still have to figure out how to use those programs, but I've learned a lot by watching."

"Well, Emmanuel, you have to see to it that Meena learns all the ins and outs," said Regina. "She's a fast learner."

"I noticed. I'm lucky to have her in the art department. Maybe we can get you on a computer tomorrow. One of the guys will be out."

"Okay," I said with a smile. "That would be cool."

"We were just about to leave," Emmanuel said. "You ladies want this table?"

"Oh, yes, thanks," said Joan. "See you two upstairs."

"Meena?" Regina motioned toward me and I quivered inside. I knew I'd been found out. I felt a reprimand coming on. "I left some things for you to proof in your inbox. I need it done by five."

Relieved by the innocuous request, I got up with Emmanuel and our trays. Dumped them and walked upstairs. But not together. I headed for the bathroom. He beelined back to his desk. And for the rest of the day, all I could think about was him—inside me, throwing my body on a bed, pulling down my thong, and ramming me hard from the back.

The days until the holiday party ticked by slower than the hands on a broken clock. We hadn't gone to lunch together since our run-in with Joan and Regina. He'd been at a weeklong art conference, recruiting new designers. So while I finished the brain-dead work of making copies, I daydreamed about my visit to his house. Visualizing which color underwear I'd slip off. Reminding myself to buy a matching bra. Shaking the nasty thoughts out of my brain until boredom allowed them to creep back in.

On the magical day, I took a cab with a few coworkers to the day party at an indoor sports park. The theme was California Christmas, and it was unlike any shindig I'd ever been to. Tents were pitched all over the venue crowded with hundreds of people, balloons, clowns, sand, volleyball nets, grills, and long buffet tables filled with seemingly unlimited free food and drinks.

At first I didn't see Emmanuel. I looked around amid the flood of folks, feeling like a raisin drowning in milk.

"Who are you looking for, Meena?" A higher-up drone, Sally Donahue, was sipping on a hot coffee. Her blond hair with red highlights brought out the hints of rouge painted atop her cheekbones. "Do you know people in any of the other Merrill Lynch departments?"

"No, just looking," I said, still surveying. "This is really nice."

"Actually, it sucks. The same food, same thing every year, but

they make us go. It's the politically correct thing to do," she said, making quote marks in the air. "I couldn't even get my husband to come this time. He thinks everyone is fake."

I laughed politely, still looking around for Emmanuel.

"Our department tables are this way," she said, pointing to the left. "Section forty-two."

I followed her to the tent, and as we got closer, Emmanuel came into sight, sitting on a bench, eating a hot dog. Relish oozed out of his mouth as he bit slowly and smiled when he spotted me walking closer.

"You're my partner in the obstacle course," he said, wiping the corners of his lips. "I can tell you're in shape. Look at those legs."

"I used to be. Don't know about now," I said. "But I'm wearing heels. Wish someone had warned me. I like to play."

"I bet you do," he said, looking me up and down. "I've seen your pretty toes. Do it barefoot."

"Um… I just got a pedicure, so I'll be running slowly."

"That's all right, I got you." He leaned toward me and whispered, "I'll give you a nice foot massage and touch-up later."

The rest of the day was a bit of a blur. I do remember being horny, drinking bucket-size cups of beer and eating seconds and thirds of chicken, hot dogs, hamburgers, and potato salad. Each time I got a nod of approval from E. "I like a girl who eats," he said, laughing. "I love that you're not shy about anything."

"I don't know about that," I replied, slowly cutting my barbecued chicken into small pieces before placing them into my mouth, conscious of his studying me, aware that I needed to appear delicate, demure. "Maybe I'm shy about some things…"

"Yeah? Like what?"

"Like when the lights come on."

"I got a nice dark playroom I can show you."

"I bet you do…"

I did a lot of smiling, and sweating, playing volleyball like a competitive medal was involved. Like I was vying for prize money. I jumped up to the net height and hit the ball aggressively, just to show off my athletic prowess to coworkers and, most of all, Emmanuel. I could feel the alcohol beneath his gaze, sticking to me like the sweaty company T-shirt they made us wear, peeling off my chest. He anticipated each move, salivating for the next muscle flex, pining, which made him miss balls bouncing his way. Pausing to give a cocky nod in my direction, the ball served from my team hit him with a blindside smack to the face. He bent over, holding his nose, seemingly expecting blood to run from the nostril. Amid a sea of coworker laughter, he sat out the rest of the game, watching me, again, with a smile. In the end, I walked to where Emmanuel sat and plopped down.

"Ooh, I drank too much," I said, taking a sip of something he handed me. "I don't even like volleyball."

"You ready to make a move out of here? I got that smoke in the car."

Our eyes met. And this time my mouth creeped into a mischievous smile.

"And you know," he said, staring at my feet. "You still got that foot massage coming."

"Yeah, but I stink now," I said, patting a paper towel to my forehead. "And my hair is a mess."

"Oh, that's all right. You smell good to me." He gave me another tissue and a cold beer. "And you look beautiful, natural. Plus, you can use the bathroom at my apartment if you want."

I didn't know about that. Even through my inebriated daze, I still preferred a room at the Hilton. "We're going to your crib?"

"Well, yeah, how am I supposed to give you a massage? In the car?"

"Yeah. But what about your wife?"

"She's at work," he said, getting up and motioning me to come with him. "Don't worry about anything, it's cool."

The ride from the company party to his apartment was awkward. Quiet. Bumpy. E and I said nothing as he drove through the streets. We dared not glance at each other as he turned down suburban avenues with meticulously manicured lawns dotted with Christmas decorations. The sidewalks looked newly cemented. The homes were pristine with upper-class statement. As he drove farther into the neighborhood and turned the corner, we eased into a new development of condos. Streets curved and circled until he pulled into a slim driveway.

"This is where you live?"

"Yup," he answered, turning off the motor. The garage door closed behind us. "Welcome to my humble abode."

Now that we had arrived, his house seemed so real. Suddenly the wet fantasy petrified me. I stumbled out the car, looking around to see whether we were being watched. Butterflies fluttered, flaming up a fire of gassy bubbles in my intestines. With my heart pounding in my throat, I squeezed my butt cheeks and took a deep breath so I could focus and not pass gas. We walked up to his door, he slid in the key, unlocked two bolts, and stepped through. I slowly followed, nervously making chitchat.

"So this is where you live?"

"Yup."

"How long?"

"Five years."

"You like it?"

"Sometimes."

"Are the walls thin?"

"No."

"Are your neighbors nosy?"

"Some." He paused and gave me a searching look after closing the door behind him. "You sound like a reporter. Are you doing an investigative story on me?"

"No," I said, with a quavering chuckle. "I just…"

"Do you want my Social Security number?"

"No," I said, before taking a deep breath and exhaling. "I just think I'm nervous."

"Why?"

"You sure your wife won't come home?"

"I already answered that question," he said, flicking on the light to his living room. "She's out of town. Come here."

His voice was inviting. I walked toward him and he pulled me close, lifting my chin up with a finger, looking me in the eye. "You're safe," he said, before kissing me on the lips. "Relax. Okay?" Then he pecked me on the forehead.

I smiled like a five-year-old, whispering, "Okay."

"I'm about to roll something to make you feel better. Get comfortable. Take your shoes off."

Emmanuel's condo was cozy, with a warm color scheme of grays and burgundys splattered across the room. An L-shaped, smoke-hued couch framed a small mahogany wooden table that sat atop a carpet adorned by brushstrokes of merlot and evening fog tones. The carpet was thin and matted, as if a day care of kids had spilled breakfast, lunch, and dinner atop its fibers. Along the walls were tall bookcases and an entertainment center holding a mixture of novels, tiny African statues, diplomas, and frames crowded with photos. I stumbled around and stopped at a collage of family pictures showing a smiling Emmanuel sitting with his son next to an overweight white woman with stringy red hair.

"Her name is Susan, right?"

"Yup," he said, sitting on the couch rolling a blunt, carefully picking out the seeds from the weed. "That's Sue."

"How many months along was she when you took this photo?"

"Oh, she wasn't pregnant in that picture," he said, laughing. "You know we like big girls in Jamaica."

"Oh, okay," I said, a touch mystified. "Ain't a thing big about me."

"Yeah, but you're sexy. Those eyes…" His words trailed off as I turned to watch him staring at me while slowly using his tongue to lick and seal the tightly rolled paper around sticky green marijuana. I sat down next to him as he lit up, took a few pulls, and passed the blunt to me.

"You should let me give you"—he started coughing out smoke—"a shotgun."

Nodding in agreement, I passed the blunt and watched Emmanuel slowly place the lit end of the cigar into his mouth. He curled his tongue away from the ashes as I placed my mouth on the opposite side. He exhaled, I inhaled, and after a few seconds backed up. As I took in the smoke, its ecstasy of herbs floated me to the ceiling. Smoke drifted out my nose and what seemed like my ears. Suddenly, I couldn't bear the overwhelming fumes and began coughing out the remaining smoke.

"Let me get you a drink," he said, getting up. "This is the good stuff. Straight from Kingston, baby."

"Thanks," I said, still coughing, choking on my saliva, sounding like an old man with bronchitis. "I'm okay."

Emmanuel cracked up as he walked to the kitchen and pulled a bottle of Guinness from the fridge. I sat still, embarrassed, eyeing the front door, wanting to leave and at the same time squeezing my vagina, trying to suck in what flowed with every thought of kissing him. I closed my eyes and took a deep breath as I felt him approach. Then it began. Softness. Nothing but his moist lips on mine. They felt sticky, yummy, sweet. The flow between my legs grew as he lifted up my shirt and sucked my neck, then my left breast and right nipple. He stopped to take a look. But I kept my eyes closed. Too nervous to make eye contact. Insecure about letting him see the weird faces I made in the midst of pleasure with the lights on. I could hear the elastic of the plastic snap around his genitals. He grabbed my legs, pulled them forward, and within seconds was inside me. *Mmmm...* It felt so good. Hard and thrashing. I could hear the juices mixing. I felt out of my mind. Completely high and groggy. Mad that I'd smoked so much, upset that I'd not kept my head and been more focused on staying sober so I could enjoy the moment. An internal conversation clogged up my brain. *Wait. I didn't want this. He's married. What am I doing? Fuck. I drank too much. Oh, God, this shit feels so good. Fuck me harder.* Dizzy, spinning like a sexual vacuum, sucking secretions and hairs and body and vagina and pelvis all in one. He knocked a family photo down while flipping me over. And then I felt sick.

"Stop," I said softly. He kept going.

"*Stop*," I said in a louder whisper.

"Come on, baby. This feels good."

"I feel sick."

He dropped my legs, staring at me as I slumped on the couch. Head limp. Eyes shut as I tried to stretch them open and lift my head. But I was too high.

"I'm sorry," I said, dizzily shaking from side to side. "I'm fucked up."

"Yeah, it's good," he said, rubbing my thighs. "Like your pussy. So tight."

I wasn't feeling like that at all. "I think I need to go home."

"Why, baby? We're just getting started," he whined. "You want another beer? Take another sip."

My eyes closed and I nearly dozed off. But I fought, holding my lids open with all of the mind strength I could muster. Something kept me awake, pushing through that super-intoxicated, spinning blur from a few puffs of weed.

"No," I said, stumbling for my bag. "Take me home."

"But I bought this weed for us."

"I'm not feeling well."

"You can take a nap here."

"No," I said, more certain now. "I need to go home. I'm going to throw up."

He sucked his teeth as his car keys jingled to the tune of something inaudibly said under his breath. The only thing I made out was "Come on. Let's go."

I could feel the thick tension of disappointment sucking the air out of the room. I stopped to pick up the Disneyland photo we'd knocked over, carefully placing it back on the mahogany coffee table next to the couch we'd had sex on. As Emmanuel opened the front door, fresh oxygen awakened my diminished consciousness enough to see him no longer looking at me like the fly young vixen he'd craved the past few weeks. When he pulled into the train station, he didn't turn toward me or say good-bye. When I got out, he was staring straight ahead. I felt guilty, embarrassed, like a failure at home wrecking.

On Monday, I called in sick. Tuesday, I dodged Emmanuel and his calls to my extension. Wednesday was the same. Thursday he confronted me.

"You okay?" He slid into my cubicle, whispering, "You seem off."

"I'm good."

"You sure?"

"Yup."

"Are you mad at me?"

"Nope," I answered, eyes focused on the computer screen.

"Well, let's go to lunch."

"I'm busy," I said, still not turning toward him.

"Okay," he said, a sulk in his voice. "I hope you feel better."

For the rest of the year, and into the new one, I found a way to never speak to Emmanuel again.

"Well, that was weird," Meredith said that weekend as I told her what had happened. She stuffed a half-smoked blunt into her car ashtray and opened a bag of Cheez Doodles. "He still wants you, right?"

"Yeah, I still get constant e-mails from him, but he's married," I said, opening my bag of gummy worms. "That's my first and last married man. I can't do that karma. I already got a family curse to deal with 'cause of some infidelity bullshit. And I wish I didn't have to go into work on Monday."

"Yo, could you please stop with the man-curse talk," she said, rolling her eyes. "Words are powerful. Words manifest. Your birthday is in a few weeks, wish for something nice. Wish to break that shit."

11

WHILE MOST TWENTY-FIVE-YEAR-OLDS celebrated a quarter-century with huge bashes, immaculate celebrations, defining vacations, and spectacular fireworks, all I wanted to do on the second day of February, my birthday, was think. Plot the future. Plan my life. Change the cycle. I gathered a stack of old magazines from the garage and began cutting out pictures and words that symbolized the life I wanted and pasted them onto a visionary poster. I'd read about making one in *Essence* magazine. How seeing images of what you want in life helps manifest them. I cut out tiny pictures of career women like Oprah and female authors, with bestseller lists coloring my poster. The words "Confidence," "Love," and "Power" curved around cutouts of married couples, smiling families, and wedding dresses. In giant letters across the top I'd pasted the word "Happiness."

I taped the finished art project to the wall next to my bed, arranging it in the middle of pictures scattered about that represented my past. Glancing over the old-school photos, my eyes rested on a shot from high school. I remembered the day, crowded at a cafeteria table, cheesing in B-boy stances for Meredith's brand-new Polaroid camera. In the picture I was standing back to back, arms crossed, with Michael Tubman, my high school freshman crush.

School was a peaceful sanctuary for me, the only place where I felt free from the constant carping at home. Between books, classes, notes, and bells, I surrounded myself with friends to channel my personal focus with gossip, jokes, and crushes on boys. I'd lost my virginity freshman year at fourteen years old. In retrospect, I was too young and immature to deal with the psychological repercussions of having sex. But at the time, on that specific day, it seemed right.

"Meena!" my friends shouted like a chorus as I arrived at our table, third from the right, next to the water fountain, across from the salad bar, in the cafeteria of building two.

"Hey, y'all, what's up?" I responded, still sluggish from the six o'clock alarm. I'd been up till after midnight talking to my second best friend, captain of the varsity girls track team, Doreen Robertson, about the same thing we discussed every day: boys, clothes, the single mothers we wanted to trade in.

"Wake up!" she snapped, before stuffing a cream cheese–filled bagel inside her mouth. I always wanted a body like Doreen's. Full 34C breasts. Jeans fitted around a plump booty. I had to tighten my belt into the last hole, waistband gathering up, just to get the fit that Doreen wore so naturally. The guys loved her.

"Wake up, so you can get your man," said Meredith, popping up from under the table. Meredith Benjamin had been my first best friend since she moved to town in the fourth grade. Always seated next to each other in homeroom, we became close because our initials were both MB. We even joined the track team together. She ran the third leg on the 4 x 400 meter relay team. I was anchor.

"Look to the east," Doreen said.

I glanced to the left and saw Carl Murphy. Head buried in a book. Sitting at a table alone. He looked up briefly as our eyes met before nervously stuffing his head back inside the pages. He'd have been a cutey if he wasn't so weird.

"That's west, girl. East, I said. East. Look to your right," Doreen said. "Not toward the geek."

I glanced to the right and my eyes met Michael Tubman's. He stretched his neck past his boys, nodding toward me. I nervously smiled back, before turning away to inspect every item in my purse.

"I love him," I said, with a Kool-Aid grin. "Is he still staring at me?"

Doreen's eyes popped out. "Girl, fix your hair, fix your hair!" She let out a boy-group-fanatic squeal. "He's walking over!"

But I couldn't find my brush. Rummaging through the tissues and papers that clogged my purse, I pulled out a hot pink comb just as he approached.

"Hey, Meena," I heard him say behind me. I could see Meredith and Doreen stretch their eyes wide as I turned to face him.

"Oh hey," I said, doing my best to feign a nonchalant tone. Meredith discreetly pulled the comb out of my hand. "What's up?"

He passed a piece of lined paper folded up into a small square. My name was written in red ink across the middle. "Let me know what you think when you read it, okay?"

"I, um…" I managed, glancing at the tiny package. "Okay…"

"I'll see you in Mrs. Johnson's class," he said before walking away. I opened the letter.

Dear Meena,
You looked pretty yesterday. I forgot to tell you that I think you look nice in pink. Call me tonight. I don't get home till after 7p cuz of practice. But my parents are out of town. Maybe you can come over since you only live around the corner. Let me know.

Michael

The table erupted into gasps.

"Oh my God," Doreen and Meredith said simultaneously. "What's it say?"

"He wants me to come over tonight," I screamed. "He said his parents are out of town."

It was like déjà vu: the table broke into gasps again.

I'd had a crush on Michael since the first day of ninth grade. Twinkling straight teeth. Chiseled chin. Long eyelashes. He was one of the few freshmen, like me, who'd managed to make varsity. He'd done it playing football. I was the occasional track star. Sharing Mrs. Johnson's first period science class together, we'd grown to know each other after being paired for a lab experiment. Homework sessions turned to long talks about life and dreams, including his hope to play for the New York Giants. He was funny and chivalrous, pulling out chairs and opening doors. He referred to me as "Beautiful." I'd never had anyone say that about me. I found myself fantasizing the entire last marking period of school, hoping to be girlfriend to the most popular boy in the ninth grade. Hoping we'd go to the same college, marry after graduation, and I'd have baby boys who'd grow up to play ball just like their daddy.

His letter, folded up tightly into a tiny Chinese star, proved that the dream was manifesting. He was finally ready to ask me out.

"What are you gonna wear?" Doreen asked. "I have to do your hair. Oh my God, are you really going over there?"

"Why are you rhyming?" Meredith asked, making us all crack up. "What the hell?"

"I don't know if I can go," I said, shaking my head. "You know my mom won't let me go to a boy's house."

"Well, you gotta," said Doreen. "I mean, this is Michael Tubman."

"Yeah, but this is Meena's mother we're talking about," Meredith chimed in. "Hitler in a skirt."

"So she needs to plan her escape from concentration camp," Doreen replied. "It can't be that hard. I sneak out all the time."

"That's 'cause your mom is cool," Meredith said, sipping the last of our shared orange juice. "You're lucky. We are not."

I gazed at Michael's letter. *But my parents are out of town. Maybe you can come over.* I kept rereading that letter, forward and backward. Michael Tubman wanted *me* to visit his house. Wow.

The loud chime of the bell ringing for homeroom slapped me back into reality.

"So you going?" Doreen asked, zipping up her backpack. "Are you gonna finally do *it*?"

"You don't have to do *it* if you don't want to, Meena," Meredith stressed. "Don't let Doreen pressure you."

"I'm not pressuring her," she snapped. "I'm just saying she needs to get on it now while the opportunity presents itself. Because if she doesn't, somebody else will."

Doreen nodded toward Michael's table, where Sheila Anderson, the class whore, was in overt touchy mode. She grabbed him tight, forcing a hug. As he put his arms around her, she rubbed his hand and eased it over her butt. He smiled and laughed while his friends clapped with approval.

"Told you," Doreen said to me. "Don't lose your chance trying to be Miss Goody Two-shoes."

"Who the hell is Miss Goody Two-shoes? And why do people say that? Who is she?" Meredith asked as she handed back my comb. "Come on, Meena, let's be out. Not only are you always late, but you always do the right thing. And you'll do it this time."

So that night, I planned my escape into Michael's arms.

11:00 p.m...

"Good night!" I screamed downstairs, making sure Mom knew I was officially going to bed. "I said, good night!"

"Did you brush your teeth?"

"Yeeees," I said, shivering with the shaky vowel. "Good night."

"How many times are you going to say good night, Meena?"

"Um... I love you!"

The sound of a metal spoon mixing sugar inside porcelain was my cue that Mom was getting ready for bed. A cup of chamomile was the last thing she drank while watching the evening news. Its warm flavors relaxed her mind and tired pupils enough to pull them into a deep, six-hour sleep. She never made it to the end of the broadcast without snoring.

I pulled the covers over me and stared at the ceiling, waiting for Mom's bedroom door to close. After twenty minutes, I began to sweat. The mixture of cheap polyester comforter fibers, unsure nerves, and the pink sweater Aunt Connie had bought me for Christmas made beads build on my chest, dampen my forehead, and moisten my neck. I pushed back the blanket, fanning myself with the sheets that felt like a used baby wipe. As soon as I heard the closing click of Mom's door, I hopped out of bed, sprayed on Victoria's Secret body spray—under the arms, over the chest, between the legs—and grabbed the plush Macy's Snoopy I'd gotten after the Thanksgiving parade. Positioning it on the pillow, I hoped that if Mom did walk into my room, she'd be too tired to see it wasn't me. Just in case, I took my night scarf, tied it around Snoopy's head, and threw the covers atop him so the navy fabric with tiny yellow flowers peeked over the blanket.

Butterflies prepared to take flight as I hopped onto the radiator, opened my window, pulled up the screen, and climbed out onto the edge of the roof. He must've been a descendant of Harriet Tubman, because Michael Tubman inspired me to escape for freedom. I could feel his warm hands wrapped around my body like it was a football, with a hug so intensely passionate and tight my bones melted. I turned back to pull down the window, glancing at the clock on my dresser: 11:42 p.m. I told Michael I'd be there around eleven thirty. But I couldn't have moved faster. The fear of Mom's wrath paralyzed me. I could see a year of invisible chains banning me from touching the TV, telephone, or going to the mall. But I had to take a stand, on a roof in Jersey, at midnight, in the cold suburban dark evening, with a patch of bushy grass to break my fall for love.

I hadn't realized that the jump from the second floor was so high. I hadn't figured out how to explain a broken leg if I happened to land wrong. But I needed to get going. So I sat on the edge of the roof, slowly, steadily, nudging my butt forward, toward the edge, till finally I had nowhere to go but down.

"One, two, three," I whispered to myself. But I didn't move, gulping, staring down at the hard, bone-killing ground. "Okay, I can do this," I said out loud. "One, two, three!"

On the last number I jumped, past the kitchen window, into the garden, atop the begonias, onto my feet, with a slight roll back to my butt. I felt like Catwoman—limber, agile, sneaky, fast. In seconds, I was up running to the side of the house, dusting the leaves off my ten-speed bike and pedaling like the mama police were in pursuit. I never looked back, speeding down the dark block, breezing through the late-night spring air. Free from Deena Mitchell's restrictions. Free to be me.

That emancipation carried me away during the short, five-minute ride while I imagined what Michael and I would do: how he'd grab me, pull my head back, caress my neck, kiss me twice, like on an episode of *The Young and the Restless*.

When I got to Michael's, I hopped off my pink Huffy ten-speed and sized up his stereotypical suburban lawn. A white fence outlined in tiny yellow tulips. A fountain with an angel spraying water from its mouth. A basketball hoop at the end of the driveway. The butterflies began to fill my right and left shoulders, fussing, whispering in my ear. *What are you doing here, Meena? Why did you sneak out? You should go home before Mom wakes up.*

But as soon as I was ready to turn around and head home, Michael opened the door. He was smiling, and his dimples twinkled, adding a sparkle to his movie-star teeth.

"Hey, Meena!" he said, standing with a phone to his ear. "I thought you changed your mind."

I paused, unsure of what to say, nervous and embarrassed by his charm and forthrightness. "Your hair looks nice."

"This? Oh, the wind was crazy…" I suddenly found the ground, the most fascinating sight in the world. "But thanks."

"You can come in, ya know," he said with a giggle. "I mean, unless you're leaving."

"Um…" I stammered, tiptoeing through the doorway, nervously looking over my shoulder. "No…"

I stepped into the porch, and he guided me through a huge family room with a black leather couch in front of a movie screen–size TV with ESPN blasting. Wedding pictures adorned the coffee table. Family photos of him, his mother, and his father at a fair, wearing matching sweatshirts. A group shot of about twenty people wearing T-shirts that read "Tubman Family Reunion."

Michael grabbed my hand and led me to his bedroom. It was decorated with a mixture of mahogany and blue accents. His Pop Warner football trophies aligned wall shelves, next to plaques, certificates, footballs, and NFL jerseys from the Giants. He walked me to the bed. "You look really pretty," he said as we sat down. "I like the way you look in pink."

"Thanks," I said, digging in my tiny purse. I pulled out a tissue and squeezed it in my hand. "Um, you have a nice room."

"Uh-huh," he said, moving closer to me, grabbing my hand. "My mom decorated it. She's good at that kinda stuff."

"So, what have you been doing?"

"Who, me?" He nudged a few inches closer, playing with my hand. "Waiting for you."

Then he kissed me. But I didn't move, stiff in shock, letting his lips do the maneuvering. Letting him slip his tongue into my mouth. Letting him run his hand up under my sweater and over my white lace bra onto my breasts. He squeezed them hard. But I didn't complain. This was what I wanted. I was going to be his girlfriend. With his other hand, he squeezed my other breast and pushed me down on the bed, kissing me and grinding. I felt him playing with my bra. Desperately trying to unfasten it. After long seconds of maneuvering, he gave up. And I felt him unbuttoning my pants, pulling down the zipper and slipping his hand under my panties. He rubbed my vagina, petting its soft virginal opening. Next thing I knew, my jeans were down and he was inside me. Burning. Pain. Like something rubbing hard on dry, broken skin. The hurt was unbearable. I gasped and tried to hold in the whimper. I didn't want him to know this was my first time. I didn't want him to realize I didn't know how to do it, that it felt like my flesh was tearing apart, that I wanted to cry.

"You okay?" he whispered.

"Uh-huh," I said, lying there, letting him push deeper inside.

He felt so big, like a tree trunk squeezing into an ant hole. I squirmed, trying to feign enjoyment, but the pain…

"Okay, stop," I begged. "Stop."

"You all right?"

"I have to go to the bathroom."

"You okay?"

"Yeah," I said, pulling up my panties. "I just gotta go real quick." Stepping inside the bathroom, I looked in the mirror. Hair a mess.

Face twisted from the hurt of each movement. When I checked my underwear, I could see blood in the seat; tiny specks stained the middle. The burning sensation between my legs inflamed my body as I peed; I held in the urge to scream, closing my eyes to hide from reality. No one ever told me sex felt this way. I thought it was supposed to be an experience that floated bodies above beds, into clouds, and across the heavens. But it was more like a torturous tearing of flesh. Right then I decided: that was my first and last time.

The next day, I limped to school. As much as I tried not to, despite the bowlegged feeling of a large crater drilled between my legs. But the soreness I felt lingered from the night before, and not just in my vagina but in my heart and head, accented with a fleeting feeling of shameful embarrassment.

"Sooooo, did you talk to Michael?" asked Doreen, smiling hard. "You go to his crib?"

"Oh, I don't know, girl. I didn't even talk to him last night," I said, looking through my book bag for something, anything. "He was at practice pretty late."

"Why are you standing like that?" Meredith sat eyeing me before getting up out her seat. "You look... crooked."

"Crooked how?"

"Like this," she said, mocking my stance, likening it to that of a constipated hunchback. "Did you fall again running to the bus stop?"

"Ooh, I remember that!" Doreen screamed, laughing. "Remember when she fell running from her dog in those white tights! And then it grabbed her purse and ran down the street?"

Meredith and Doreen busted out laughing.

"I'm good. Thank you for asking, *stupids*," I said, rolling my eyes. "I... just... hit my knee this morning."

"You are so clumsy, *damn*." Doreen pulled out a compact to comb her hair. "Better not let Michael know that. He likes them model-looking girls. You could be one, but you need to learn how to walk, instead of tripping all over the place. And you need to put some makeup on. How come you don't wear makeup?"

"I can't be a model. I'm too short."

"You don't have to be tall to be a model, Meena," Meredith added. "You could do catalogs. You're pretty, you got the look. All skinny and everything. Long neck. Nice smile."

"Whatever," I replied, attempting to slowly sit, before feeling the pain of the squat and deciding to stand. "I'ma go to the bathroom."

"Good. When you come back, be off your period," snapped Doreen. "Crankiness doesn't look good on you."

I turned to walk toward the girls' room when my eyes met Michael's. He turned away quickly. During Mrs. Johnson's class, he did the same, rushing out of the classroom before I could speak

to him. I wondered whether he was embarrassed, too. Perhaps he
didn't know how to talk about it either. So after lunch, I decided to
go to his locker. As I limped down the hallway, I saw a congrega-
tion of the football team standing next to him. The closer I got, the
more they snickered. I smiled at Michael as I walked up.

"Hey," I said, smiling. "What's up?"

"Oh, what's up?" he murmured, not even looking at me. "Yo,
I'ma talk to you later."

"Um, okay," I said, watching him walk away. His boy Rex put a
heavy arm around me. "So you gonna let Michael hit it again?" He
smiled hard, the gap between his teeth whistling an air of unsaid
words that read across a devious smirk.

"What?" I looked up at him, pushing his oversize bicep away.
"Get off me."

"Don't play stupid. I'm his boy. I know what happened," Rex
said, removing his arm from around my shoulder. "You did a
booty call. It's cool. All the girls do it. Besides, you know what they
say about girls who don't have their daddies around. I know you
couldn't help it."

I glanced back at Michael and found a smug look of triumph
on his face.

"Trust me. I understand," Rex continued, pulling out a notebook and pencil. "What's your number?"

I turned to say something but couldn't muster it up. Instead I
speed-walked away, into the school library, where the only other
person I noticed, hiding in an aisle, was Carl Murphy. I tiptoed
past him, sitting in the comic book section.

He glanced up. "Hey, Meena."

Holding back tears, biting my lip, I gave a little nod. As I
whisked away I faintly heard him say, "I like your dress…"

But I couldn't hear any words of praise. Ashamed, embarrassed, praying I wouldn't develop a "reputation" like some of the
other girls who'd slept with football players at school, I stayed hiding in the library for the rest of the day, reading astrology books

on Michael's two-faced sign of Gemini. Relieved that spring break began the next day. I called Michael three times over vacation. But the asshole never called or spoke to me again.

⚬⌒⚬

All these years later, as I sat remembering my first time having sex, sad thoughts of that painful past made me rip the picture with Michael off my bedroom wall and trash it. Then the phone rang.

"Happy birthday! Why are you awake?" Meredith asked on the other end. "Thought you'd be sleeping in since you took your special day off. It's snowing outside. Good day to just stay in bed."

"Thank you. But I'm not awake because I want to be," I answered, shoving the picture deep in the garbage. "Mom woke me up making unnecessary noise this morning. I feel like she did it on purpose."

"You and your mother…" Meredith said. "Was she talking to herself again?"

"Yeah, about her and Aunt Connie. They always fight."

"You all should go to family therapy."

"Yeah, okay." I laughed. "Like they'd talk about their issues to a professional."

"I think they might talk to me. I'd serve magic brownies and write a prescription of a dime bag of weed so they all could just smoke together, laugh, and love and calm down."

"What?" My face was twisted up, looking at the clock. "It's ten a.m. Are you high?"

"Girl… brownies. I had some last night. I mean, I made them for you. And I sampled some. And man, they just stay in your system forever."

We paused for a second of silence before cracking up together. Meredith always made me feel better. Like life was to be enjoyed and laughed at. Like giggling at yourself and taking a deep breath were essential keys to sanity. Like everything would be all right.

Growing up, she was the only one who ever said that: "Everything is going to be all right." She was the sister a lonely, only child like me had always wanted. She was my support and backup to the bullshit of life. She was my conscience and voice of reason even when I didn't listen. As she placed me on hold to run to the bathroom, I glanced at her smiling picture from last summer's family reunion, surrounded by my cousins; she fit right in with the crew: Bernard, Bishop, Tommy, Winnie, and me. Meredith was the one who suggested we all take a walk that day. It was during that family walk when I realized how deep the curse ran.

⚬⚯⚬

Escaping from the reunion, we'd taken off toward a dead end that led to a short path, looping around the perimeter of a lake. Across a tiny bridge was a recreation area packed with kids on swings, a crowded basketball court, and families splashing in the swimming pool. We sat on a bench, watching an old lady throw slices of bread at pigeons.

"Hey, have you guys heard of some curse on the family?" I asked, watching a little girl with braided pigtails bouncing atop her daddy's shoulders. "Some man curse we're supposed to have?"

"Oh, hell yeah," said Bernard. "Mom talks about it all the time." He looked at Bishop, who nodded his head in agreement. "She says that's why my dad cheated on her."

Bernard and Bishop's father, Jonathan, was a cop with the Philadelphia Police Department. After they were born, Aunt Cece pushed for marriage. But when Jonathan finally agreed, she hired a private investigator to conduct her version of premarital counseling. Hiring a friend who had once worked for the Philly PD, his inside sources found out that Jonathan was sleeping with a female cop on the force. "Well, I don't know about a curse. My dad says it's a bullshit excuse for being single," said Winnie. "He says the reason why so many women in this family have no man is because they're too mean and angry. Too hard. He said they're all looking for a man to make them happy."

"Haaa!" Tommy let out a loud, drunken laugh that made him stumble to catch the fence before he fell.

"Before my dad died, he said he felt sorry for the women in the family," Tommy said, dusting himself off. His words suddenly seemed more sober than ever. "He said that even though he didn't get along with his sister, Grandma Fey, he felt sorry they were all alone. I remember him saying that it was strange how all of his female cousins and aunts never married and would get into a relationship with a man who abused them. If he didn't beat or cheat, he'd usually up and die before marrying them."

"That's crazy," I said under my breath. "I didn't know about the dying part. But now I'm freaked out thinking about that guy Aunt Connie was supposed to marry, until he was killed a week before the wedding by a stray bullet."

We all shook our heads in unison.

"Ooh, and you heard about one of the Camden cousins? I think her name is Diane?" Winnie asked, looking around for someone to recognize which cousin she was talking about. No one knew. "Anyway, she had to get her tubes tied and she can't have babies 'cause some guy gave her an STD and she didn't know."

"Damn," said Bishop and Bernard in unison.

"Maybe the curse is true," said Tommy with a little giggle. "But it do be mean women in this family. Like you, Meena, lookin' at me mean all the time. Haaaa!"

I caught myself giving him a repugnant look, nose wrinkled, smelling the nasty aroma of nonsense coming from his mouth. My face only softened when I realized everyone was staring at me, stuck on the verge of laughing.

∽•∾

"Yeah, I learned a lot about you and your family that day," Meredith said. "It explained why you think the way you do. Date the guys you do. Oh! And speaking of dating someone. You know who I saw the other day?" she said excitedly. "Joey Williams."

After losing my virginity to Michael, I stayed away from boys, especially him, for the next two years. By the eleventh grade, I'd decided I wanted an older, more mature boy, Joey Williams. A senior, he went to the alternative school for bad kids after fighting got him expelled from everywhere else in the district. After passing each other while walking home from the bus stop, we realized this shared route was magical destiny and immediately became a couple. It didn't take long for afternoon phone calls to escalate into after-school visits. He treated me like his thug queen. Hanging out at the mall holding hands. McDonald's Happy Meals every day after school. Random gifts, teddy bears, and candy; he even let me wear his Africa medallion. Joey was a regular guest before Mom got home from work. We'd bump and grind, like the horny teenagers we were, on my bed, on the couch, or on the floor. At sixteen, sex didn't hurt anymore. My painful experience freshman year with Michael became a fleeting thought of the past when Joey came into my life. He slowly wooed me into sleeping with him. Soft, careful, and tender, asking every few seconds, "You okay? You all right?"

I'd nod my head, lying still, breathing deeply, imagining the faces of pleasure I'd seen on late-night HBO. Beautiful women enjoying the moment of sex. I wanted to be like them—gorgeous, fabulous, and masterful in bed.

I used to let Joey follow me into my bathroom, lock the door, and grind on me, atop the fluffy blue rug beneath the sink. We did it standing up, lying down, out of breath like two playful, raw puppy dogs. He'd exhale whispers of how I was the best. I'd make small noises, like the ladies on HBO. And this was our routine, for months, until my mother came home early from work one afternoon.

I heard the grumbling car pull up to the driveway, and fortunately, the entrance to the basement was inside the bathroom. As my stomach flipped into butterfly-fluttering mode, Joey and I flew across the bathroom, gathering our clothes, buckling pants. I fixed the rug. He grabbed his sock. Pants half-buckled, he fled down the basement stairs and out the cellar door, running across the back-yard. Watching him escape, I turned to fly up from the basement and close the door. I was about to walk out of the bathroom as Mom met me at the threshold.

She marched forward, nudging me back with the strength of a soldier. I could have sworn she sniffed the smell of sex in the air.

"Did you have someone in the house?"

"No."

She looked around, surveyed the bathroom, checked the trash, opened the toilet, looked behind the radiator—and there, crumpled up, with a tiny brown stain in the crotch, was Joey's underwear. Fuck.

"Tell me the truth, Meena."

"Ill, what's that?" I said, feigning dumb. Hoping to win an Oscar. "Meena…" she said, holding the underwear with her two fingers at the tips, nose turned up. Suddenly the floor, my toes, anything besides direct contact with her eyes became interesting.

Still, I knew it was better to lie. Being honest was a death sentence; the truth was something she wouldn't accept or believe anyway. She always thought I was lying, even when I wasn't, so I self-fulfilled her prophecy by becoming a vivid storyteller.

"Did you have sex?"

"No."

"Did you have sex, Meena?"

"No," I repeated a little more passionately, yet not too sassy for fear of encouraging a slap.

She picked up the air freshener and sprayed. Sucked her teeth and hissed under the breath, "Stay here."

Left alone for a long, uncomfortable stretch, I waited with knots tangling my insides. Mom returned with a small box. "I want you to use this."

The word "douche" stood out in black letters between her fingers. "Read the directions and use it to clean up." She waited for the words to sink in. "Go ahead. Do it now!"

I hurried to pull down my pants. She watched, closing the door behind her. "I'm so disappointed in you. Don't think about watching TV. Unplug that phone and put it on my bed."

Standing in front of the toilet, I stared at the instructions, following the diagram that showed how to squeeze the vinegar mixture between my vaginal walls. Pulling out the plastic device, I stuck the contraption between my legs. It felt strange, like the cylinder of cardboard holding a tampon in place. I squeezed the device as cold liquid poured inside me, dripping into the toilet water. When done, Mom opened the bathroom door. I handed her the empty box.

"Go upstairs," she said. "And unplug that video game, too."

That was the last thing she said about the situation. After thirty days of punishment, void of phones and the ability to venture anywhere, I never called Joey again, dodged his calls and after-school doorbell rings. Taking an alternate route home from school, I felt ashamed of being caught. Embarrassed about having to use vinegar to clean. Scared of my mom's wrath. So I simply didn't call Joey. Our love faded away into oblivion.

"Yeah, I remember Joey," I said to Meredith with a deep sigh. "He was actually pretty nice."

"So how come you didn't ever call him back?"

"Scared of my mom."

"You never call the nice guys back," she said, laughing. "Remember poor Monster?"

Beenie Wilson. One of the linemen on the varsity football team, he was six-two, 290 pounds, and dark as a skid mark. His overwhelming weight at sixteen made room for the nickname "Monster," especially since you could hear his heavy wheezing as he carried himself to class.

"I dare you to kiss him," Doreen said one afternoon at lunch. "Not a peck. But tongue and all."

"Ill," I said, feigning vomiting. "Why would I do that?"

"Because it's a dare!" she said, smacking my arm. I lost balance and tripped down the hallway. "Girl, if you trip again... You need to loosen up. It's just for fun. There he goes..."

Monster was leaning on his locker, breathing as if he were on a ventilator, wiping sweat from his forehead.

"I can't just walk up and kiss him," I said, turning up my lip. "I need to get to know him a little."

Doreen sighed. "What is this?" She looked as if she couldn't believe me. "You are so corny. Catch up to the times," she said, rolling her eyes. "Just kiss him. If you do it, I'll buy you lunch for a week."

Doreen knew I hated packing my cold, mushy peanut butter and jelly sandwich with a plastic bag of potato chips every day. Always envious of those who bought pizzas, hamburgers, fries, and tacos, I'd borrow a dollar from different people daily, just to get a plate of hot cafeteria food. Mom never gave me an allowance. But I knew whose parents did.

"Okay, I can do it," I said, watching Monster talk to his friends. "But in my way. Watch..."

I followed Monster into the stairwell and tugged on his shirt. "Hey, Beenie," I said, smiling brightly. "Is that Polo?"

He seemed surprised, eyes lighting up, euphoric that a pretty girl would talk to him.

"Um, y-yeah," he stuttered. "I got it for my birthday."

"Okay! What's your sign?"

"Virgo."

"Uh-oh, perfectionist. I'm an Aquarius. We're supposed to be good together."

He laughed out loud, obviously not expecting that.

"Well, you look nice today," I said, rubbing his arm. "That shirt brings out those muscles. I'ma call you later."

He did a double take. "You got my number?"

"Not until you give it to me."

Beenie moved faster than I'd ever seen: throwing off his backpack, kneeling down, ripping out a notebook page, and scribbling his digits on a piece of lined paper in huge numbers across the center of the page.

That night we talked, laughed, and gossiped like two lost friends who hadn't spoken in years. I was surprised as we moved from sports to music, TV, movies, and parental complaints. Not only did the conversation flow, but he even brought up things I'd said in class a year ago. Apparently Beenie had a crush on me since the seventh grade. He admitted to being jealous and angry when he heard about my incident with Michael Tubman freshman year, while his teammates snickered about me in the locker room. But they didn't think of me as a slut, I was relieved to hear him point out. I was just another girls' track team challenge achieved.

By the end of the week, I asked him to be my boyfriend. Each day, he bought me lunch, shunning his friends, sitting with mine, giving me doting attention. Doreen would snicker and stare. Meredith kept a confused look on her face. And the moment he walked away, they made me feel embarrassed to be with what they saw as a monster.

"You like him?" Doreen asked, checking herself in her compact mirror. "You're like Beauty and the Beast. You can do better, girl. Don't settle."

"You two are an odd couple," Meredith chimed in, looking at me with what had come to be a familiar perplexed expression. "But if you're happy…" Her words trickled off into a place of uncertainty.

"Oh my God, she is not happy." Doreen laughed out loud. "She's a genius. Meena is working for that free lunch."

"Well, he buys me lunch every day," I said, digging in my bag. "He's actually kinda nice."

"Girl, please. He just wants some coochie. Have you even kissed him yet?" Doreen waited for an answer, tapping her foot.

"No, you haven't," she said. "That's what I thought. 'Cause he wouldn't be all up on you like that. I mean, the whole point of the bet was for you to kiss him."

"You'll know if it's meant to be," said Meredith. "If the kiss is right, you'll know…"

"And if not, cut your losses," snapped Doreen. "Be out."

After lunch, in the northeast stairwell, I moved next to Beenie for our first kiss. Grabbing his arm, I pulled him close. He opened his mouth wide and with a jolt forward threw his tongue down my throat. The Monster grabbed tight, bumping his teeth into mine, swallowing my mouth, touching my gums. I couldn't breathe. His breath smelled of salt-and-vinegar potato chips covered in ketchup. Globs of saliva covered my lips as he woofed them between his sticky smackers. Instinctually I moved back, nearly falling down the stairs, until Beenie caught my arm and pulled me up. Saved by the school bell, I ran to class without a word. That night, I ignored his phone call, feigning sickness to avoid him. And the next day, in that same kiss-of-death stairwell, I killed our short-term romance.

"This isn't gonna work," I said. "We're just… different."

His eyes flooded with tears; he was like a giant teddy bear begging for a hug.

"Beenie was nice," I said, glancing at his picture on my wall, phone cradled next to my ear. "I shouldn't have done that to him."

"Yeah, well, we were stupid in those days," Meredith said, as I stared at a picture of her, Doreen, and I dressed as sexy cats at the junior-year Halloween party. "I mean, it is what it is. But breaking up with a nice guy like Beenie wasn't you. That was Doreen and her peer pressure. She was so mean and fake. Negative and manipulative. I'm glad we're not friends with her anymore."

"Amen."

"Although…" Meredith's words trailed off. "What?"

"I heard she just got married."

"Doreen? To who?"

"Your old boo."

"What? Who?"

"Jason Novack."

I glanced at a group picture of the girls' and boys' track teams. The lone white guy, in the middle of a group of brothers, was Jason. At six four, he was not only the tallest in the school but one of the most popular. A junior who'd made his way to being a standout starter on the boys' varsity basketball and track teams, he hung out with all black guys, listened to hip-hop music, and seemed more like a brother with soul than a white boy with Czech roots. He wasn't known for dating anything other than blondes until the day his sister Jennifer gave me a ride home after track practice. Since our after-school schedule coincided with that of the basketball team, Jennifer scooped Jason up and dropped me off on the way to their house. I'd never noticed him until he opened the car door for me, grabbed my bags, and escorted me to the steps of my porch. Before then, he'd been just a beige blur in the hallways. But the flirting turned to late-night phone calls, inschool letters, and a card and carnation on the day he finally asked me to be his girlfriend.

Things began well between us. On rare days when we didn't have practice after school, I'd go to his house and laugh as he'd sweat. Exuding nervous shivers, he'd turn red as I took advantage of being more experienced than him; I was his first sexual encounter. I sucked on his neck and slowly kissed his lips. I pushed myself onto his body, pressuring him to have sex with me. His pale skin would turn reddish purple with a short, sixty-second suck to the neck. And I loved it, enjoying the power of control over a boy who hadn't gone all the way with anyone other than himself. He fell in love, calling me nightly to share his heart. Things changed when he invited me over to meet his parents one evening.

"So, Meena, what does your mother do?" His mom asked this while cutting her chicken into tiny pieces. "I believe Jason said she works in finance. She deals with money, I assume?"

"Oh, no, she just answers the phones," I said, dousing my chicken with salt, thinking Mrs. Novack must've forgotten to season the food. "But she's trying to get a new job at another company, 'cause she wants to make more money."

"Oh." She smiled, sipping a glass of white wine. "Well, what does your father do?"

"I don't know," I said, shrugging my shoulders. "I haven't seen him since I was a baby."

Silence followed that answer. There was an awkward tension as the Novack family—Jennifer, his mother, and father—looked down at their plates simultaneously. Nervous gas bubbled in my belly. I went to grab the salt again, but Jason's mother gave me a sharp cut of the eyes that sliced my pride I slipped back my hands and retracted them into my lap. I couldn't wait to leave.

Later, Jason admitted that he'd gotten into a major fight with his parents after his mother began lecturing him about "black people."

The only thing I remember him saying about that conversation are the words his mother apparently screamed across the dinner table: "This is a white family!" She threw Jason the subtle reminder when I walked out the door. She reminded him again after seeing his hickies and running from the table in tears. He, in turn, ran the other way, out the house and down the street to a pay phone, where he called me.

I wanted to understand him and not be offended. I knew this was his parents' ignorance and no fault of Jason's. But at seventeen, I didn't know how to deal with what I felt. Embarrassment? Shame? I wasn't sure, but I couldn't get over the reality that I was dating a child of racists. The anguish and emotional uncertainty of having never dealt with racism projected my anger onto Jason with a fury of mean insults. I began to act out toward him, the way my mother treated me: nagging, complaining, verbally abusing, and publicly humiliating him about everything—from his clothes to the way he walked. Suddenly he became a corny white boy in my eyes, not cool enough for me. Not deserving of my respect and attention. Becoming aware of our differing skin tones brought on embarrassment. Suddenly I noticed people staring at us. We'd walk in empty spaces, and I'd drop his hand when anyone we didn't know approached. And eventually, I broke up with Jason, publicly, so everyone would know, picking a loud fight in the hallway and berating him in front of the school. The result was a beet-red shade I'd never seen his face turn. He hung his head low and ran into the boys' locker room. We never spoke again.

"Jason Novack…" Meredith's words trailed off. "I will never forget that breakup. That boy almost cried in the hallway. He really loved you."

"I know," I said with a sigh, staring at an old Valentine's card he'd written that still hung on my wall. "I still feel bad about that. But his parents… they messed everything up. What the fuck? Do you think that's man-curse shit?"

"No, that's racist shit."

"How does a bitch like Doreen get to marry a nice guy while I keep attracting these assholes?" I said, shaking my head back and forth.

"Well, she got pregnant. And you know he's Catholic. He's likely doing what he thinks is the right thing."

"What? Pregnant?" I sighed, staring at my visionary poster. "I don't know. I've got to figure this shit out. I need a new job. I need a new man. I need to move out of this house."

"You need a new perspective," Meredith said, cutting me off. "'Cause this man curse is all in your head. You made your goals. So believe, wait, and they'll manifest. Do you believe you can have what you dream of?"

"Yeah."

"So you will. It's that easy," she said, "Power of the mind, Meena. You'll see."

"Birthday number twenty-five," I said, closing my eyes to pray. "Dear Lord, thank you for the day. Please bless me with success, happiness, and love. Amen."

⟡

The next morning I overslept. A night of partying with Meredith left a hangover that made the sound of a chiming phone rock me awake with a throb of my head. In what seemed like an early-morning haze, my phone echoed from a faraway place deep down in the black hole known as my pocketbook. I messily dug in my bag, looking for the cell. Pulled it out. Dropped it. Slowly picked it up. Stretching my eyes wide to see the fuzzy vision of a 212 number. Who could be calling me from New York? Bill collectors? No, that would be an 800 number. Maybe it was Dexter calling, taking a trip to the city to get me back? No. Fuck him. Then it hit me: *Buzz*.

Buzz had been the hottest magazine on the entertainment scene the past year. I remember seeing their TV commercials; covering everything from music and fashion to TV and film, *Buzz* was always on the pulse of what's hot and not. Thanks to a hookup from her cousin, Meredith and I had volunteered two summers ago during their *Buzz* music seminar week. Picked as gift-bag stuffers for a celebrity fashion show, she dragged me as her plus-one to all the hot parties, where we brushed shoulders with celebrities, drank free liquor, and grabbed expensive swag bags. Loving the fast, superstar lifestyle, I made business cards at Kinko's with my name and number and handed them to everyone I met.

"Hey, well, here's my card," I'd say to whomever I bumped into at the bar. "If you're looking for a good assistant, let me know."

Stuffing bags at the *Buzz* office, I walked around and passed out my contact information. Smiling. Talking. Chatting. Making sure each person at that magazine knew my name. And for every business card I received, I sent a personalized follow-up e-mail to touch base. Three months ago, I had submitted my résumé in reply to a job-listing e-mail I'd received from someone I'd met at the seminar. *Buzz* was searching for an executive assistant. A few weeks later I was called in for an interview, but I'd nearly given up hope after several follow-ups and no returned call. But now, ninety days later, maybe they were finally getting back to me.

I cleared my throat.

"Hellooo." I let the *oo* ring out like a morning cheer. "This is Meena."

"Meena Butler, please."

"Speaking."

"Meena, this is Denise Banor from *Buzz* magazine. How are you?"

"Hi, Denise!"

Denise Banor was the new editor in chief of *Buzz*. She'd written for all the mainstream magazines in the country, had interviewed nearly every major celebrity on earth, and was queen of the publishing world after her fiction novel became a bestseller. I remember her being one of the less snooty ones at *Buzz*. She never talked down or made me feel like a peon, never gave me the once-over look that most in the industry would give. Denise was warm. Familiar. Cool. And I was honored to have received her call.

"Meena, I'm sorry it took so long for me to get back to you," she said, Busta Rhymes playing in the background. It was a song I hadn't heard before. Had to be new. "We just closed our biggest issue of the year, and—"

"Is that a new Busta Rhymes song?" I cut her off, regretting it the moment I opened my mouth. But I couldn't help it. I loved hip-hop, and if there was anything I knew, it was rap music. "Sorry, I didn't mean to cut you off."

"No, it's cool," she said, laughing. "Yeah, a new single that drops next week. You like hip-hop?"

"Yeah. *When Disaster Strikes* is one of my favorite albums at the moment."

"Good. You need hip-hop knowledge if you're gonna work with me. But I need an assistant ASAP. I want you. If you're ready…"

I didn't know how to answer. Stuck in shock, the moment slowed down.

"Hello?"

"Um, hello," I replied. "Um, yes."

"Meena. You okay?"

"Yes."

"You want to work for me? Help me get things right?"

"Yes."

"Can you come in tomorrow to fill out paperwork?"

"Yes."

"I assume as my assistant you'll be saying more than 'yes'?"

"Yes. Ooh, I mean. I'm sorry. I'm just… um… wow! Yes! I can start whenever. I am so ready. Thank you so much, Denise."

"You're welcome," she said, cracking up. "But I'd rather you thank me by being a great assistant and holding me down."

"Oh, I will. I'll be the best ever."

12

THE NEXT DAY, I was up at six and on an eight o'clock train to New York City. I sent a quick e-mail to Merrill Lynch, letting them know I'd found a full-time gig in lieu of the freelance work they offered. And the best part was that I didn't have to be at work until ten, per entertainment industry hours. But I wanted to get there early. Squeezing between a small, skinny Indian man with a pocket protector and a large, bald white guy with a beer belly, my legs curled to the side in a ladylike position. Hardly able to move, my knees knocked with one passenger. My bag brushed stomach fat. But I didn't care. I was going to work for *Buzz* magazine. I was going to be in "the industry."

The New Jersey Transit train pulled into Penn Station. I bustled my way through the fast-moving crowd onto a platform that spilled out of the train tunnel and onto the cold, icy February street. Pushing my way through everyone, I became part of a marathon of hungry, workforce runners vying for the top position. Speeding to escape the freezing wind that slapped our backs and pushed us along. I slipped my way onto Eighth Avenue. Bumped into one man. He nudged me with his shoulder. Tripping, I stepped on the foot of a lady. She whispered an insult. And in a domino effect I fell forward into someone new.

"Oh my God." I sighed in frustration, pausing on the sidelines and telling the man I bulldozed as I picked up his dropped book, "I'm sorry."

When he turned around and stood up straight, time stopped. He was like a god, sparkling on the outside. The sun's light shined on him with such beauty and ease, bouncing off the muscles that protruded through his shirt. Cornrows tightly braided, neatly crisscrossing back into fine, ripe elements. His eyes glistened as he looked down upon me. My face was confused, in awe. Mouth numb, partially open, eyes stretched in a rush of excitement.

"You all right?" he asked, his voice smooth and relaxed. Assured and calm.

"Yeah," I said. "I just feel like I got brushed up into a tornado or something. And I didn't mean to step on your shoes. I'm so sorry."

"It's okay, nothing polish won't take care of." He pointed down Eighth Avenue. "You headed this way?"

"Yeah," I said, walking. "I'm a few blocks that way."

"Well, I'm going in the same direction, so I guess I'll be watching you stumble down the street."

"Probably. I need to pack my sneakers tomorrow. Thought I'd be cute today, but I obviously need better traction to handle these folks in New York."

"Where you from?"

"Jersey."

"Oh yeah? Me too. I live in Brooklyn now. Was visiting my family this past weekend in Newark."

"For real? I was born at Beth Israel Hospital."

"Wow, me too. Maybe we were babies in the same ward. And now we're reunited," he said, straight-faced. "Although, wasn't everybody in Newark born at Beth Israel?"

I laughed but stopped short. Careful not to crack up too loud and make him think I was trying too hard. We talked and walked all the way to the *Buzz* building.

"This is my stop," I said, wincing on the inside, hating that I used a cliché film line. "It was nice meeting you. What's your name?"

"Sean. Sean Baxter." He grabbed my extended hand, held it for a few moments. "You work in this building?"

"Yeah."

"Which floor?"

"Fourth."

"Interesting," he said with a furrowed brow. "That's where I'm going."

"*Buzz* magazine?"

"Yeah, I have an appointment with the editor in chief."

"Interesting." I grinned. "So do I. What do you do?"

"I'm a writer. What do you do?"

"I'm the editor in chief 's new assistant. Nice to meet you." We stared at each other. Marinating on the moment. "Hmmm," he said, opening the door for me. "Interesting."

"Talk about six degrees of separation," I said, giggling. "I mean, I thought the world was bigger."

"No," he said, not smiling, rubbing his goatee. "It's not."

When I looked at him from the side, he was still furrowing his eyebrows. Serious, perplexed, in deep thought. We were silent the entire elevator ride up to the *Buzz* offices.

⁓

Stepping off the elevator was like walking onto the set of a TV show. Large, colorful framed photos of celebrities lined the walls. Each had been featured on *Buzz* covers. Will Smith, Tom Cruise, LL Cool J, Mary J. Blige. A neon-blue light outlined the reception area. Ceilings and floors glowed with a fantastic blue haze. Long, black couches curved with every slope of the oval room, forming a U-shape design. A sixty-inch flat-screen TV flashed a mix of music videos, fashion shows, and movie trailers. Mase, Puff Daddy's newest protégé, blasted from speakers jutting out of the corners of the ceiling.

"Here's my card," Sean said, as he nodded at the receptionist. "Although I'll probably be seeing you again."

"And here's my info," I said, digging in my bag, anxiously feeling around for my card. But I couldn't find one. "Hold on a minute, I know I packed them."

I took the bag off my shoulder, set it on a table, and began desperately digging past tissues with lip imprints, pens missing tops, dirty brown envelopes with cell phone bills inside, a raggedy checkbook with the top page falling off, strands of hair, old panty shields falling out of the pink packaging, empty sandwich bags, hairpins, and makeup containers—and then, deep inside a hole ripped through the lining, I felt a card.

"Here ya go," I said, passing it to him. "Sorry it looks a bit bent, it's my last one."

"It's cool," he said, checking it out. "It's got all the info I need, Miss Butler."

I smiled, watching his tall, lanky body casually stride to the couch and sit down. He crossed his legs into a manly, ninety-degree angle and flipped open an old issue of *Buzz*. Pointed at the table of contents, his fingers were beautiful, long and precise like his body. Probably like his...

"Excuse me..." The receptionist's voice snapped me back to reality. "Who are you here to see?"

"Oh, I'm, um... sorry."

"I know." She laughed. "He's a cutie. Beauty and brains."

I suddenly began to sweat. Red flowed to my cheeks. Taking a deep breath, I exhaled. "I'm here for Denise Banor. I'm Meena Butler, her new assistant."

"Ohhhh! Hey, mami!" she said, smiling a toothy grin. "Remember me?"

I looked at the receptionist carefully. Her yellow arms had two tats apiece. One near her shoulder read "Nay-Nay." Around her wrist was a hemp leaf. On the other arm was a vine that twisted around the muscles to just above the elbow. She wore a rhinestone butterfly ring with rainbow colors. Her long, black, shiny hair was cut to frame her round face. And her cotton midriff top was cut low enough for cleavage, highlighting the cat paws protruding from the neckline of her teeny white V-neck T-shirt. I didn't recognize her.

"Girl, it's me, Carmen! Remember we worked the *Buzz* music seminar? Summer of '96? All those damn gift bags we stuffed? You were with your friend."

My face went blank before suddenly attempting to cover. "Meena, remember when we got lost trying to find the Puffy party 'cause we were so damn high off some weed your friend had gotten from some Jamaican?"

Still nothing. I think the weed was affecting my memory. "Remember I used to break-dance?"

Slowly it all came back. Carmen Mercado, the skinny Puerto Rican mami from the Bronx. She had a deep, beautiful voice that she'd use to bust into a rap at the drop of a beat. I remember at one party, she began dancing in the middle of the floor better than most B-boys in music videos. She was the one who always set it off. But that Carmen was a skinny, flat-chested, five-two girl who dressed like a boy. Now she was a busty bombshell advertising all her assets.

"Yeah, I know I look different," she said, looking down at her body. "I had twins. And an idiot husband for six months. So that's three kids. Gained a lot of weight." She sucked her teeth. "Left his lazy ass. Now I got a girlfriend, gay and proud."

I busted out laughing. "You look fine," I said. "Although all the cleavage and tats made it hard for me to remember. But you look good. All thick and sexy."

"Thanks, mama," she said, smiling. "You got the gig, huh? That's hot! We gotta go to lunch, yo. I can tell you everything about this place." She rolled her eyes and adjusted her headset as the phone rang. "Good morning, *Buzz* magazine."

I was impressed at how her slang and voice morphed from Webster Avenue, Bronx Boricua into eloquent, college-bred professional. "Absolutely, sir," she continued in her nonregional diction. "Let me transfer you." She gave me a wink, knowing her power, playing the game. "Good morning, *Buzz* magazine. Mr. Jacobs, how are you, sir? How was your long weekend? I assume fabulous?"

"Miss Meena Butler."

I turned around to see the source of the voice behind me. Stepping off the elevator was the queen herself, Denise Banor.

"Hey, Denise!" I didn't mean to sound so excited. But I was. I had a job working for the most powerful editor in the entertainment business. "Cute shoes!"

"Thank you, lady," she said, grabbing the *New York Times* off Carmen's desk. "You ready?"

"Yup."

"Cool, come on."

We walked through the couch area. She whizzed past Sean, stopped, and did an about-face.

"Mr. Sean Baxter," she said with a half grin. "Bright and early."

"Well, when I have a meeting with the queen, I aim to be on time."

"Good, now if we could just get you to do that with your assignments, we'd be good."

Sean shot a quick, embarrassed look at me, and then said to Denise, "Um, yeah, I'm on that. That's why—"

"Sean, I just got in. Lemme get settled, show this girl around, and I'll have her bring you down. This is Meena Butler, my new assistant."

"Yeah, we met," he said, shaking my hand again. I plastered a big grin on my face.

Denise squinted her eyes. "Okay, missy. No fraternizing with the help. Let's go."

She turned for the stairs and I was at her heels, taking one last peek at Sean as I walked downstairs. At the bottom was a scruffy man, with an unshaved goatee, dirty Timberland boots, and a New York Giants jersey hanging to his knees.

"Griffin, this is Meena Butler, my new assistant." He shook my hand. "Please give her whatever she needs for the desk."

Denise informed me, "Griffin runs the mail room. Sometimes that reggae he plays is too loud," she said. "But whatever you need, call him."

I nodded.

She pulled out her key card and opened the door. Inside was a large room filled with cubicles. Some empty. Others occupied and cluttered with old magazines, empty boxes, Xerox paper, and outdated computers. A few folks popped their heads over the top of the divider. Others stood stiff as Denise whizzed by. It was like a scene from *The Devil Wears Prada* where Meryl Streep's character scares the office straight, stopping all idle chitchat. Denise dressed like a *Vogue* editor: slinky black Chanel dress, mile-high bright red stilettos, and a large vintage Gucci bag that matched the Gucci scarf swinging from her neck. But unlike *Vogue*'s editor in chief, Anna Wintour, she was abruptly sassy, with a warm, down-to-earth mix of sarcasm that melted any ice some might assume she'd convey.

"Good morning, everyone," she said, walking to the center of the cubicles, stopping to stand in an empty aisle with a large cabinet in the middle. Atop it sat a fax machine and a tray of scattered, disorganized cover sheets and confirmation pages. "I want to introduce you to Meena Butler, my new assistant."

The office cheered and clapped.

"About time," said a tall, skinny man with a purple ascot. He had one hand on his hip and the other in his blazer pocket. "That temp was the worst. Can I get a meeting now?"

Everyone laughed.

"We'll do that today, Francois. Now, some of you may or may not remember Meena from working the *Buzz* music seminar. She's visited periodically, so she's already been a member of the family. You know she's solid, because I hired her. So if she looks lost in the corridors, please help her out. Okay?"

Some nodded their heads affirmatively. A few looked me up and down, analyzing my outfit, studying, probably wondering how long I'd last. I planned to stay for the long haul. I was confident on the outside. But insecurity shook my nerves. Everyone at *Buzz* seemed so fashionable and fly. White, stiff, clean, uptown Nike sneakers. Fly knee-high boots. Fresh new Gucci bags, Prada this, designer that. And here I was wearing the flyest outfit I could afford from The Limited—a pair of khaki-colored pants in the winter and a striped black, white, and brown shirt to match. My shoes were cute black heels with a tiny bow at the top that tilted to the side. I got them from Bakers—affordably fly, thank you very much.

"Meena," said Denise, grabbing my hand. "Lemme show you my office and where you'll be sitting."

She headed down a hallway, waving at passing offices. Some had music blasting from doorways opened to messy, disorganized desks. Others were meticulously clean with layouts of the magazine adorning the walls. Another office was covered with large color proofs showing pictures of the magazine, models, and celebrity types, with large red pencil marks circling unflattering parts of their bodies.

Denise walked me into her zone. Half of the office was covered in magazines, old issues of *Buzz* with pages turned, ripped out, and curled at the corners. Some magazines looked as if they'd been read a million times, others were crisp and clean. Stacks of paper sat messily atop her desk next to empty water bottles and coffee cups with lipstick on the rims. Pencils, pens, markers, mail, tissues, makeup-stained proofs—Denise's desk looked like the inside of my purse. "I don't expect you to clean my office. You're not my maid," she said, taking a seat. Throwing her purse on an anonymous pile of papers, she glanced at the computer and moved the cursor back and forth. "I don't want an assistant who wants to be a secretary forever." She picked up a proof and peered at it in distaste. "I want someone who wants to grow with the company and do bigger and better things. Not saying being my assistant is not a good thing. But it's just a start for you. You're talented. That's why I hired you. I remember your hustle at the *Buzz* music seminar and it was fabulous. That's the kind of energy I want you to bring with this job."

I nodded affirmatively.

"Just two words of advice for you. One: Don't tell my business. Everything in my life and what I tell you is confidential. Never tell anyone where I am. And two: Don't tell your business. Everything in your life is confidential. This is a small industry. Word travels fast. You don't want people all up in your shit."

She looked at me straight-faced with her arms crossed.

"You got all that?"

"Yeah. I got it. I don't like people in my business anyway. If I tell you something, it's because I don't care if you know. I'm careful with what I share."

"Good," she said. "Now, Griffin is out there setting up your desk. He'll bring you a computer and show you how to log in, set up Outlook, and how to use the phones. If my door is closed, it means I'm busy. Only you can knock or buzz me to check if I want to be seen or take a call. If it's an emergency, definitely knock.

"Right now, I need you to put your bag down and lock it in the file cabinet. Not saying people here are thieves, they're not, just always be safe. Then go upstairs, get Sean, and bring him down. Afterward, go to the business department, get your paperwork done, your key card programmed, and then I need you to make copies of a few articles, hand out some memos, and check my voice mail. At eleven, we'll have an editorial meeting, I'll need you to take minutes. After that, we'll go to lunch and…" She paused. "Do you need to write all this down?"

"Oh, yeah, I should." I rummaged through my pocketbook. "Lemme just find a pen." I looked inside, pushing aside the random papers and makeup and receipts, dollar bills, wallet, tissues, everything I needed for my bag. But I could feel Denise's impatience. Out of the corner of my eye, I saw her face, twisted and staring, as a tiny smirk opened her mouth.

"Take this," she said, holding up a purple pen. "And use this notepad. When we're done, go get your supplies from the mail room."

I grabbed it and wrote everything down, speaking out loud as I scribbled. "Sean, supplies, copies, minutes, key card, paperwork, messages, meeting at eleven, minutes, lunch." Then I looked up. "But not in that particular order. I just wanna make sure I jot it all down before I forget."

She smiled. "Yeah, you're gonna work out. I gotta check my e-mails. So you go handle that, get Sean, buzz me thirty minutes after he's been here, and when it's ten forty-five, give me a heads-up so I can get ready for the meeting. And close the door behind you."

I left the office, placed my bag in the file cabinet next to my desk, and, before heading to the lobby, I scoped out my cubicle. A dirty, bland white, with dust outlining where the computer was to be placed. Still I smiled, because it was mine. My area. A spot at *Buzz* magazine. A warm, tingly thing did a rhythmic happy dance in my stomach, making my cheekbones stretch with wide contentment, making me exhale with sighing relief. Maybe I could be happy.

13

Sean Baxter. Writer.

His card, with a Brooklyn address and 718 area code, had a brown recycled look and feel to it with a cute pen-and-pad logo. I unfolded the edges, wrinkled after a tumble in my purse, and stared at the words that scrolled across the bottom: *Thinking. Dreaming. Creating.*

I'd heard that writers were intellectual types—smart, well read, full of worldly knowledge. At the time, I'd never dated one. I didn't know if the stereotype was true for any writer other than myself. But after meeting Denise, the staff of scribes at *Buzz*, and Sean, the wordsmith description seemed to be true. I was happy to be among likeminded people.

Sitting on the train back to Jersey, watching the outline of trees blow in the dark, a momentary doze led my mind to drift. A dreamy vision of me sitting at a laptop, pregnant, feet propped up on a wicker stool, computer nestled on a small stand. And there I was, tap-tapping keys, two hundred pages along, pounding letters into my next bestselling manuscript. The nanny would call, letting me know my son had been picked up from school. At six, I'd make dinner. At seven, my soul mate would arrive home from work. And at seven thirty, we'd have family dinnertime. By ten, my husband and I would be laughing, talking, foreplaying into passionate lovemaking. That was true north. A dream I knew would come true. But who would play the role of soul mate? Sean, perhaps? He was a cutie, knew the entertainment business, and wanted to take me out. I wondered, *Maybe I should call him.* The thought lingered as my phone buzzed with a new text message: *In the morning, stop at Guy & Gallard and order a fruit platter for the meeting tomorrow. Pay for it with the credit card when they arrive. Denise, EIC.*

Seconds later it buzzed again.

Oh, and good work today. Your first day at work and you represented. So happy to have you on the Buzz team. Gnite.

And then a third buzz.

Hey beautiful, so when are we goin out? Italian? Chinese? French?

It was Sean.

I texted back: *How about tomorrow after work?*

Sean: *Ok. Let's do La Petite Maison. Lincoln Square. 730p.*

Me: *Ok. :+)*

The next day. 6:45 p.m. Buzz offices…

I was sitting at my computer, waiting for Denise to finish her meeting so I could leave. Trying to stop myself from watching the clock, I watered and adjusted the fern next to the computer. Looked back at the clock: 6:47. *Shit.* I needed to leave by seven to get to the restaurant on time. On tarot.com, I began reading the plethora of Aquarius horoscopes offered: daily scope, love scope, monthly scope, weekly scope, feng shui tip of the day. I got up, went to the bathroom, and stared in the full-length mirror. My white skirt flared at the bottom. Short and sweet, it crept above my knees in a schoolgirl fashion. My matching top had spaghetti straps embroidered with small gold flowers crisscrossing the shoulder blades. I touched up my brown shimmery lipstick, pranced back to my desk, and prayed the meeting would be done. I could hear the editors loudly debating.

"That is not *Buzz* magazine," said Denise. "I'm not going to have a feature on some chick famous for sleeping with lots of rappers."

"But she's hot right now."

"She does look good," somebody else chirped.

"She's a whore," Denise snapped back. "What talent does she have other than being able to fuck rich MCs?"

"Well, I heard she was starting a new fashion line," Francois, the style editor, sang.

"Oh, that's original," Denise shot back. "If y'all want this chick on the cover, tell me something I haven't heard before. You better wow me."

"And I heard she's got a new perfume coming out," someone else added.

"Called what?" Denise asked, giggling. "Eau de ho?"

Everyone laughed, including me; I let out a small snicker that I tried to catch by muffling and clearing my throat. "Meena! Meena Butler!"

I jumped with each syllable of my name that Denise enunciated. Hopping up out of the chair, heart beating quickly, I shivered into her office.

"Meena," she said, "have you heard of Abby Tulip?"

"Yes."

"What do you think of her? Would you read a story about her?"

"Well…" I paused, searching for the politically correct thing to say. "I, um…"

"Meena," Denise said with an impatient exhale. "First rule of journalism: Be honest. Speak your mind. Be an opinion maker. Speak the fuck up."

"Okay." I took a deep breath. "Everything I need to know about Abby is in the tabloids. She used to be a porn star. She sleeps with all the rappers, actors, ball players. And now she's got a new album, lingerie line, and perfume coming out. She cut her hair off bald, and copycat girls are cutting theirs off, too. I think she's a horrible example to women who want to make it in this world without sleeping around. I think she's a floozy and I have no interest in her at all. I don't care about her. But I did hear *Playboy* was putting her on the cover. *Buzz* is always the first to the hotness. So I'd be surprised to see you come behind a magazine known for showing naked women."

"Tell us how you really feel," Francois said, smiling. He looked at Denise and added, "I like this one."

"That's why I hired her. She's honest, knows the magazine, and she gave us the lowdown. Sam, why didn't we know she's on the next *Playboy* cover? That's your job. Are you not the music editor?"

"Well," he said, sweat beading above his eyebrow. "That's not confirmed."

"It's a rumor we need to investigate. I hired you to stay on top of that kind of shit. We were about to put this little naked girl on our cover *after* a tramp magazine like *Playboy*? That would have killed us! And then I would've fired you."

Denise looked at me. I held my breath.

"Thank you for that, Meena. That's all. You can leave now. I'll see you tomorrow." She got up and closed the door as I walked out.

Smiling, I unlocked the file cabinet, grabbed my bag, logged off, and speed-walked to the elevator before Denise changed her mind. Time check: 7:05. My date awaited.

14

SEX WITH SEAN WAS AMAZING. As his pelvis jutted out, back and forth, he thrust his package inside me. He rolled his back in a way, with slopes and peaks and valleys arching me into a shape that rolled with him, like a rowboat, over and over through rapids and shores far away, sailing my insides to a place where I could soar with the wind, feel the warmth of the sun, shout and scream. I could moan without the fear of someone hearing. I could moan in a way that felt like a fabulous, sweaty workout that tensed, stretched, and worked the muscles. It was so beautiful and wonderful. So wet and sticky; I oozed with sensual satisfaction between my legs that seeped down, dripped on the thigh, and lathered tiny hairs on my vagina into white, wet follicles filled with excitement, lust, love, and passion. I felt his fingers below. Inside my pussy. One. Two. Three. Pushing. Shoving. Digging. Twisting. Gushing. I whimpered a tiny yelp of delight and nudged forward so he could dig deeper, far enough for fingers to touch my uterus, to puncture deep and push it to the side so he could reach my heart. Touching it slowly and poking it with a reminder that the connection between mind, body, and soul can come with the best orgasmic release that blows up inside you and bursts like the hot ash and flames of a volcano. It's not just a sexual connection or the release of endorphins that connects you heart to heart. It's the synergy of a mind-to-mind connection. A yearning of mental stimulation that morphs into emotional love. That can turn the simplest chance meeting into an eternity of togetherness, of unity of enlightenment, and growth, and happiness. A lifetime of one. Being one because of the unity of two. So wonderful. So beautiful. Sex.

"Next stop, Seventy-second Street."

The train operator's muffled announcement woke me up from my momentary nap. Wet in two spots, I wiped slobber from the side of my mouth, realizing I'd dozed off in the short ride from *Buzz* to Lincoln Square. Standing up, wobbling, I felt the weakness of wet dream legs. As the train slowed, I checked the window's grimy reflection. Moist down below, horny as an inmate who hadn't had sex in months, I casually turned to make sure there wasn't a tiny circular wet spot on the back of my skirt. That's all I needed: to walk into my date looking like I'd sat in a puddle of vaginal secretion. Gross.

I adjusted myself, twisting and turning. Taking out a compact, I dabbed oil from my T-zone, then pulled out a comb to adjust stray stands. When the train doors opened, confidence spewed with each wide step I took in my fly black stiletto heels. I felt like Naomi Campbell, supermodel with an attitude, beating down any who dared stare at my high steps of self-love. Men broke eyeballs. Ladies sucked teeth. I giggled at the fellas. Smirked at female envy. Meena Fey Butler was feeling herself. Headed toward the exit and grabbing the railing, I walked up the stairs. When suddenly, time slowed. Stubbing my toe on the first step, I fell like a deflated balloon descending from the sky. The trip forward left my butt hanging in the air, left leg dangling. No one stopped to offer anything other than a snicker as they grazed by, nearly stepping on my black Gucci bag. My right knee was slightly skinned, a burning sensation oozing from an ashy-white skid mark. My white skirt was bruised black, spots of subway residue speckled with dirt. I took a deep breath, sighing a loud, groaning yoga-release of stress, when I heard a voice. "Are you all right?"

Turning around, or rather, flipping over with my palms, I held myself up the best I could. Struggling for my clothes to no longer touch the nasty steps, I was helpless, like a baby learning to walk, plopping down unsteadily back onto the floor. When I looked up, there was Sean, staring down at me, smiling.

"You tripping again?" Holding out his left hand, he seemed to do his best to restrain a burst of laughter. But his silence only lasted five seconds, broken by my sad face turned upside down as I cracked up, howling. Echoes of our unified laughter bounced off tagged-up, underground walls. Minutes later, we sat in that moment, no words, just staring at each other, cheesing. I took out my sanitizer, squeezed it slowly onto my hands, offered him a few squirts, and we were silent again, rubbing our hands with Purell.

"So..." I said, "you've seen it all. You know the truth. I'm a klutz." We both cracked up again.

"Don't worry, I won't tell anyone. Although..." He pulled out a small notepad from his back pocket and slid out a tiny pencil stuck between its spirals. "I may have to write about this one day. I mean, it won't be you, per se. But it will be your actions. This whole scene is inspiration for a great movie."

"Oh, so if I read something about a girl who busts her ass in front of the guy she's supposed to meet for dinner, then I should assume that's a version of me and this episode today?"

"Exactly," he answered, nodding his head.

We both cracked up again as he pulled me up off the steps. "Well, the good news," he said, helping me to steady myself, "is that your legs still look great even when they're slightly ashy."

I looked down to see white lines grazing my front shins and knees.

"Oh my God! I am so embarrassed," I said, covering my face. "This is a nightmare."

"It's okay. You're still beautiful. I mean, your beauty is amplified by the way you're handling the situation."

I looked at him. "You think?"

"Oh, absolutely. Like, the typical girl would get all weird and have an attitude 'cause she got a little scuff on her heels or black mark on her white skirt. But you…"

As he paused, I looked down to see a scuff on the back of my right heel. My white skirt had tiny spots of dirt throughout. I sucked my teeth and exhaled silently.

"But you, you're taking this whole thing in stride. You're still walking your model walk. You're smiling. You're sparkling. The fact that you can laugh at yourself is absolutely beautiful to me. It says you're humble. It says you don't take life too seriously. I mean, shit, sometimes you gotta laugh at yourself. Right?"

"I guess," was all I could say, nearly at a loss for words as my eyes sparkled like a fanatic spectator's. The air around him rippled in a haze, like a mirage in desert heat. I mean, was this man actually speaking all of this chocolate fudge sundae sweetness? Yum. I'd never heard a guy speak with such warm, rhythmic beauty. My ears melted slowly, dripping with sexual tension. And I stood there in awe. Deaf to the A train pulling into the station. Blind to the tiny piece of tissue sticking to my heel.

"Let me get that for you," he said, bending down as I lifted up my foot. He pulled the tissue off, throwing it to the side. Slowly standing back up, eyeing my calves, knees, thighs, body—and finally whispering into my ear, "Beautiful."

As the A train doors opened, Sean glanced at a tall blonde with supermodel features stepping off. I could've sworn he smiled as their eyes met when she pranced onto the platform. Moments later he refocused on me, grabbing my hand and pulling me toward the exit. "Let's get you some food."

Sitting at La Petite Maison, a sexy French café quietly tucked away on a side street, I twitched and turned. Nervously arranging and rearranging the napkin on my lap, I suddenly felt weird in my own skin, fidgety, itchy. Bladder felt full. I kept taking regular bathroom breaks, only to return and fumble with my silverware. It was Sean. The way he didn't stare at me but through me, like a journalist studying an interview subject, looking for quirky tics to color his story. I reached for a sip of Zinfandel, dying to relax, focusing on holding my wineglass stem without shaking, without sipping it and having drops drizzle down my chin onto my dress.

"You've got something here," he said, pointing at his nose and doing a wiping motion.

Oh my God! I have a booger. The words ran across my brain as I wiped. He motioned again. I wiped again. He shook his head in the negative. I wiped a third time.

"To the left," he instructed. I wiped to the left.

"Okay, now you moved it to the right." I wiped to the right.

"It's not cooperating," he said. "It likes you or something."

I pulled out my compact to see a tiny white piece of tissue, lingering on the side of my nose.

"I bet you thought it was a booger, huh?"

I looked at him, rolling my eyes with a giggle.

He laughed. "I promise I'd have told you if it was. You can always tell your friends, because the fake ones will let you walk around with a booger in your nose. You'll be smiling hard, taking pictures, working the room, then hit the bathroom and see a giant snot ball in your nose, wondering, 'Now, how long did I have this here? And how come no one told me!'"

We both laughed. Hearty and loud. Relieving my tension. He grabbed the check before it hit the table, and minutes later we were on the sidewalk amid billboards aglow, people jaywalking, and horns blowing, large drops of rain splattering on the pavement in the background. He pulled me under a tiny convenient store awning. Caressing my arms, protecting me from the coldness of nature's wet spasm, he kissed me. Slowly. Delicately. Carefully.

"I love rain," he said, lifting his face high, letting drops splash off his forehead. "It's renewing. Refreshingly romantic."

He stared into my eyes. "Something about the backdrop of water to a first kiss, undisturbed, immune to the lights of a busy sidewalk corner attracting millions of people. It's amazing. Beautiful. Like our own world."

He kissed me again. And my legs began to buckle.

"Well, this is the first time I like rain," I said, looking around at the splashing, nose turned up, toes shivering and crunched up. "It's always been depressing to me."

He pulled me closer, turning my head toward him, asking, "You depressed now?"

I smiled, shaking my head until he kissed me again.

"I didn't think so," he said, stepping to the curb and waving down a cab. After three empty cabs whizzed by, I slowly joined him at the curb, and finally a driver stopped. Opening the door while using his jacket as an umbrella, he guided me to a warm seat. Once I was inside, he took his hat off, held it like a flag, and waved good-bye as the driver departed for Penn Station. The moment was monumental. And minus the falling and tissue stuck to my nose, it was the best date I'd ever had.

15

"I'LL PUT THIS OLD TOKEN HERE to symbolize you coming back."
Sean's words were the musical soundtrack to his methodic, sexy
motions, placing an old New York City token on a mahogany
mantelpiece. It sat atop a candle and a small bowl with scented oil.
"There's power in this."

"What is that, voodoo or something? What are you, Haitian?"
I sarcastically quipped, reaching for a glass of wine while eyeing
the tiny Haitian flag sticking up from the soil of a potted plant.
"Are you about to start chanting?"

"Nah, I'm just gonna place this here to make sure you come
back. It's symbolic," he said, staring at the dull coin's positioning. "I
do this with Haitian pride."

"You always do." I giggled. "*Sak pase?*"

"*N'ap boule,*" he replied, grabbing my hand, pulling me close,
and kissing me.

* * *

I'd learned a lot from Sean during the six weeks of random dates
after work. This was my first visit to his apartment in Flatbush,
Brooklyn.

Above the mantelpiece at his home were posters of Bob Marley, Wyclef Jean, and Marcus Garvey. Seashells were strewn out on windowsills, next to fresh green plants towering like trees, while a creeping vine crawled across the floor. His office was on the left side of the living room, featuring a carefully built L-shaped Ikea desk. Above it, countless books stacked up, touching the ceiling. Old magazines sat in a mile-high pile crowding the floor. His desk was meticulously neat. Scant items atop it seemed strategically positioned at ninety-degree angles. A yellow No. 2 pencil positioned bone straight, next to a small reporter's notepad, was placed in the center of the desk. To the left, in a corner, was a coffee cup filled with black ballpoint Bic pens. In the opposite corner was a bottle of hand sanitizer. As Sean squirted a few drops and rubbed his hands, I watched a black piece of lint bounce down a wall.

"Yeah, I'm a neat freak," he said, grabbing an old newspaper, rolling it up, and smashing what I thought was lint, crawling toward the floor. "My work space has to be in order before I can create. Before I write, I clean like Arm and Hammer. It clears my thoughts."

"So…" My words trailed off as I stared at the mangled insect carcass. "Is that an isolated roach problem?"

"Yes! Damn roaches," he muttered, using a tissue to wipe bug blood off the white paint. "Fucking building is full of them, so even if I keep my place neat, the neighbors' dirt issues invade my space. And the landlords don't care."

I watched another crawl up the wall. He grabbed a shoe and smashed it twice, screaming, "Fucker!"

"Why don't you move?" I said, turning up my nose. "That's one thing I don't do: roaches."

His eyes furrowed like a madman's.

"This place is rent stabilized. I've been paying the same price for five years," he said, cleaning up the mashed insect with a paper towel. Remnants of roach legs imprinted the wall. "If I move, I'll be raped."

"I guess you get what you pay for. Cheap rent. Mad roaches."

He looked at me and sucked his teeth. "You know what? You've got a roach on your shoulder."

I jumped up and nearly fell off the couch, rushing to brush my shoulders as fast as I could. I spun around, looking back and forth, a shrill, squeaky scream came from my throat.

"Sike!" Sean cackled like a warlock. "Gotcha! Smart-ass…"

"Oh, you think you're funny," I said, plopping back down onto the couch. "I bet you'll find it funny when I don't come back."

"Oh, you'll be back," he said, yanking me up out of my seat. "It's just a matter of time."

"Yeah?" I asked, a seductive few inches from his ear. "How do you know?"

"Because I cast the spell already. The token is on the mantelpiece. It's done."

"I thought you said that wasn't voodoo."

"It's not voodoo. It's my magic. A little special thing I do." He bent over and kissed me.

"Call me when you get home, beautiful," he said, walking to the closet and grabbing my jacket. "Call me when you're coming back."

I floated back to Jersey, drunk from punch mixed with Sean's euphoric lips, tasting of sweet dreams.

After an hour's ride, I stepped off the train into suburbia. Looking for an available cab to ride home, I spotted a familiar vehicle. Green. Tinted. Shiny rims. Spotless tires. Hyundai. The window rolled down, and a small, tiny head popped out.

"Hey, pretty lady."

"Dexter?" I winced, face twisted into confusion. "Hey…"

"How was your day?"

"Um, good. What are you doing here?"

"Well, I was thinking about you. Hadn't heard back. Did you get my messages?"

"You called?"

I knew Dexter had been trying to contact me. And I was consistent in not calling back. Disinterested in talking to him, I'd left Maryland behind with no interest of ever returning. He must have broken up with his side chick because lately his calls had been constant, every other day, painful reminders of an ugly past I didn't want to relive.

"You know I called. But it kept going to voice mail. You know I don't leave messages." He smiled a half grin. "I even called a few weeks ago to wish you a happy Valentine's Day. You know that's your favorite holiday."

"I do not. I hate V-Day."

"Whatever. Lemme give you a ride home."

"Oh, I was gonna take a cab."

"Meena. I drove all the way from Baltimore to see you. You really think I'll let you take a nasty cab? Come on, I wanna show you my new sound system. Plus, we need to talk."

"Talk about what?"

"About us, Meena. Don't tell me you got all industry on me now," he said, stroking his chin.

"Industry?"

"Industry. That's what you call it, right? When people who work in the entertainment biz forget where they come from. Act all stuck-up. Don't wanna be down with the people they came up with. You used to always talk about that. You forgot?"

I couldn't believe this was happening to me. "Okay, come on."

As I stepped into Dexter's car, a chill flooded through my body. He blasted his music at full volume, nodding his head to the Nas blasting from floor to ceiling. "You hear that bass, Meena?" He shouted over the beat. "That's some real shit. And it didn't come cheap."

Riding with Dexter was like walking in time backward toward blind, young days of dysfunction. I felt like a new woman working at *Buzz*. Independent. Confident. Sophisticated. On it. But with

Dex, I was feeling a familiar tension. Anxiety. Always a word away from an argument or a scream at the top of the lungs.

"He reminds me of your father." I would hear my mother's words during Dexter's worst outbursts. She'd be chopping up carrots for a cake, glancing up at me with a concerned half smile, mixed with worry.

"Really?" I asked, anxious to know the genetics of it all. "How?"

"Just that cocky, short-guy complex. Your father was like that."

"Well, is that a good thing? My dad was abusive, right?"

"I just said he reminds me of your father. That's all. He's not your daddy. And you said he treats you well, right?"

"Yeah, I love him."

"Okay, then. My experience is not yours. Hand me some more carrots, Meena. I got to make two cakes for the potluck at work."

And that's all she'd ever say to me about Dexter. "He reminds me of your father..."

Dex turned onto my block. Pine trees covered the streetlights and a dark, eerie, eleven o'clock black coated the walkways. It was the end of March. But the shadow of winter's chill still floated through the air blocking heat from the sun.

"I just want us to get back together," he said. "That's all."

"Dex, I told you we can't get back together. All we do is fight."

"Yeah, well, all couples fight. We can work it out."

"We've tried to work it out so many times. It always ends in screaming."

"Yeah, but I love you."

"I know you do."

"Do you love me?" he asked, looking sideways, studying my response. "I know you still do."

"Dex," I began, "I..."

"Just say it."

Glancing at his eyes and his forehead, I saw a tiny speck of sweat formulate, and his eye seemed to jump. He put his hand on my arm, making me freeze.

"You're scaring me, Dex."

"I'm scaring you? Why?"

"Well, you come here unannounced. You meet me at the train station. You don't know when I'm coming, so you just wait. How long were you there?"

"Only an hour or so. But I know what time you get off work. And since I missed your birthday last month, I just wanted to do something with you."

"How do you know what time I get off work?" I asked, knowing we hadn't spoken in weeks.

"Your mom," he said, shrugging his shoulders. "I called earlier and she told me."

I could hear his words in the background of my momentary daydream. An out-of-body moment recollecting the call I'd taken from Dex on my birthday. I accidentally dialed his number, drunk and high that night off some brownies cooked with weed Meredith had gotten from Brooklyn, to celebrate. He called me back. And we ended up talking on the phone for two hours. Like old times. Laughing and gossiping. The way it was when we first met. Before the fights. Before the angry emotional outbursts. The call ended when his phone rang at two a.m. He clicked over. Kept me on hold for sixty seconds too long. And I hung up. Knowing what a call at that time of night meant.

When I sobered up and woke the next morning, I regretted every second; he spent the next few days buzzing and beeping me. Calling the house phone. Talking to my mother. Blowing me up despite my ignoring the calls. As if we were back together. As if I'd forgotten why we broke up. And here he was. Stalking. Again.

"You didn't know what time I was getting home. So this is crazy, Dex." I crossed my arms and stared out the window. "You drive up from Baltimore and wait somewhere for me? You just sit and wait for an hour? What the fuck?"

"Well, I came from Maryland and I stopped in Philly to see my dad. And when I leave here I'ma sleep there and go back. I came to tell you I'll be moving to Philly and staying with him. I'll be close. Only an hour and a half away. Not two and a half like Maryland. So we can see each other."

"We're not together anymore, Dex!"

"But, Meena…" he whined, glossy-eyed. "Come on, we can be. If you just try. I can't let you go." His eyes began tearing up as he inched closer, grabbing my arm.

"Let me go!" I yelled, yanking away from his grip and jumping out of the car. "What the fuck?"

By then he'd pulled up in front of my house. There were no lights on. The porch was twenty meters away. I thought about sprinting to freedom but knew that Dexter's ex-soldier calves, bulging atop his cross-trainer Nikes, might catch up to my heels. I grabbed my scarf and wrapped it around my face. Arms crossed. I looked up and down the street at utter emptiness. Like a horror movie, like a scene from *A Nightmare on Elm Street*. My worst fear flashed through my brain: chased by a serial killer and no one to hear the screams but me, dying to the bloodcurdling echo of my own voice in the distance.

I knew by now that Mom was probably dozing to the evening news. So when I got out of the car, I did the safest thing I could think of, which was to stand in the middle of the street, under a lamp. Its brightness glared, stretching my shadow long and dramatic, like the moment.

"Why are you standing there, Meena?" Dex asked with a sinister smile. "Aren't you cold? Why don't you go in the house?"

"Because I don't feel like it. I feel better standing here in the middle of the street under the lamp, where I'm safe. Where people can see and hear me if something should happen."

"And what's gonna happen to you?"

"I don't know. Hopefully nothing as long as I stand in this spotlight."

"I'm not gonna hurt you, Meena. I love you."

"Well, you're scaring me. And if you love me, you'll drive off, go home, and leave me alone."

"I'm not leaving, Meena."

"Well, I'm not going in the house then, and you don't love me."

"I do love you."

"Well, then leave."

"I'm not leaving. I wanna talk to you."

"Leave, Dex. You wanna talk on your own terms. This shit here is spooky," I said, crossing the street. "And you don't care. That's some selfish shit."

"Where are you going now?"

"To stand in the light in front of my neighbor's house. They're awake. I can see lights on and the TV playing."

"I can't believe you're acting like this."

"Leave, Dex. You're scaring me."

"Meena…"

"If you love me, you'll leave."

"I do love you."

"So leave and stop scaring me."

"Meena, come on."

"*Leave.* How many times is that now?"

"I just—"

"Leave!" I screamed it down the street. Icicles shivered from the limbs of tree branches as dogs barked and the squeak of my neighbor's screen door crept open. A little girl poked her head out.

Dex and I turned to see the baby standing there under the porch light. Slippers on. Head full of barrettes. A Barbie doll in hand.

He sucked his teeth and turned on the ignition. Placing his hands on the steering wheel, Dex exhaled a long, hard huff before screeching off. I waited ten minutes in the street, anticipating his return, fingers numb, white air blowing from my lips, staring at that little girl. Feigning a smile, I waved. She looked back, bewildered, combing doll hair with a perplexed smile on her face.

"Girl, get in the house," said Maryland Phillips. My lab partner from the tenth grade. She and her daughter still lived next door. Once a skinny girl with big boobs and a butt, she now wore a size twenty. "What are you doin' out here? It's cold."

"Combing Tee Tee's hair. We want to see the snow."

"It's not snowing tonight. Get in the house," she said, pushing the little girl inside. Looking up at me, she waved.

"Hey, Meena!" She peered at me over her glasses. "What are you doin' out in the street?"

"Oh, just taking a walk."

"You like this fake spring arctic weather?"

"Not really. I just need to clear my mind."

"Okay, well, be careful, it's late," she said, looking up and down the block. "Oh, tell ya mom I want some more of those cupcakes she made for the church."

"Okay," I said, slowly walking up my driveway. The minute the screen closed behind her, I broke into a full sprint toward the front porch, speed-unlocked the front door, and slammed it behind me. Walking through the house, teeth chattering, I turned on all the lights, locked each window, and ran upstairs.

16

I COULDN'T WAIT for the *Buzz* magazine Memorial Day power mixer party. Timed yearly to take place at the end of May, it was the most talked-about event in New York, when the new issue was unveiled in a room packed with shakers and superstars of the entertainment industry. The weekend prior, I'd gotten the perfect outfit—all white fitted pants, fluffy ruffled shirt scooped to the neckline, revealing a tad of cleavage. I'd packed my black heels, with the straps across the ankle, and a tiny clutch to accent.

The party, carefully planned to coincide with when our workload was the lightest, took place after we'd shipped the newest issue to the printer. The office was less crazy and tense. Denise would take out-of-office meetings with long lunches—some business, others personal. Editors would cram into the IT office, fighting for the remote to play the newest video game that hadn't hit the market yet. And I spent my downtime on the phone with Sean. Placing him on hold, in between taking calls for Denise's office.

"I need you to dial a number for me," he asked one afternoon. "I'll give you the digits."

"What's this? A three-way call?"

"Yeah, but don't say anything when they pick up."

"Okay, cool. Who is it?"

"Just someone I was supposed to call and didn't get a chance to," he said. "This will be quick."

"Better be. Denise's phone rings like a broken record." I dialed the number Sean recited.

"Hi, this is Kelly Jones. I'm away from the office now. Please leave a message."

"You can hang up now," Sean said before the beep. "She must be in a meeting."

"Who was that?"

"I told you about Kelly. She works at that entertainment news company EURweb. I'm supposed to call her about a story."

Pause...

A moment of déjà vu set in. I began to feel the insecurity and remember what my mother had said more than once about women in my family. Most women in general, as a matter of fact. "We always know, feel, or sense when something isn't right."

In the Mitchell family, a lie is the highest form of insult. It's like spitting at someone, or throwing a shoe at the president. And even "lawyer lies," passive-aggressive fibs that tell part of the truth, while purposely leaving out pertinent info, didn't escape our loathing.

"Did you have sex with her?" I asked, deciding to be frank instead of playing mind tricks with myself. "I mean, it's cool if you did. I'm not your girl. And I know there were women before me."

Sean paused. Void of the typical quick-witted response.

"Uh," he began, clearing his throat. "Well, yeah, we dated a little. But it didn't work out. She said I had too many female friends. And I was busy, and couldn't be there when she needed me. Some emotionally unavailable self-help female bullshit. Blah, blah, blah. Didn't make sense."

"How long ago was that?"

He paused.

"You can't remember?"

"About six months. Maybe a little less. I don't know." He awkwardly paused again before continuing. "She said she didn't want to bring me into the New Year with her. She wanted to start the year fresh and clean. I still think she was seeing someone else. I mean, how could she stop seeing me like that? Why couldn't we still be friends? Had to be someone else."

"Well, for the record, I'd never ask you to call my ex on your phone. That's just rude."

"She's not my ex!"

"You just said you used to date her."

"Yeah, but she was never my girl. You're my girl."

This time I paused, only for another reason entirely. In the nearly four months that had passed since I'd met Sean, he had never referred to me as his "girl" before. We talked for hours and went on weekly dates. The sex occurred once or twice a week, multiple times a night. But I was careful not to think he was my man, since he hadn't mentioned it. I hadn't fully opened my heart to Sean. He was a workaholic. I knew about the female "friends." And I refused to be hurt again. But his new revelation was a first that made me do ecstatic inner somersaults.

"Oh, I'm your girl?"

"Well, yeah, if you want to be. Do you?"

"Yeah."

"Okay, then. You are."

"As long as you don't have me calling chicks on the three-way for you anymore."

"Done." He laughed.

"Deal."

The party that night was at Tavern on the Green. White lights adorned trees, hanging with elegance like on an angel's harp. Countless buffet tables filled with assorted breads, shrimp, salmon, beef, salads, crackers, and cheeses highlighted varying spots of the venue. Waitresses sashayed in sexy white heels, carrying platters of champagne. Waiters in tuxedos worked their best to elegantly sweat while rushing to appease the demand of a thirsty crowd salivating for enhanced inebriation.

I arrived with my cousin Bernard, who'd just moved to New York from Philadelphia. Looking to break into the photography world, he'd packed his camera and made a point to take shots of all my coworkers. In between his playing paparazzo, we walked the length of the party, nodding our heads to Biz Markie's live DJ mix. It didn't take us long to find the perfect spot at the bar, situated on a stage of sorts, where the entire view of the party could be had in one glance. Bernard maneuvered, taking pictures of my sexy pose with a glass of champagne. I simply nodded, sipped, admired, and watched the view until my pupils focused in on him: Sean. Standing in the middle of the floor talking to her: unknown. She was fairly cute. A short cut cropped to her head. A beige blouse and flowing skirt that fell below her knees. Something about her style was wholesome and churchlike. From the dainty flats she wore to the frumpy top and matching skirt seated on her calves.

But the way Sean watched this girl, standing less than two feet away, her head tilted, laughing bashfully, made me jealous. He carried a Heineken, whispering in her ear. She held on to her wine, blinking slowly with a seductive stare.

"Who are you looking at like that?" Bernard picked up his camera, hoping to get a good shot. "You look disgusted, like…"

"Like what?"

"Like you want to cut somebody."

"Oh, I'm staring at Sean all over this girl."

"Which one?"

"See the chick with the beige skirt and red flats?"

"The one with the beige shirt looking like it's a size too big?"

"Exactly." I laughed. "He's standing way too close to her."

"Well, go get your man. Take his attention off her."

"You're right," I said, putting my empty glass down on the bar. "But you have to distract her. Go flirt or something. Take a picture. Get her number. Something. Just keep her away from him."

Bernard took his orders, marched over, and like a good photographer asked whether he could take a picture. Of course she obliged, put a hand on her hip, and posed. In the meantime, I walked up to Sean.

"Hey, handsome."

He turned around. "Wow," he said, mouth wide open, looking me up and down. "You look beautiful."

"Thank you," I answered, grabbing his hand. "Let me get you a drink."

I pulled him as he followed, mesmerized by my smooth, brown legs in super-high platform heels.

"Vodka tonic, right? Here ya go. On me." He laughed. "The bar is open, ya know?"

"Oh, is it?" We looked at each other as I maintained my most seductive gaze. "You should take advantage. What are you doing after this?"

"No plans. Figured I'd head home and do a little writing since I am on deadline. I shouldn't even be out tonight, but I needed to get a drink."

"Yeah, well, don't let Denise see you."

"What? Why?" He looked around, face full of alarm. "Where is she?"

"In the VIP section, surrounded by too many people," I said, pointing at a crowded corner blocked off by a red velvet rope. "But she's distracted and she's drinking, so you're good."

He exhaled and smiled at me. "So what are *you* doing after this?"

"Going home with you."

Pause...

I'd never been this straightforward before. But then again, it had been a long time since I'd been at an open-bar *Buzz* event drinking King Arthur–size goblets of wine and champagne. The fermented grapes affected my confidence, giving me super-man-size balls to take verbal risks without a thought. I was feeling myself, Sean, and the moment.

"You ready?" I asked, before guzzling down my glass. "Let's go."

"Are *you* sure you're ready?" he said. "Because with the way you look… and it's a full moon."

I grabbed his hand and stumbled out of the party. As Sean tried to hail a cab, I texted Bernard.

Gone to Sean's house. Spending night. Thanks for keeping that bitch off my man. Talk to you tomorrow. Gnite.

He texted back.

Damn, you got your man. Ok, cuzzo. Wish I could find somebody as fierce as you. And that bitch's name is Kelly Jones. Works at some entertainment company. You know her?

The minute I got into the cab I was all over Sean, caressing the small of his back, nibbling his ears, unbuckling his pants. I didn't care that the driver was watching from his rearview mirror. Wine, bubbly, and hormones had given me the confidence to be a swinging exhibitionist in a dirty yellow taxi. It gave me the will to ride him as hard as I could, on the floor, next to the futon, and eventually across his bed in Brooklyn. He grunted and moaned. I screamed and scratched, down to do anything to make him, and me, forget about Kelly Jones.

17

THE NEXT EVENING, I sat in the doctor's office, eyes long and droopy. Half falling asleep. I'd spent the last thirty minutes nodding in and out of rapid eye movement. The day had been a never-ending episode. And the night before with Sean hadn't ended till five. I was thirsty, hungry, hungover, and under-rested. Not one to both cuddle and sleep simultaneously, I found myself having an uneasy rest at Sean's. Tossing and turning, wiggling and scooting, aiming for the far side of the bed, away from his body. Two feet from the stifling sweat of an unmovable snuggle. I mean, I love cuddling in a man's arms. But after the sex is done and the moment has passed, I need my own space and place to sleep—my own side of the covers, corner of the sheet, and long length of the bed.

The night and morning were long. Asleep at five thirty. Up at seven. More sex till eight. Shower. Quickie sex in the shower. And on the train from Brooklyn to Manhattan by ten. Or rather, 10:11. I was blessed to have a job where I didn't have to report at nine o'clock. The entertainment-industry late start was perfect for someone like me who was prone to sleeping in and running ten minutes late. Always rushing.

Denise hated this lateness even though she had a punctuality problem herself. When I was hired, she'd said I didn't need to get to the office before ten. But over the past month, she was in "acting like an editor in chief" mode, getting to work at nine thirty. And I knew I should be the dutiful, diligent, reliable assistant by her side at all times, even before ten. And I planned on it. But this particular morning, it wasn't easy.

The night before, I'd seen Denise laughing loudly in VIP, guzzling down glasses of red wine. I was sure there was no way she'd be in the office at nine thirty. So I aimed to be there by ten—or rather, 10:11, which was on time in Meena world.

When I walked in, the office was a vacant room of silence. Late nights didn't work well for magazine editors, or their assistants. I dragged myself to my desk and sat down; my phone rang. Clearing away the tired, overnight cobwebs in my throat, I smiled to adjust the tone of my voice and answered, upbeat, "Denise Banor's office."

"Meena."

"Hey, Denise."

"You on vacation today?"

"No, why are you calling the office line?"

"Because I've been ringing your cell phone and paging you for the past thirty minutes."

I looked at my cell. It had five missed calls. None I heard, because I'd forgotten to take the ringer off silent from the night before. "You didn't tell me my nine o'clock breakfast had been moved," Denise continued. I could hear the siren of a fire truck in the background. "I'm in the street, rainy as hell, looking like a fool, lost."

"Where was the meeting moved to?"

"You're supposed to tell me, Meena. That's why you're my assistant."

I suddenly remembered the call, the day before, from Clive Owen's assistant, requesting the meeting be changed. But after being on the phone with Sean, caught up with his three-way to Kelly Jones, and his telling me I was his girl, I'd forgotten to write it down. The butterflies in my stomach fluttered. Gas bubbles formed.

"It was changed to Café Jule on Forty-sixth Street," Denise said. "But I was at the Kitano on Park. So I was thirty minutes late, and looked like a fool walking in. This was an important meeting, Meena. I need to confirm this Whitney cover. But we only got to meet for fifteen minutes because I was *late*. And now he's leaving the country on vacation and I won't be able to meet with him again until next month. After July fourth, damn near two months, Meena."

"I'm sorry, Denise. My phone was on silent, and I overslept and—"

"Meena, your phone should never be off when you work for me. And you know I don't like being late. We'll talk about this when I get to the office."

And she hung up.

An hour later, when Denise arrived at work, she didn't address me directly. Her communication came through memos and to-do lists she'd throw at my inbox. They all came with Post-its stuck to them and instructions in capital letters written with red pen:

"PROOF THIS."

"PASS THIS OUT."

"READ THIS."

"REMIND ME OF THIS."

"SAVE THIS."

"FILE THIS." I was happy to leave at five for my doctor's appointment.

"Meena Butler."

I'd nodded off after filling out the health insurance paperwork. During that groggy daze, I sort of watched *Jeopardy*. Alex Trebek questioned a contestant who answered, "What is sleep?" Or maybe that was a dream.

"Meena Butler."

The second call of my name made me jump out of my seat into an upright position, where I instinctively wiped slobber off my face. Stumbling toward the nurse, I picked sleep out of my left eye and mumbled, "Sorry. I didn't hear you."

Her reply: a fake smile.

She led me down a pristine white corridor to Dr. Patel's office. His room was clogged full of book cabinets stacked with old medical manuals. The dark, olive walls featured crooked framed certificates of degrees and specialties. Atop the desk were stacks of papers, pens, pencils, sitting next to tiny trinkets and colorful toys that looked out of place in a medical room decorated with various vaginal diagrams. Next to the toys sat a bowl filled with shiny peppermints and other candies.

In an effort to stay awake, I popped a red-and-white-striped candy in my mouth. The smell of it opened my eyes and nose, helping me breathe deeply and awaken to my surroundings.

"Hello, Ms. Butler."

"Hey, Doc."

Dr. Patel had been my gynecologist since I first got my period at thirteen. He was my mother's gyn and knew all the intricate family details, vaginally, that a family gyn should know. He was a short, skinny brown man with two patches of gray hair on both sides of his head that framed a brown birthmark shaped like a halo. His eyes were small and beady, and he had a large gap between his front two teeth. I always made my yearly appointment at the beginning of summer.

"Well, you're all healthy, blood work came back fine." He pulled out the paper to read from. "Negative for HIV, HPV, chlamydia, gonorrhea, syphilis, herpes."

"Well, that's good."

"But the images from your uterus came back showing you have a growth."

I sat up straight, chewing the mint. "A growth?"

"Yes, something on your uterus. A mass of some sort."

"Do I have cancer?"

"I don't think so. But you'll need to go to a specialist. She's a good doctor, I know her father. She'll tell you more. But you may need to get a laparoscopy."

"A lapa what?"

"A laparoscopy. An exploratory test where they'll make small slits on the sides of your stomach," he stood up to use his pelvis as a diagram, "slip tubes in, and see what that growth is."

"Whoa, Dr. Patel." I was nearly standing now, wide awake. "I just started a new job a few months ago. I can't take off."

"Well, you need to have it sooner than later. And it may be nothing. But the laparoscopy will help us know for sure. You'll be out a week, two at the most."

A week or two was like an eternity in magazine land. That was one-third or half of the period it took to close a magazine from Word document to final shipment to the printer. A week or two was the period of time it took for Denise to realize her last assistant sucked. And now, with her pissed at me after messing up the last meeting with Clive Owen, that teetering feeling—Denise miraculously made everyone feel they were her most loved, yet still on the edge of losing their jobs—had my stomach doing backflips.

I massaged my temples as Meredith pulled up. Her car huffing and puffing like the anger I felt at life's monkey wrench. Like the aftereffects of the blunt sizzling in the ashtray that I was happy to see and need. We pulled into our usual spot at the playground near my house. I kicked my feet up. She popped in my advance copy of Outkast's new CD. *Aquemini.* The funky Southern drawl of weird loops and psychedelic pops fit my scattered mind, half-tired, half-high, half-confused about what to do about my latest health dilemma. "Well, can you avoid the surgery?"

"I guess, but it's a damn mass. Fucking tumor. What if I have a tumor?"

"What if you don't?"

"What if I do? Cancer at twenty-five. That's some bullshit. Still living at home. I need to move. I'm moving to Brooklyn."

"When?"

"As soon as I get this surgery shit over with. I have the money saved. I don't need a car in Brooklyn. I was saving to buy some old used thing when I can have my own space and peace of mind, instead of buying a ride."

"And you can be closer to Sean…"

Sean. The other reason being away for two weeks scared me. More than a week was too long not to sleep with a man. That was more than enough time for him to miss me, get horny, and run to what's-her-face, Kelly Jones. My being around made it harder.

"If he wants to cheat, he'll cheat," Meredith said, shrugging her shoulders with a lip turned up. Exuding the throw-away-a-man confidence I always admired. She never held on too long. Never had drama. Was always ready to walk away the minute they acted up. The lucky product of a functional two-parent household. "You can't make a man stay. You can't make a man not cheat. But you can definitely push them away by being all on top of them. Calling and texting all the time."

I let the words seep in as Andre 3000 rapped so fast, I couldn't understand what he was saying.

"You think I'm chasing?" I blinked slowly, already knowing the answer, but in a mirage of dry, parched, weed-induced famine that made me hunger for Doritos flavored with answers to my problem. I was thirsty for juice that contained vitamins of common sense.

"I mean… yeah. That's what you do. But you don't know it, and I really think you can't help it. I mean, even when you aren't physically chasing, you're mentally doing it, thinking about him with this scheme on how to get him. Wondering if he wants you," she pointed out to me. "I say, fuck him. If he wants you, he'll come get you. Easy. You don't have to do much of anything but be your-self. Mind your business. Return his calls. My mother always told me that. She said she didn't have to do a thing to get my dad. He always just kept showing up. Calling up. Hanging around like a little puppy. Making plans. Treating her nice. Giving her attention. So she finally picked him."

I let the words sink in. "She finally picked him." Wondering why I always felt like I was the one being chosen. Like I had to prove myself. Elated over some guy liking me and wanting me and noticing I was pretty. Where did I get that from?

Meredith dropped me off at home and I walked through the door. Mom laughed loudly. Cackling through the corridors. Not even acknowledging I'd gotten home. I knew who she was on the phone with. After all these years, she and Larry were still going strong. She was still the side chick. He was still about to leave his wife.

"Oh, baby, you are so funny." She giggled as she closed her bedroom door. "You better call me back this time. Uh-huh... uh-huh... excuses. Okay, well, then call me Saturday."

A minute after she hung up the phone, I heard her pick up and dial.

"You didn't tell me you loved me." Silence.

"Say it!" She giggled like a high school kid.

"Okay, okay... I know you gotta go. I love you, too." And she hung up.

I called Sean. The phone rang five times. Voice mail. I hung up and dialed again. He picked up on the third ring. "Hello." He was short. Exasperated.

"Heyyy..." I said, trying to sound relaxed. Wanting to jump into spilling the breaking news on my surgery. But needed to build up to it. "What are you doing?"

"Writing." Short again. Attitude.

"Why do you sound like you have an attitude?"

"I don't," he said, aggravated. "What's up?"

"Yeah, so I just came back from the doctor." Silence.

"And... well, yeah. I have to have surgery."

"I'm sorry to hear that." I could hear him stabbing a computer key. Repeatedly. Killing a button. "Delete, delete, delete. Shit!"

"You all right?"

"I just can't get this together. I'm just…" He sighed. This time it was frustration. "Yo, can you come over?"

"Well, I'm home. It's already eight. I wouldn't make it out there till eleven if New Jersey Transit acts right. And you know MTA runs slow at night."

"Yo… lemme call you back."

"Um…" My words trailed off. "Well… okay."

I turned the ringer up, ready for Sean's call. Laying back, I closed my eyes and visualized a Brooklyn brownstone with my dream apartment on the second floor, before drifting to sleep.

18

THE SURGERY TOOK PLACE IN JULY. Right after July fourth. Even though the mass was found to be nothing but an insignificant growth of tissue left over from birth, I was out of work for two weeks. Spent three days in the hospital. And a week and a half lying in bed with stitches on my pelvis and large sterile pads taped to me. My mother played nursemaid.

"You hungry?"

She brought a tray of pancakes. Scrambled eggs. Potatoes on the side. Biscuits. I sat up in bed and smiled.

"Wow. Thank you."

"You know you're my baby."

My mother was a sucker for helping people. Saving the downtrodden. Codependent at times. But it was all about love, in her own way, of course. If you fell? She might not give a hug, but she'd bandage you up and make you a nice meal. If you cried? She might not kiss your forehead, but dinner would feature your favorite entrées. Took me years to realize this and understand her love language and figure out that cooking food and the act of doing someone a service were her ways of showing love. Rolling out of bed to whip up pancake batter, scrambling a few eggs, buttering a pan of biscuits, and frying a few potatoes was the equivalent of "I love you." Some gave gifts, others complimented or showered you with affection, many like myself preferred quality time and attention, but my mother's love language was an act of service. I remembered reading about it in Gary Chapman's *The Five Love Languages*.

She went downstairs and I picked up the phone tucked under my covers; I sucked my teeth when I saw a missed call from Dexter. Damn stalker. I hadn't spoken to him since his crazy sighting at the train station months ago. He didn't call as frequently as he had. But every few months, I'd see a little check-in and missed call just to spook and remind me of his presence still lurking somewhere.

I dialed Sean. Said I wouldn't. Said I'd wait for him to call me. Chase me. Check in on me. But it was like an annoying addiction. I couldn't wait. The anxiety was overwhelming. The yearning to dial seven digits and talk to him. Go to him. It was like a crackhead hearing a pipe calling his name. Abandonment issues. Insecurity and the fear of feeling the disappointing possibility that he might not call me. I had to take control.

"So you coming to see me today?" I asked, sitting up in the bed, waiting for an answer. I hadn't heard his voice in a week.

"Nah, I'm on deadline," he said to the tap of a keyboard. A bag of chips ruffled in the background as he crunched on the phone. "But you're better, right?"

"If I was better, I'd be at your house," I snapped back. "And you said that last weekend, 'Nah, I'm on deadline.' "

"Well, this is what I do, Meena. I'm a writer. I have deadlines. What the fuck?"

"What the fuck? Um… maybe your girl had surgery and she's in need of the same TLC you give your damn computer. Maybe if I had circuits I'd get some attention."

"Oh, come on now. Are you on your period?"

"Don't insult me with that sexist bullshit."

The truth was that I was menstruating. The first day was the worst, heavy, bloated, crampy, and irritated. The insecurities that hormonal shifts evoked were uncontrollable. I was horny as hell. Couldn't have sex. But needed some love. Some quality time. Tears welled up in my eyes.

"I miss you and you don't care. I feel like I haven't seen you in forever, you don't call, you work all the time. You haven't come to see me once. You say you care, but you don't. I'm all alone."

"I do care, Meena. Come on. And you're in another state. *Jersey*. I care, I mean… why are you crying? I can't talk to you like this."

"Like what? What is 'like this'? Explain that shit. What am I like?"

"Nothing. I mean, like crying… and sad. Like… Meena, come on, babe. Not now. This is a cover story for *Buzz*. *Your* people. I'm almost done. Don't do this to me right now."

"You know what? This is why I'm moving to Brooklyn."

"You're moving to Brooklyn?" He sounded nervous suddenly. Serious. "When?"

"Soon. Because *Buzz* is my job. *You* are my boyfriend. But no one would know since I just had my uterus dissected and stitched back together with a million threads, big-ass gauze of puss oozing on my stomach, and you keep talking about yourself. 'I'm on deadline…' "

"Listen, if I can finish this draft today, I'll try to come out there tomorrow, okay? Since you way in Jersey and all. Is that all right?"

"No, it's not! Fuck!"

And I hung up.

Tired of the monotonous murmur of TV voices, I needed to see my man, my love, needed the quality time with his presence and touch. That was my love language. But I didn't know how to express it; my naggy insecurities came out in jumbled, wrongly positioned words fueled by frustration and uncontrollable emotion.

The next day Sean didn't call. I sent him a text.
Hey you.
No reply.

A day later. No reply.

As much as I wanted to pick up the phone and blow him up, I didn't. I wasn't going to act crazy. So instead, I suffered the misery of burning separation anxiety on the insides of my stomach, consuming it with a fear of loneliness because he hadn't called. Because he hadn't come to see me after surgery. Because he wasn't trying. I sat in bed full of heated fury. Finally, I grabbed the phone and turned off the ringer. Silencing the alert signal, ending the bells and whistles when someone texted or e-mailed. I was tired of waiting for *him*. Tired of wanting *him*. I scrolled down my contacts list and deleted Sean's number from the call log, incoming, outgoing, contacts, everywhere, so I couldn't call *him*. I was tired of chasing and needed to make sure I couldn't follow, even when the urge erupted. But twenty-four hours later, the first thing I did was wake, turn on my phone, and eagerly check texts and voice mails, looking for signs of my missing man, missing me, missing the sound of my voice and heart and warmth and spirit. But nothing. When the phone did suddenly ring, a burst of anxiety traveled through my valves. Making them pulsate and leap like a classroom of kids anticipating Santa's arrival. It came from an unavailable number.

"Hello," I said calmly, trying not to sound excited.

"Hey, sick girl," said Meredith, the only one who called regularly just to say hello. "What's up?"

"Oh," I said, deflated. "Hey."

"Well, damn, you could at least fake like you're happy to hear from me. Damn."

"Nah, I'm fine."

"I didn't ask if you were fine. But I do want to know how you're doing. Why do you sound like that?"

"Nothing."

"Nothing?"

"Nothing." I paused. "Why is your call coming through as 'unavailable'?"

"Oh, I forgot to tell you. I found this block-number feature on the phone and I wanted to try it out. I see it works. That's good for if I need to stalk."

I didn't reply. Making a mental note of needing to see whether my phone had that feature.

She was quiet before continuing. "Sean come see you today?"

"He was going to, but he's on deadline. So…" The words drifted off before I sucked my teeth. "And I understand that. I mean, if he doesn't turn in his cover story to Denise on time, he won't be writing for *Buzz* again."

"Uh-hm."

"What does 'Uh-hm' mean?"

"So he hasn't come to see you after you've been in the hospital and had surgery?"

"Well, he's on deadline. And it takes a lot of transcribing and time. I mean, I'm cool."

"Cool? So you're okay with that?"

"Yeah. I mean, of course I want him to see me. But I also don't want him to resent me because he came, and then got back to his computer and couldn't write. You know when writers get into a rhythm it's hard to really get them out of it."

She paused for a second.

"That's some bullshit," she continued. "And I don't like him. I can't wait till y'all break up."

Meredith. Always quick to call my men out and express her opinion. She'd always been right. Anyone she didn't like typically didn't last. But I never listened.

"I need to take some more painkillers. I think it's been six hours, stomach is starting to sting."

"No, stay away from that addictive crap. I'm coming over to see you. I got some medicinal marijuana to cure your pain."

"I could use that…"

"I know. See you in a few minutes."

The hemp smoke tasted fabulous floating through my lungs and out my nose. My head and mind opened up my body to thoughts of relaxation and contemplation. Clarity. A third sensory eye. Meredith and I sat in her car, smoking up the windows. Nodding our heads to Big Pun's *Capital Punishment*. My pink bunny slippers perched on her dashboard as I reclined the seat back to a 180-degree position. I was glad my mother had gone to work. Relieved to be alone to smoke, giggle, and be relaxed long enough to let the truth speak freely.

"Last night, I had a dream that Sean was cheating on me," I said, after blowing out a long cloud of white. Clearing my throat and pulling again. Smoking in silence was our way of taking it all in.

"I was standing there, watching him hugging this girl. He hugged her, kissed her, put his hand in her pants. And I started crying."

I took another pull before passing the blunt. Holding the smoke in my mouth, I saw visions of the dream drifting in my head. The fear in my heart skipped along like brain zaps on a hospital monitor.

"And you remember what I told you about women in my family and dreams, right?"

Meredith nodded her head as she pulled on the joint. She'd rolled it smooth and tight.

"Yeah, the women in your family are psychic," she said. "Y'all see the future."

"It's crazy. I hate when I have the cheating dream," I said. "It's always a sign. Always comes true."

"That's crazy. So what are you gonna do?"

"I dunno, girl. I love him."

"You are always in love, Meena. You better stop falling in love before you really know and trust these guys. Protect your heart."

"I know. I try. But the sex makes all the walls I put up come right down if I see relationship potential."

"And if he's not, you can fuck him forever and not feel a thing. I know. I get it. But love is not enough to make a relationship work. Just because you love somebody doesn't mean you're supposed to be with them," she said. "Both of my parents told me that. They say it all the time."

The words seeped into the clouds of smoke. Her mother and father had remarried each other after both of their failed first marriages. Meredith came a few years later.

"Like when you fall before you know someone well. When you don't trust your instincts, sex dulls them even more, love blinds you altogether, making it hard to tell truth from fantasy. You start doubting yourself, doubting your soul. Living without integrity to your own damn self. Literally lying to yourself. We can't do that as women. We always know. I mean, I always know when a man isn't being honest with me. I think every woman does. And I know sometimes you can't control who you feel love for, but you can control who you give love to. You can control who you're in a relationship with."

Meredith rambled on, making all the sense in the world. She tended to do this when she was high. First being quiet, like a therapist taking notes. Then talking a mile a minute. Morphing into superintellectual weed-smoker mode. Pontificating on the ways of love, where her words ran into one another with no periods, occasional commas; her points ran on. When Meredith finished, she took a long pull, held it in for ten seconds, and exhaled. "So what are you gonna do?"

"I don't know, girl. I'll figure it out."

"You need to snoop," she said, smiling. "Get your private investigator on. Next time you go to his house, look around. There are always signs."

"I need to move to Brooklyn."

"Whatever. Doesn't matter where you live, if he's a cheat," Meredith answered. "Just do the digging."

I could see the sense of that. My dreams usually manifested, like instinctual infidelity premonitions. When it came to the women in my family, we never knew if the nightmare we envisioned meant the cheating would occur in the future or if we were seeing the past. Regardless of when the transgression took place, we always found out, in the most blatant manner.

19

MY FIRST DAY BACK in the office at the end of July, and I was greeted with a present—a mile-high inbox. Paper leaned sideways like a raggedy tree. Tiny, hot pink Post-its with Denise's red writing twinkled like old Christmas tree ornaments. But I didn't mind, getting to work fifteen minutes early, logging in, and spending all day reading and responding to the hundred e-mails I'd received over the past two weeks. Pure heaven.

I'd missed the loud creative hustle of an office full of artistic minds on steroids. Biggie blasting from one speaker. Mary J. Blige blaring from another. U2 and Bob Marley echoing from the mail room. Someone unabashedly yelling "Fuck!" after hanging up the phone and screaming, "I hate fucking publicists!"

That was the life of working at *Buzz*. This was the real world. *My* real world. Not one of being locked in a house on an empty side street in Jersey, watching *Rap City* on BET. By the end of the day, I'd happily gotten through all of my e-mails when a new message pinged my inbox, titled "Beautiful Return."

Dear Lovely Meena,
Welcome back. Your missing presence left a gaping hole in my
heart. One where my mind craved for the beauty of healing
that only comes from the soft caress of a woman such as you.
                                                    Sean

I smiled so hard that I didn't realize someone was standing behind me. Timberland boots, a crisp, new tan pair, baggy jeans, and a polo shirt. I nearly fell out of my seat when I realized it was Sean holding a bouquet of mixed flowers next to a crooked smile. He looked half-embarrassed, half-nervous.

"Wow," I said, wide-eyed. "Just got your e-mail."

"I know. I just sent it. I was standing over there," he said, pointing toward the elevators. "I wanted to watch you open it."

"Are you stalking me, Sean Baxter?"

"I will if you don't pack up so we can go eat."

"Cool. But I'm still on that medication, so I can't drink."

"It's okay, more for me. Come on, lady."

～

The rest of the summer seemed perfect between Sean and I. Romantic dinner dates, boat rides, long walks, days spent sleeping at his house with random clothes stuffed in my own drawer. It was like the surgery and time apart had been a blessing to bring us closer together. I was in love. He was my king. And I was the happiest I'd been in my life.

By the fall, we were in a routine, with Friday date nights to see the newest movie release. On one typical evening, I logged off, grabbed my bag, locked Denise's office, and headed to the lobby with Sean. We stood at the elevator, smiling, brushing shoulders, until the door opened and a girl stepped out.

I recognized that familiar face. Young and bright. Ballerina hairdo with a bun at the top. Flowery ruffled shirt falling from her shoulders. Same church skirt worn at the *Buzz* mixer, hanging below her knees. Kelly Jones.

We stopped short. She paused, gaping at Sean. And out my side view, I could see his eyes stretched wide. He'd stopped breathing.

"Um, hey, Kelly." His voice quavered. "You know Denise's assistant, Meena Butler, right?"

"Oh, yeah," she said, forcing a smile. "I heard about you. Hey."

I thought about not replying. But for the sake of fakeness and professionalism, since we were in the *Buzz* offices, I forced myself to mutter one word.

"Hey," I said. Blank face. No emotion. Cold, icy, and stiff.

Tense silence followed the end of that one word. She kept staring at Sean, me, and back to him again. Breaking the stagnant energy, I stepped onto the elevator. Sean followed, dropping his head like a kid, mumbling at Kelly without looking at her, "A'ight then," he said as the doors closed.

Our eyes met, she the bitch in a church dress, me the bitch with the man she wanted. We'd meet again.

"What's that company she works for?" I asked Sean when her face was out of sight. "Did you say it was *EW*?"

"No," he said, staring at his phone, trying to look busy when he wasn't. "EUR."

"Oh, right, they're always clogging up the fax machine with their blasts."

"Yeah, she writes all their little updates," he said, checking his phone twice for a reply. "They're funny. Kinda quirky. I look forward to those blasts every day."

"I bet you do."

"What does that mean?"

"I just thought you weren't into entertainment gossip stuff," I said, pressing the button for the first floor after realizing we hadn't moved. "You always say it's so trivial and a waste of journalism. What did you say again? 'A tool to distract the masses'?"

"I mean, yeah, it is. But I didn't say I don't sometimes read them when I need a convenient distraction."

I sighed at his obvious lie. "What's wrong now, Meena?"

"What do you mean, 'now'?"

"I don't know, seems like something is always bothering you."

"No, something is not always bothering me, Sean."

It was his turn to be annoyed.

"Listen, I'm hungry," I said, exiting the elevator into the lobby. "It's been a long day, I got here crazy early. Let's just go eat. I may have to have a sip of wine. I need it."

After an Italian dinner of ten words and a bottle of wine, I woke in the middle of the night at Sean's house. We were coupled up on the bed, atop the covers, holding hands, asleep in each other's arms. Had to have been the wine. I drank so many glasses after my run-in with Kelly Jones; compensating for insecurity with inebriation seemed the only thing to do. After we got back to his place, made sloppy sex mixed with the taste of fermented grapes and vodka, we passed out, holding each other like cuddling babies.

The discomfort made me sweat. Sean's arm around my neck and his sticky, hot fingers nestled into my palms. I felt a tiny cramp bubbling up my spine. A little woozy from all the wine, I pried myself from his grip and crept to the bathroom. Even on my tiptoes, the floor squeaked. I stopped walking, trying not to wake him. He snored so loud that the pencils on his desk rolled to the side. The movement was a reminder: investigate. A reminder that Sean wrote a biography of dates on his jumbo desk calendar. Each box had an important deadline or meeting. I took a moment to reacquaint myself with a map of where he'd been.

I squeaked to his desk, reading carefully. Due dates for October magazine assignments, *Buzz*, *Entertainment Weekly*, *Rolling Stone*, *Vibe*. And then my eye stopped on the weekends. "Meet Kelly," read one date outlined twice with a star. The following Sunday, "Meet Kelly for brunch." I looked at the calendar closer and flipped back to July during the weeks of my surgery. "Meet Kelly. 7:30 p.m." was written with an exclamation mark on two separate dates. My heart throbbed with infuriation that rammed into my throat, wanting to scream, fighting my need to stay silent. I wanted to be destructive, pull the calendar off his desk, scribble cuss words across it, crumple it up, and light it on fire. But then I heard a loud snore, and Sean coughed himself awake. Bed springs bounced with a tiny squeal as he tossed. And with each sound, I tiptoed back to his bedroom, slid under the covers, and lay on my back with my eyes wide open. Maybe he'd met her for a casual meeting of writers. Perhaps he was schmoozing, hoping for more work with her company. One side debated: *There has to be some explanation.* The other side ached and seethed: *He's cheating. Fuck him!*

He turned over and put his arm around me. I wanted to bite it and spit angry venom on his wrists. But instead, I let it lie atop me, feeling heavy, hot, like an anchor confining me to this bed of disloyalty. *Had he fucked her?* I pondered the question until I fell asleep. When I awoke two hours later, I rolled off the mattress, hopped in the shower, double-scrubbed my vagina, and knew for sure what we needed to do: take a trip to the STD clinic.

20

I DIDN'T REALIZE HOW LONG my shower took that morning till Sean knocked me out of a daydream.

"Uh, did you drown?" he said, banging on the door. "I have to pee."

"What time is it?"

"Eight thirty. Thirty minutes past the time you got in there." His voice sounded muffled. I could hear the vibrating bass of the Red Hot Chili Peppers blasting from his stereo system. "You want some eggs or a bagel? I was gonna get breakfast."

"Nah, my stomach is bothering me."

"Okay, I'll be back."

As the door slammed behind him, I stood in the shower, numb to the touch of water bouncing off my body. Tiny drops steamed up the small, square window above the tub, allowing specks of sunlight to poke through the glass. Past the smears were the sights of overhead subway lines, a random rooftop, grime, and pigeons flying. As I stared out that window, all I could see was Sean fucking Kelly. Tossing. Turning. Grunting. I know it was a daydream. I knew it was a thought I shouldn't have. But I couldn't help the boil of envy, the seething resentment of knowing that he had made time to meet with her, while on deadline, but couldn't come see me in Jersey—his sick girlfriend, sewn up from surgery. How fucked-up was that?

I felt the burn of tears welling in my eyes as I stood under the showerhead, forcing myself to let the water hit my face and slap me around for being a blind, bumbling idiot.

"Hey, I got you a jelly donut," Sean said as I turned off the shower. "And tea with milk and sugar. I know you're not hungry, but you might be later."

"I hate jelly donuts. I told you that. And is it soy milk?"

"No. Since when do you like soy milk?"

"Since I decided to be a vegetarian."

"When did you decide that?"

"When I was sick in bed in Jersey," I said, leaving the bathroom with a large black towel tied around my body. "You'd have known if you'd visited me."

"Oh my God, you bringing that up again?" Sean sipped his tea too fast, burning his lips, wincing in pain. "Shit!"

"Uh-huh, God don't like ugly. Especially with that selfish shit coming out your mouth," I said, a tiny smirk on my face. "I'm so embarrassed to tell people you didn't come visit me after surgery that I lie and say you did. They'll go, 'Oh, he's such a good boyfriend'…"

"You know what, Meena? I told you why I couldn't come. So deal with it." He sat in his chair and turned on the computer. "Why can't you just stay in the moment?"

"Why couldn't you come see me? Oh. Right. 'Cause you were on deadline. You had people to see." I picked up my tea to check it, slowly envisioning myself splashing it across his desk. "What's that you say, 'I have things to do, places to go, people to see'?"

"I was here writing."

"*Right*," I said, spewing sarcasm. "Just you and your lonesome computer spending time together."

"You know what? I see you're trying to be funny."

"Not at all. You said you were here both weekends, right?"

"No, I didn't say that. But yes, Meena, I was."

Lie. I thought this to myself, wanting to spit out the word onto his damn calendar. But I didn't need to. The look on my face spelled things out.

"You think I'm lying?" Sean glanced at me and back at his computer with an aggravated smirk. "Obviously you do by that look you're giving me."

"I think we should go to the STD clinic."

He looked up, eyes dazed, confused, like a drug addict.

"You know there's one a few blocks away from the *Buzz* office," I continued, "so we can go one morning before work, get in there early, beat the crowd, and get out in a few hours."

"Well, uh…" he stammered, like the jelly donut was lodged in his windpipe. Finally he managed to say, "Well, why do we need to do that?"

"I always do this with my boyfriends. We've been together eight months. You say I'm wife material, so let's go do what committed couples do—go to the doctor and get checked together."

"I haven't been to the doctor in a long time," he said, looking expressionless at the laptop. "Man, I don't even remember when."

"Which is why we should go. Like, when's the last time you got checked for STDs?"

"Ooh," he said, scratching his neck, voice in a low mumble. "I don't remember that, either. Years."

"What's that you said?" I asked loudly. "I couldn't hear your last words there."

He cleared his throat. "I said, 'Years.' "

"Wow, so how do you know you don't have anything? If you've been fucking for years, how do you know you're not giving me something from all that raw sex?"

"I mean, I'd know," he said, his voice in a defensive high pitch. "It would be a brown color or burn or something."

"Not all the time. Sometimes these STDs are colorless and have no smell."

He took a deep breath and sighed. "Okay..." The word trailed off till he whispered three more: "We can go."

"What was that you said?"

"We. Can. Go." He enunciated, straight-faced, aggravated.

"Well, I knew I was going," I said, back in the bathroom, fixing my makeup. "Just wanted to make sure you were coming with me."

"When you wanna go?"

"Today. As soon as I finish getting ready."

"Wait," he said, picking up his planner and turning the page. "Today? Why the rush?"

"Why wait? If we're thinking about it, we might as well go before we talk ourselves out of it. I'll just text Denise, tell her I had an emergency and needed to go to the doctor."

"Well, won't that make her ask questions?" He nervously began cleaning up his desk. "Don't tell my business."

"Sean, don't insult me."

"I feel a little insulted." He got up and walked to the bathroom door. "You think I have a disease or something."

"And I'm insulted and suspicious that you don't want to go. What are you scared of?"

"Nothing, I just don't like doctors."

I adjusted my hat, blotted my lipstick with tissue, and took one last look at the mirror before brushing past him and squeezing my way out the bathroom door. He stood there, hunching. Gone was the confident, upright strut of a Leo man. Replaced with a slight frown below eyes of fear. I turned to grab his waist.

"Come on, baby." I felt his tightness melting in my palms, muscles relaxing. "You know I love you. I just wanna do things right. This is the right thing to do."

I looked up, chin on his chest. He looked down, halfway smiling, before folding his lips inside his mouth.

"See, you're lucky you're cute." He pulled away, marching to the couch and grabbing his backpack. "I wouldn't do this for any other girl."

He grabbed his keys off a hook and opened the front door.

"Why are you standing there?" he asked, walking out. "Let's do this before I change my mind."

21

THE CLINIC ON TWENTY-THIRD STREET in Manhattan was the filthiest health facility I'd ever seen. The middle of the front lawn was littered with papers, bottles, miscellaneous junk, and a sign reading "Helth Clinic." The line of would-be patients arriving early, hoping to be seen first, trailed out the door and down the stairs. One woman with a tattered leather jacket yelled at her kids for picking up bottles off the grass: "Get over here! Shit!" Another, with a toe hanging out the top of old, decrepit, laceless Adidas sneakers, made his way down the line, asking, "Do you have a cigarette or spare change?"

"Is it always like this?" I questioned the guard giving out numbers. "What's the wait?"

"Yeah, right after the weekend, it's crazy," he said, rolling his eyes and shaking his head. "You lucky you didn't come after Halloween. You should definitely give yourself two to four hours today."

I looked at my watch: nine thirty. My immediate text to Denise read: *At doctor. Won't be in till after lunch.*

I knew I was safe today. The magazine was in the early weeks of its next issue. Things were less hectic, allowing Denise to busily edit and not take any calls. She texted me back: *No worries. Hope everything is ok. See ya then.*

After an hour, Sean and I finally made it to the waiting room. We passed time by playing tic-tac-toe and hangman while snickering at the poorly written and acted "safe sex" movies flickering on an old TV. Doing our best to hide giggles when watching the craziest of the city walk into the waiting room. Two hours passed before we were seen. Sean was called first.

"Fifty-two. Number fifty-two."

He looked down at his creased cardboard numbered square to make sure it was his. And then he stared at me, pursed lips and nervous eyes reminiscent of an eight-year-old.

"Good luck," I whispered with a smile. "It's gonna be all right." He slowly got up and followed the nurse down the hallway. I took out my journal and wrote:

At the STD clinic with Sean. I'm sooo glad he came with me today. Maybe he isn't cheating on me. I mean, this is a step in the right direction. The fact that he came with me at the last minute, when I was sooo bitchy this morning. Think my period is coming. I hate when I PMS. But that shit with Kelly. That name on his calendar 4 times? WTF?! Nah, for real, if that asshole has anything, I'm killing him. I mean, not for real (in case something happens to him and the police read this journal for evidence. I would never kill Sean. I love him). But nah, I'm definitely breaking up with him. And I'm confronting that Kelly bitch. But wait, I'm getting ahead of myself. Lemme relax. He's here with me. He came to the STD clinic. He loves me. Relax.

"Number fifty-three. Fifty-three."

I dropped my journal on the floor. The pen rolled under the seat in front of me, and I bumped into a homeless man moaning and gritting his teeth as he dozed in and out of sleep.

"Ooh," I said. "I'm sorry, sir."

"Motherfucker! *Shiiit*," he yelled. "Can't even get some sleep at the damn doctor!"

He grunted, crossed his legs to the right side, and fell back asleep. As I rushed out of the waiting room, Sean walked in, face full of fear.

"What happened?" I asked, grabbing his hand. "You okay?"

"I hope, just waiting for my results."

"How long?"

"They said like twenty, thirty minutes." He glanced at the waiting nurse. "Your turn?"

"Yeah. Wish me luck, babe."

I hated the doctor's office. Any of them. It was never comfortable, always tense and cold. Same gown open in the front so your breasts and pubic hair flashed the world. Same embarrassed thought of *I should have shaved before I came here*. Or *I should've put some Vaseline on my legs this morning*. Same nurse questions, like "When was your last period?"

"Are you on any medication?"

"Why are you here today?" She scribbled something down on her pad. You never knew what, even though she was staring at you like a specimen waiting to be felt up. And in came the doctor with his investigation.

"Have you had any discharge?"

"No."

"Itching?"

"No."

"Burning?"

"No."

"Good, lie back and relax."

Out came the big silver tongs after he snapped on his gloves, with my legs wide open, vagina hanging out, and lips parted for the world to see. The entire moment was straight from Eve Ensler's *Vagina Monologues*. Minutes later it was done.

"You can get dressed," the doctor said without looking at me, dropping the tongs into a sink. "Go back to the waiting room, and someone will call you in twenty or thirty minutes with your results."

Back in the waiting area, Sean was reading *The 7 Habits of Highly Effective People.* I slid beside him. "They call you back yet?"

"Nah, just waiting with the crazies," he said, as a white lady with a raggedy ponytail and dirty cast limped by with her giant pocketbook bulging from clothes falling out the broken zipper.

"Number fifty-two."

Sean's head shot up like a frightened deer's.

"You want me to come with you?" I asked, grabbing his hand again.

"Um, yeah," he said, squeezing it back. "I got nothing to hide." We were following the nurse down the hall when I was stopped by a counselor.

"Are you two together?" she asked, looking down at us from her size-thirteen, five-ten frame.

"Yeah, I'm his girlfriend."

"Let me discuss a few things with him in private, and then you can come back," she said. "I'll get your results, too."

My exit left Sean with a pale, empty look. Like a sick person, about to vomit. The counselor closed the door behind her as he walked inside the office.

Fifteen minutes later...

"Number fifty-three."

I followed the social worker to the end of the corridor toward a red door. Inside, the beige room was covered with STD posters full of statistics: "15 million Americans become newly infected with an STD each year."

"Untreated, chlamydia can lead to severe health consequences for women, including infertility."

"Condoms are not 100% effective against pregnancy." Pictures colored these stats, featuring graphic images of warts framing chapped lips. Crusty, peeling sores on bald vaginas. Gashes out-lined with dry blood on penises. It was like sitting in a room of sexually repugnant erotica.

I looked at Sean. He didn't acknowledge me, instead leaning to the side, crossing his legs and uncrossing them.

"So, ma'am, how's your day?"

"It'll be better when you tell me my results. I know you want to build rapport, but the wait is killing me."

"Very well." She opened up my folder and chart. "Your results came back clean. Your chlamydia, gonorrhea, syphilis, HPV, her-pes, and HIV all came back negative."

"Oh, that's good." I breathed a sigh, smiling at Sean, who con-tinued staring at the floor.

"Um, sir, did you want to discuss your results with her, or…" Her words drifted off, and Sean slowly turned to face me.

"They sayin' I got gonorrhea or something."

"What?" My face was stuck in a position of solid stupidity and disbelief. "Wait." I gathered my thoughts. Swallowed. Took a deep breath. "So how do I not have anything and he does?"

"Well," the nurse began, ruffling through her papers, "he could be a carrier and not have passed it on to you yet. Has there been unprotected sex?"

"Yes," I snapped without a thought. "Sometimes."

"Well, consider yourself lucky."

I turned to Sean, who had the stupidest expression that reminded me of Big Bird, only with a long beak of lying Pinocchio bullshit.

"We're going to give you both a prescription of medication that works to clear up gonorrhea," she said, nodding toward me. "For you, it's just to be safe."

⌀⸺⸾

At the diner down the block from the clinic, the food looked like gonorrhea. Green slimy crap splattered across the plate. The putrid eggs smelled like ass. The greasy bacon sat to the side, cold, crusty, and decrepitly crass. The grits looked like cold, white shit with specks of black stool. As Sean ate, he slurped with his tongue, slithering hissing saliva over each morsel. The bacon didn't crunch inside his mouth. Instead, it was sloppy and chewy, melting from the acid of his gums.

Everything about that man disgusted me. He was like a virus, full of puss, bloated and swollen like a whitehead dwelling on a skin's surface. My eyes were razors, sharp needles waiting to burst him—the pimple—and watch his blood splatter across the glass where the stench of his remains would smell worse than gas passing through intestinal membranes. Worse than the Newark extension of the New Jersey Turnpike. He swatted away a gnat as he put a fork full of grits into his mouth.

"So you're not gonna say anything to me?" He said this with his trademark half smirk, scraping the last morsel off the plate. "Meena, I'm sorry. I really didn't know."

He took a sip of tea. A tiny drop dripped from his lip as the sip burned his tongue. "What do you want me to say?"

"Something."

"Something like what, Sean?" I sat there waiting for an answer. "Oh, I know, um… you're cheating on me."

"I'm not cheating on you."

"So how do you have full-blown gonorrhea and I don't? We use condoms most of the time. You're fucking someone else."

"I don't know, maybe I already had it. We only been together four months."

"Eight," I spit back.

"Four. We were just hanging out for the first four."

"You know what?" I shook my head and sat back, crossing my arms. "You're lying."

"Okay, so who am I fucking?"

"I don't know, um, Kelly Jones, maybe?"

He paused too long, grabbing a piece of bacon by way of distraction.

"I'm not sleeping with her." He looked down at his plate. "That's not true."

Silence. He chewed till there was nothing else on his plate. Then he slowly looked up.

"She is just a friend, someone I've known for a few years. We're just comrades in this writing game."

"Then why do you have so many meetings with her on your calendar?"

"'Cause she wants to get into freelance writing for magazines, and she's been asking me to look over some of her work."

"Oh, she needs your help, how convenient."

"Meena…" He realized something all of a sudden. "How do you know what's on my calendar?"

"You know what?" I grabbed my bag, preparing to leave. "This isn't going to work out. I can't be with you anymore."

Sean looked up at me. His droopy, puppy-dog eyes were the first sign I'd ever seen of defeat. It gave me confidence, so I continued.

"I don't trust you. And I just can't be with anyone I don't trust. I mean you've got an STD, from this girl I feel you're spending time with. I think we should take a break."

He looked down at his cup and whispered, "Okay."

We sat there in silence, avoiding each other's eyes. Looking around, uncomfortably, waiting for the slow waitress to drag her fat ass to the table and bring the check. Minutes later we parted. He to Brooklyn, me to the *Buzz* office. Fuck him. I needed to deal with Kelly Jones.

22

A WEEK LATER I began to look for a new apartment. Searching in the *Village Voice*, pulling out a checkbook when interested, I took only two weeks to find the perfect spot. A one-bedroom in a four-story walk-up in Bed-Stuy, Brooklyn. Word was, Biggie used to live around the corner. The apartment Lil' Kim grew up in was a block away. The wild days of crack-fueled gunfights had calmed down into a gentrified, cleaned-up area that was on the rise as far as overpriced places to live.

But it didn't take long for me to regret moving to Brooklyn. Weeks of not speaking to Sean had me yearning for home and wishing I'd picked Jersey City, instead of a borough that reminded me of *him*. After a long November weekend, a friends-and-family production of unloading boxes and furniture into my tiny spot, I trudged down the chilly block to the C train. Observing gloomy clouds and couples skipping with the promise of falling in love, my heart withered with blackened anger and moldy envy. I noticed the dead leaves turned inward, spotted crisping branches and potted plants suffocating from a craving for water. At work I sat hard, motionless, like a corpse in rigor mortis. The words on the computer screen were blurry to me, meshing with its blue background into a mirage of letters on the horizon of sleep. I dragged on tirelessly to the promised land, the land of the finished task—proofreading documents, typing memos, sending e-mails, making copies. I could see completion in the distance, but getting there was an upward hike. Something was holding me back, for days, weeks. The heat of depression, anger blazed across my brain like an oppressive heat wave—thick and pressured—sitting on triggers igniting my migraines. Tension in my stomach built, blocking my appetite, mooching my smiles, robbing me of all happiness and love. Damn that evil man. The aftermath of my breakup with Sean was murdering my soul.

"Meena!"

I jumped out of sullen inertia and found Denise standing over me with a confused look of concern on her face.

"Come in my office," she said, before placing yet another pink Post-it with a to-do list atop my inbox pile and walking back into her office. "Get an intern to answer your phone."

I took a deep breath and dragged myself behind her.

"Close the door," she said, sitting at her desk, typing an e-mail. "Let me ask you something…"

The thoughts inside me ran in frenzied, circular disarray. *What did I do now? Sean cheats, damn near gives me an STD, and now my boss wants to fire me. Fuck.*

I plopped down on her white leather recliner. In front, atop a marble table, my eyes focused on a dying bouquet of roses turning brownish black, a tiny petal hanging like my heart from its tall glass vase.

"Okay, what's going on, Meena?" Denise walked over and sat next to me. "You're starting to depress me. Did something happen?"

"No," I answered in a monotone, eyes fixated on the dead flowers, concentrating on keeping tears from flooding my eyes. "I'm just tired."

"Meena, come on now. Been there, done that," she said, placing her lipstick-stained, tall cup of coffee on the table. "What's up? How are you and Sean doing?"

Priding myself on being private, I hated that everyone knew Sean was my boyfriend. It was as if he'd made a point to tell every single writer, editor, and publicist in New York City that we were dating. He had to find a way to let people know our ups, downs, and outs. I'd run into people on the train and they'd say, "Hey, are you okay?" With a sad, pouting look of apology they'd add, "I talked to Sean."

But Denise wasn't sitting there pouting. Instead, she held a pinkie to the side while sipping a hot latte. I could feel her studying me, hoping to connect and understand. For the first time, I didn't see my boss. I saw the big sister I'd always wanted. She sat with her legs crossed, patiently waiting. Her pager buzzed across the room, e-mails chimed in her inbox, and still she didn't move, staying focused on me. "Listen. If he's not making you smile, it's not worth the stress," she said, taking another sip. "We women have a tendency to put so much into relationships, losing our souls. And when we're so busy doing that, we can't enjoy the success that we have in life. The success and happiness we've created by ourselves, without a man, goes unappreciated, unnoticed, and unenjoyed because we're so busy focusing on him."

"I know," I said with a sigh. "I just love him. And I want it to go right."

"Meena, you have so much going for you right now. You're doing an excellent job as my assistant. Everybody loves you. The big dogs that call always tell me how professional and efficient you are. I can't run this without you. Even though I know I'll have to promote you soon."

I perked up. Eyes wide open. Like a jolt of caffeine running through my veins, giving an adrenaline pump of electrified interest.

"Soon," she said, with a smile. "But see that energy there? The way you sat up straight, alive, eager? That's the type of energy I need. Not that mopey shit."

She returned to her former point. "I don't know what's going on. But if he's not treating you right. If there's another girl…" Her words drifted off as our eyes connected in a moment of under-standing. "If you think there's another girl, listen to your instincts and do something about it. But don't let it hold you back and affect what you do here or anywhere else. Business is never personal. Walk into your job, forget about the outside world, and you'll do fabulous. Fuck him."

She let that idea marinate.

"It's hard being a woman, all emotional and full of moody estrogen. We need to have tunnel vision like these men. Focus. Forget about the outside till we get outside. Does that make sense?"

I nodded in agreement.

"Good, now clean your desk. It'll help clear your head."

"Thank you," I said, walking toward the door. "I needed that. A nice kick in the ass."

"No worries. Been there, done that," she said, smiling. "Close the door on your way out. E-mail my messages and don't disturb me for a few hours. I need to get on this editing."

I walked back to my desk renewed, refreshed, refocused. Picking up the pile of papers in my inbox, I shuffled through the stack of Denise's Post-its, differentiating between what needed to be handed out, copied, typed up, and filed. Making my rounds, I proofed a few documents, sent them back to the managing editor, cleared my inbox, and finally got to file a stack of writer contracts. Pulling open the heavy black drawer, I found each space was filled with overstuffed manila folders. Determined to be productive, I alphabetized and updated each section until I got to the bottom of a disorganized stack. Then I picked up the final contract, and a name in blue ink was written in capital letters: KELLY JONES.

The phone rang.

"*Buzz* magazine," I snapped, not realizing I'd answered my personal line and not Denise's.

"Uh, Meena?"

The familiar voice was strong, soothing, and melodic like a latenight radio DJ's, making my heart melt with a romantic R&B serenade. It was Sean.

"Hey, babe," I said instinctively, missing that man I hadn't seen in forever, loving him.

"Okay, that sounds better. What are you doing?"

I looked at Kelly's contract in my hand and felt the wall build up again.

"Filing. And I'm kinda busy. What's up?"

"Damn, and you are kinda bipolar right now. You on your period? PMSing?"

"I have to go…"

"Okay, okay, I was just calling to see if you wanted to come over after work. You know, I was gonna pick up some salmon or something. Make you dinner. Haven't seen you in… too long."

"You wanna cook for me?"

"Um, yeah. I miss you. And I wanna talk."

Ice melt. My heart was cold, but the charming heat in his voice turned my mind to mush.

"Well," I said slowly, fighting the soft urge to give in, failing at the need to be hard. "I guess we can do that."

"So when you get off, and you're on your way, call me. I miss you." I was silent for a few seconds. Letting his words percolate inside my body, sinking emotionally, chemically, appeasing my addiction that had caused painful withdrawal. Pissed that he sounded like nothing had happened. But his words said he acknowledged it. We had talked easily, a familiar pull of affection and friendship.

"Hello?" he asked, a tinge of doubt in his voice. "You there?"

"I miss you, too," I said, looking at the address on Kelly's contract. "But I have to go now. I'll see you later."

632 Greene Avenue. Brooklyn, NY.

I knew that address. Kelly lived around the corner from my new apartment. I could reach out and touch a bitch. We'd probably been on the train together and not even known. Taking out my planner, jotting down her address, I filed the contract and sat at my computer to open a new document. It began with two typed words: "Dear Kelly…"

23

I HATE BREAKUPS. That fucking yearning to want to be with someone you have no business being with, but you can't get his damn face out your mind, the feeling of his body, his touch. So addictive. Thoughts that make you pine with sweat, your vagina vibrate with wet daydreams. I know why I did it. Because I loved him. Because my self-esteem was wastebasket low; because I subconsciously believed I couldn't do better, that I had to prove myself, chase love, show my worth. Because I hoped that by doing it, by being the best at it, he'd be satisfied and not want anyone else. I thought I needed this attention, needed his love, needed him. I thought sex was the cure.

On a table next to the bed, a brown prescription bottle from the STD clinic lay sideways, empty. Still there even though he'd finished it weeks ago. Next to it was an empty condom wrapper. I picked it up for inspection, making sure it wasn't expired, reading: "Durex. Made in India. Effective against pregnancy, HIV (AIDS), and STDs."

I was lucky not to have gotten gonorrhea from Sean. But the mystery of where he'd gotten it made me delirious. We'd used condoms some of the time—we'd had several drunken slipups. But was he cheating? Or did he have the infection before we met and I'd been blessed by God not to have contracted it? In my head I did

the math: Two weeks of no sex after my surgery. Two weeks of seeing Kelly Jones on weekends. Those recent dates on the calendar.
He had to have gotten it from her. It was a fact that nearly every
woman I knew, including myself, and except Meredith, had a man
cheat on them. That didn't automatically mean Sean was doing the
same. But my faith and confidence were screwed up from years of
being told about "the curse." From years of hearing that all men
were dogs. From trying to block the seeping generalizations of men
that poisoned my mind and suppressed my confidence in making
the right choices. But I was still determined to break the bullshit
line. Maybe there was still hope. Maybe he would change his ways
and we would get married and live happily ever after. We'd look
back and tell people the dramatic stories about how many times
we broke up and got back together before deciding to finally stay
together. It could happen. I could manifest my thoughts. But to do
that, I had to trust him. The vision of Kelly Jones stepping off the
Buzz elevator, and that uncomfortable triangle of tension between
her, Sean, and me. I couldn't shake it. I wish I hadn't found her
contract. I wish I could get her out of my head.

"What are you thinking about?" Sean said, his hand rubbing
my stomach. "You look angry."

"You," I said, grabbing his hand and holding it close. "You, me,
the possibilities…"

"I didn't do it," he said, laughing and squeezing my left breast.
"I'm innocent."

"Didn't do what?" I let go of his hand. "How do you know I
was accusing you of something?"

"I'm just playing!" He laughed and kissed my lips. "Relax,
babe."

"I know, sorry," I said, snuggling up and kissing his neck. "Let's
play hooky today. We can stay in bed, play, take a break. I can make
you some lunch. Play some more. Then I'll make you dinner. Give
you some head."

"Well, I got plans tonight," he said, pulling away a bit. "I got a meeting."

"Yeah, about what?"

"Oh, I've got a follow-up with Puffy. You know, for that story I'm doing for *Buzz*."

"That's right! You got the cover again! Congratulations, babe."

"Yeah, thanks." He smiled. "But I'm supposed to meet with him and then talk to the writer doing the sidebar and give some info to help with that."

My ears perked up. I was like a dog hearing the sound of a whistle miles away in the wind.

"Oh, okay. When's this happening?"

"Tonight."

"Who's the writer?"

"Um... Shawn Garrett, you heard of her, right?"

Shawn Garrett was the biggest lesbian in the freelance writing game. She dressed and walked like a boy. But despite her manly stance and swag, from the neck up she looked like Tyra Banks. Her niche was reggae and world artists. A piece on Puff Daddy seemed strange.

"Anyone else working on a sidebar?"

He was quiet for a long, contemplative moment. As if he couldn't formulate the words. As if he didn't know what to say or do.

"Hello... did you blank out?"

"Um, nah," he said, getting out of bed. "I'm not sure..."

"Not sure of what? The sidebar?"

"Why are you asking so many questions? Damn, you're like five-o," he said, putting a leg into his sweat pants. "What the fuck, Meena. We're sitting here, having a good morning in bed, and then you're cross-examining me."

"What the fuck?" I asked this while jumping out of bed. "Where's my bra?" I started walking around feverishly, looking for my underwear. I had to get out of that place. "Where's my panties?"

"Where you going, Meena? I'm sorry," Sean said from across the room. "I'm just hungry."

"Something came up," I said, sitting on the bed, putting on my socks. "I forgot I gotta go to the office."

"So no hooky day today?"

"Nah, I gotta do something for Denise." I pulled my blouse over my head. "I need to get to the office. I just remembered."

Sean watched as I rushed and stumbled to get dressed. His face was perplexed. I ran out of his house, caught the train, and made it to work in thirty minutes flat. Eight thirty. Ran upstairs, flew past the security guard, got to my desk, and with my purse still on my shoulder I opened the file cabinet and pulled out a contract. It said what I'd suspected: "Kelly Jones Assignment: Puffy sidebar. Word count: 250 words."

"Lying-ass motherfucker," I said out loud.

I slammed the cabinet closed, sat and turned on the computer, pulled up the document in my files, and began typing:

Dear Kelly,
You don't know me well. But I think it's time we talk woman to woman...

24

I DID NOTHING THE ENTIRE WEEKEND but obsess over "The Kelly Jones Letter." That's what I called it, like it was an FBI or CIA document. This letter was the truth. My truth. The only truth I knew how to express written out fully, typed carefully, double-spaced, spell-checked, and grammar-proofed. I'd spent my Saturday and Sunday rereading it out loud to myself and over the phone with my editor, Meredith. She was my partner in the premeditated scheme to get rid of that bitch, Kelly Jones, once and for all.

"Wow..." Meredith said with a laugh after hearing my final recital. "It's good. Deep. I wish I could write like that."

"She needs to know the truth," I said. "I'm not the only one Sean fucked up."

"True, but can she use that truth against you?"

"How could she do that?"

"I mean, she could save your letters, make copies, send them around to people, publish that shit," Meredith pointed out. "She is a journalist."

"Do you really think she wants to publish what's in this letter? I mean, really? It'll make her look not as squeaky clean as she appears to be," I said, dumping the filling out of a cigar. "I don't care how low her church skirt swings. She's just as dirty as Sean, gonorrhea and all."

"That's true," Meredith said, screaming over DMX barking in the background. "But how are you going to get it to her?"

"I'm bringing it to her house."

"You sure that address on the contract was the right one?"

"Yeah, it's in her handwriting, all bubbly and shit."

"Ill, she has bubbly handwriting? With big loops all around? Like high school?"

"Yes," I said with disgust. "And her name underlined with a curvy line."

"She doesn't dot her *i*'s with hearts, does she?"

"No," I said, laughing. "She's got a thing for butterflies, though."

"What? Ill…"

"Yeah, she's whack," I said, breaking up weed on my living room table. "I'ma take it to her crib and slide it underneath her door."

"And what if she has a doorman? How are you gonna get by?"

"Girl, please, I got this," I said, rolling up the blunt. "Security guards are easy to get past. All you gotta do is smile, look confused, and be like, 'I need help.' "

"Yeah, some men are stupid like that. But still, I think you need to plan it. Say it out loud to manifest it. Know your route."

"I *got* this, son."

"Son?" Meredith's question trailed off into a pause. "What? You move to Brooklyn and you're Mobb Deep now?"

"Um, they're from Queensbridge," I replied. "Step up your hiphop knowledge."

"Bitch, I mean, son… you're from the suburbs."

"Whatever," I said, busting out laughing. "Son…"

Monday morning I called in sick, dedicating the day to delivering my truth. At eleven thirty, knowing she'd have been to work by ten, I walked down the block with fluttering things moving and curving in my intestines. The orange juice I'd drank bubbled and bounced, gurgling with each step I made toward Kelly's building. As I made my way to Greene Avenue, I kept seeing doppelgänger versions of her walk by—same light yellow complexion, same short haircut, same Catholic-length skirt. They glared back at me with red in their eyes, hot lasers staring me down as they walked by.

When I got to her street, I stood at the corner, like an FBI agent doing surveillance. Monitoring the building. Keeping account of how often people walked in and out the front door. And how many used the driveway. It was a quiet residential Brooklyn block. Diversified to the fullest. A white dude with a Mohawk and Converse sneakers walked his ten-pound dog. An Asian girl with her fuzzy-haired, caramel-complexioned son waited at the bus stop. A brother with his dreadlocks braided into cornrows whizzed by on his ten-speed. Dressed in all white, he sang along to the Bob Marley record blaring from a little boom box fitted into his bike's front basket.

Kelly's building looked fake in Brooklyn's Clinton Hill section. The olive-green building was accented with a pink awning and matching window frames. Little begonias and yellow tulips lined the makeshift garden in the walkway. The small, five-story apartment complex looked out of place on a block of brownstones, like a Barbie house tucked in the middle of a gentrified 'hood.

I got to the door as someone was walking out. The momentary opening allowed me to slip in without having to ring a bell. The doorman sat at the desk, reading the *Daily News*.

"Hi," I said, smiling brightly. "I'm going to Apartment 512. Kelly Jones. I have to drop something off for her."

"Is she expecting you?"

"Oh no, it's a surprise, for her birthday," I said, still grinning. "I figure she's at work by now, and I want to slide this under her door. She's not home, is she?"

"No, this building pretty much empties out by nine," he said, brushing the powdered-donut sugar off his hands. "Sign right here."

Nervous about being asked for my signature, I quickly scribbled something as illegible as possible, without adding the date or time, and walked away down the hallway and around a corner, out of sight. After I pressed the button for the elevator ten times, it seemed to take an hour to come. When I finally got to the fifth floor, I followed signs to 512, down a long corridor, where the vomit-green walls rolled up and curved into a funnel-like appearance. Her apartment sat at the far end: 512, in giant numbers. Things felt like a blur as I moved closer, hot and shaky. I gulped in the heat, wishing I'd packed a bottle of water, hoping no one could hear the loud pounding in my heart. Praying no one would see Denise Banor's assistant trespassing along the corridors of a private residence.

When I got to Kelly's apartment, I placed my ear a few inches away from the door. Standing still. Listening. It was like a silent meditation, waiting for the faintest sound or movement that might point to her being home. The questions came: *What if the guard was wrong and she is home? What if she forgot the stove was on and comes running down the hallway? That would be awkward.* I envisioned myself giving her the letter in person and saying, "Hey, girl. Um… yeah, you might wanna get checked for gonorrhea. I wrote about it in this long-ass, well-written, four-page letter." Or something like that.

Back in reality, my heart screamed in anxiety. Standing, holding my breath in the best stillness I could find despite my shaky, sweaty palms, I slowly moved my arms, fearing someone might hear bones popping from tension as I dug in my bag and pulled out the envelope. It was bulky and wrinkled, bulging from words of truth pushing to be released. I stuffed it under the door parallel, but it wouldn't fit. I pushed. Nudged. The envelope began to wrinkle into a raggedy lump. So I slid it the long way, perpendicular, pushing slightly till the letter was gone. Taking a deep breath when the covert operation was done, I did an about-face and nearly ran out that building onto the street. The sun shined. A slight breeze blew through my hair. A sense of achievement glowed through my cheeks. And I smiled. Mission accomplished.

25

Twelve hours later...

THE SADNESS WAS INTENSE, as if my heart had plummeted through veins, blood cells, vessels, and muscles. It felt like a putrid moldy apple, imploding and shriveling into a nonexistent space.

I hated him for the lie he'd spit in my face, stomping my love and shitting it out like an assful of bull misconstrued as vibrant, monogamous love. But it was nothing. Nothing more than darkness—a dark magic cursed with the death of love and life.

I dragged myself home from work and sat for hours in front of a blank TV screen, staring past the actors, the color schemes, the fuzzy lack of cable, and commercial jingles into my own oblivion. Rehashing and revisiting the coulda, shoulda, wouldas on replay like a syndicated show, like a rerun of a bad episode of love. The evening's breakup scene recurred in my head, drowning obsessive thoughts into thinking of nothing more than his voice and the pain he brought.

Two hours earlier...

"Why did you do that, Meena?" Sean's voice was aggressive and intense, waiting for a response. "Hello? What, you can't hear me now?"

"Do what?" I replied, feigning innocence. "I don't know what you're talking about."

"You know what the fuck you did."

"Sean…"

"No, don't come at me with that Sean shit. You did some *crazy* shit." He was breathing fire into the phone receiver. "You snuck into her building? And then you… wait, how the fuck did you get into the building?"

"The doorman let me in."

"Yeah, but how? You don't know her. What did you say to him?"

I was quiet before answering. Contemplating if I should be honest about my method, or deny, deny, deny. "I told him I was her friend and she'd asked me to leave her something."

He laughed cryptically. "Crazy shit, Meena. Crazy. So you get in the building and leave her the letter. Where?"

"Under the door."

"What the fuck, Meena! And then you tell her our business? You fucking tell her about the STD clinic and the gonorrhea? The private shit I'm not proud of and haven't told anyone? You told her *that*?"

I was silent.

"Why, Meena? Why did you do that?"

"Because…" I felt like an eight-year-old caught in an interrogation. "Well…"

"Because what?"

"Because of you."

"What the fuck did I do?"

"You know what the fuck you did," I said, fed up with his game of nonacceptance. His annoying habit of continually acting as if he were the innocent party angered me. "You fucking cheated with her." He was silent a few seconds. I could hear him loudly tapping his pen on the desk.

"You know what, Meena? Yeah, I did it. I fucked her. Won't happen again 'cause she's not speaking to me. She's saying I put her health in danger. Saying I burned her. Saying I ain't shit…" His words trailed off into an incoherent mumble.

"I…" I went blank, unable to get my thoughts together. "I just… well, now it's out and—"

"And you know what? I ain't shit," he said out of the blue. "Both of you are right. So I'ma do you a favor and say, 'Stay away from me.' Or to make it politically correct, 'This isn't going to work out.' That crazy shit you did tells me that you're on some other shit. I can't trust you. You're selfish, sneaky, and I'm not down with that. So don't call me, don't text me, don't e-mail me. Stay away from me."

And he hung up. And I cried.

And life ended.

Fuck him.

26

"THAT'S RIGHT, FUCK HIM."

Meredith rolled her eyes. I sat at a booth. Checking my cell. Secretly hoping to see Sean's number. Watching phone calls from Dex. From Mom. I couldn't be bothered. The only voice I wanted to hear was Meredith's. She'd met me for lunch in the city after her interview at Columbia University. She was med school–bound. Psychologist in the cards. I was glad I had her appointments for free. "I love you. And I'm glad you texted me. I was worried when you told me you'd been out of work a week."

"Eh, it's holiday time. Everyone is taking off. Shit, I don't even feel like being here today," I said. "But I need to take my mind off everything. Do I look like I've been crying?"

She sized me up, then glanced at her phone. "No."

I knew she was lying. Meredith had a particular way of saying no when she really meant yes. That look in her eyes of insecurity, hesitation, was out of character for her. She was normally quick with a witty reply. When Meredith paused, the answer that followed was always the opposite of what she said.

I took out my compact and opened it up. My eyes were swollen like an abuse victim's. I looked as if I'd been socked in the pupils by a demented madman, face left puffy and round. The rings under my lower lashes were slightly masked with dabs of cover-up. But

I hadn't spent much time and care on my face this morning. I'd woken up at five, after a long night of crying until three. I'd reluctantly boo-hooed myself to sleep, trying to hold in tears, working to not let salty liquid roll down my cheeks, penetrate, and puff up the skin under my eyes, making them tight and protrude like a water balloon about to burst.

I took out a bottle of Visine, stretched open my lids, and squeezed in a few drops. The saline usually worked to open up my red, squinty, marijuana-affected lids. At times it helped decrease the swelling of my eyes after crying.

"You don't look that bad," Meredith said. "If you're concerned about it, just stay at your computer all day and work. Keep busy. Keep ya mind off that asshole."

Her phone rang and she glanced at it, then at me, then at it, wanting to answer, knowing she should, but being an amazing friend.

"I know you have to go," I said. "It's cool. I just needed a hug."

"Girl, this rut. This pain you feel? It's necessary. It's part of the process of healing. I know the holidays make it worse. But if you don't feel it now, you'll feel it later," Meredith said, looking me in the eye. "Be brave. Deal with the darkness. And know that it will get better. You will move on and make it back to the light. Promise."

She called the waitress over, paid the check, then motioned for me to stand up to give a tight, embracing hug.

I moped back to the office, slumped in my chair, logged on the computer, and typed one-word responses as e-mail replies.

From Meredith: an attachment of the song "Don't Worry Be Happy."

My reply: *Thx.*

From Denise: *Remember to remind me to remind my mother to mail me that banking info.*

My reply: *Ok.*

From the fashion director, Francois: *Is Denise still having an editorial meeting this afternoon?*

My reply: *No.*

From the managing editor, Michelle Chin: *Can you see me in my office?*

My initial reaction to this e-mail was one of worry. Michelle Chin was the guardian of the editorial offices. She wrote and signed the contracts. Kept the magazine production schedule on time. Slayed passive editors who couldn't control their writers or meet deadlines. She hired. Reprimanded. And after two strikes, eventually fired those who didn't live up to *Buzz* standards. On the outside, she was a skinny five-three with a smile that evoked memories of a giddy schoolgirl opening gifts on her birthday. But on the inside, Michelle wasn't about laugh-out-loud jokes. She was about business, professionalism, and punctuality. She was about snarky, sarcastic comments projecting waning patience. She was about direct words and tense tones with no chaser. An e-mail from her brought chills and anxiety to stable bank accounts. Michelle was the career judge, the budget cutter and job slasher. The editorial warrior princess. I arrived at her office door sixty seconds after opening the e-mail.

"Hey, you said you wanted to see me?"

"Yeah," she said, looking up from her planner. "Close the door." With my stomach in knots, sentences ending in question marks flew through my head. *Damn, why does she want me to close the door? What did I do? Am I about to get fired? Wonder if I can sneak out and talk to Denise? Does Denise know about this? Did Michelle call Denise before I came in her office? Fuck.*

I sat down as she began.

"Meena, I planned to have this meeting with you Tuesday, but you were out. I wanted to talk about your work performance. Your tardiness. For the past several weeks, you've been late most days. It's becoming a nuisance to Denise. There's no reason she should be arriving to work before you. There's no reason she should be having meetings and not have anyone to greet her guests or answer the phone. She depends on you and when you're not there on time, all the time, it affects her and makes us look unprofessional. Why are you always late?"

I sat in silence, thinking about my habit of going to bed at three in the morning. Up all night watching TV, lying under the queen-size covers, tossing and turning, mind racing and rehashing: Sean, the four-page letter, the breakup, the man curse. I'd wake in the morning, sun shining through the blinds, and only one word would come to my head that I'd scream out loud: "Fuck!"

In that moment, sitting there with Michelle staring at me, waiting for words to come out of my mouth, I had an epiphany: I needed a change professionally and personally. I needed to stimulate my mind more and be excited about getting up in the morning and getting to work—on time. I could do this job with my eyes closed, cartwheeling down a hill. I needed more. And I needed to get over that asshole. But I didn't say any of this to Michelle.

Instead I replied, "Well, I'm misjudging my time. I just moved to Brooklyn last month, and I'm having a hard time figuring out how long it'll take me to get in to work. Sometimes the trains don't run on time and I'm stuck underground, with no signal, and can't call to say I'll be in late. I guess I can work to leave earlier and prepare for a slow train."

She shook her head, staring through me, peering for honesty. What I said was partially the truth. I mean, I did have a problem organizing my time properly. I did underestimate my travel time from Brooklyn to Manhattan. But I also had a sinking feeling that I wanted a new job. I was tired. Tired of the same old shit. Tired of the ten o'clock call time. Tired of answering phones, ordering lunch, cleaning up crumbs, and making photocopies. I needed a new life.

"Okay, so this is what I'll do, Meena." She took out a lined notepad. Pulled the cap off a ballpoint pen and began jotting notes. "I'll tell Denise we met. And that you're still in transition and working on it." She scribbled something illegible in doctor's handwriting. "But this is the first warning. I don't do late. I don't do unreliable.

I don't do excuses. So I need you to get your schedule together, get to bed earlier, get up earlier, leave the house earlier, and do whatever you need to do to get to work on time. You've been here nearly a year. I know you can do better. You know how things go here. *Buzz* magazine didn't get its name or a reputation for being ahead by being late. Understand?"

I nodded quickly. Half with understanding. Half with relief. I wanted to know what she was writing. I wished she didn't have such messy penmanship, so I could read her words upside down. She underlined something all hard, dotted an *i* like she was stabbing it, ripped the paper out of the notebook, then patted it with one hand as she said, "Okay, Miss Meena. I have a meeting after you. But I think we're clear, right?"

I nodded up and down like an obedient child just removing a dunce cap.

"Good," she said, closing her book, smiling a sweet, sinister I-could've-fired-you grin. "I'll see you at the editorial meeting."

"Um… that's canceled." My voice shook, as I remembered I'd forgotten to tell the staff. "I was about to send an e-mail to everyone." Michelle opened her notebook and jotted something again. "Oh," she said. "Huh. Well, okay. Make sure everyone knows. Thanks, Meena."

I nodded like a scared idiot, stood up, and gave an uncomfortable thumbs-up before walking out of the office. My heart sank. I cleared my throat, swallowing sore, swollen glands, thinking one thing: *Today sucks.*

⸎

A few days later, I called in sick. Sniffling. Stuffed nose. I opened my mouth to see a red, oversize esophagus sprinkled with nasty white dots. Turning off the alarm clock, I picked up the phone and dialed

Denise.

"Damn, girl, you okay?" Tupac blasted in the background. "You sound bad."

"I feel like shit," I hissed in a hoarse tone. "And I texted you, didn't get a reply, so I wanted to call."

"That's because you need some sleep," she said, phone ringing in the background. "Tell that Sean character to bring you some chicken noodle soup."

"Oh, don't make me think about him." I managed a dry, painful cough. "Just wanted to let you know I feel like crap."

"Ooh, you do sound bad," she said. "There's a bug going around. A nasty Christmas gift of disease. Take care of yourself. Get some sleep, and keep me updated. I gotta take this call." And she was gone.

I turned over, pulling the covers over my head, lying there looking out the window. Raindrops bounced off the screen, pattering against the windowpane. Sean thought rain was romantic. Our first kiss was in the rain. My eyes welled up with tears, angry at Denise for bringing his name up, while mourning the thought of what was lost and never to be found again. My phone vibrated with a text.

Sean: *Hey, you got my hat?*

I pursed my lips. Half annoyed. Half excited. My heart began to beat nervously. I wasn't going to answer. Pulling the covers over my head. Turning the phone upside down. But I couldn't help it. Something was pulling me to reply. The urge was unbearable. But I kept it under control by typing one word: No.

Sean: *You sure?*

Me: *Yeah.*

Sean: *You check your overnight bag?*

I pulled myself out of bed, limped to the closet, and dumped the contents of a bag I hadn't used in weeks, since breaking up with Sean. My Nike duffel bag flopped onto the cold, mahogany floor. Nothing but dirty panties and a pair of flip-flops.

Me: *No hat. But I did pack your flip-flops by accident. Sorry.*
No reply.
Me: *I'm home sick today. My throat is killin me.*

I waited ten minutes. No response. Maybe he'd gotten a call or something. I texted again: *I could use some chicken noodle soup.*

Sean: *I got that. But you gotta come over here to get it. I'm on deadline. Can't move the groove.*

I didn't reply.

Six minutes later my phone vibrated. Sean: *You comin?*

I sat there. Staring at his selfish text. Cussing him softly for demanding an immediate answer. For not caring about my state, my body, the fact that my throat felt fat and raw, putting heavy pressure on my tongue, forcing enunciations into lisps. For reaching out like he always did after weeks of not speaking and acting like nothing had happened.

"Can't move the groove" was his asshole comment. Meaning that if he stopped his writing flow, he might not get it back. Did he stop that flow for Kelly Jones when he was fucking her with his gonorrhea dick? No. Fuck him.

I hopped in the shower to cool my angry fumes. Got out and stared at the phone across the room. Scared to stare at it. Scared I'd do the wrong thing. I could hear and see it vibrating again. I walked over and looked.

Sean: *Bring my flip-flops when you come.*
Me: *Ok.*
No reply.

I hated that no-reply crap. Rude. Thoughtless. It was the epitome of bad texting manners. If someone texts you, text them back. Easy method. I'd just had this same conversation with Meredith. She'd met a handsome, intelligent, accomplished dentist. They'd had a wonderful weekend bar hopping, restaurant stopping, kissing, cuddling, and a little touching of the fuzzy bunny. The following Monday evening she texted him a sweet thank-you ending in "xox." Twenty-four hours later, he still hadn't replied. What the fuck does that mean? Is that some weird, manly detachment phe-nomenon? Whatever. It's some bullshit. And I hate it.

I dragged myself to the closet. I threw on a fedora, didn't bother with makeup, strapped my Timberland boots on, slipped on a pair of jeans, hoodie, and headed to Sean's house. It was a rainy, cold day in December at thirty-seven degrees. The trains were delayed, as usual. New York's transit system seemed to always fall apart when the weather went sour. The largest city in the world couldn't prepare in advance for a rainstorm. Today's commute to Sean's house took a ridiculous hour and a half. Flooded tracks. When on a normal, drama-free day it took thirty minutes.

I got off the D and dry-coughed my way up the subway steps, cussed Mother Nature and her bitchy moodiness under my breath with each incline, and went into the torrential rain. After sliding up a steep hill to his house, I finally made it to the front door and rang the buzzer. Oversize drops splashed across my red nose. I waited sixty seconds. No answer. Buzzed again. No answer. I glanced at my cell phone with 9 percent battery left. No text.

I typed: *I'm here. Downstairs. Where u?*

Two minutes later. No answer.

The heat boiled in my belly. Images of me thrashing him came to mind, as if he were a slave and I was giving him fifty lashes. *This nigger knew I was coming. Where the fuck is he?*

I rang his cell. No answer.

The rain fell harder. I coughed and squinted my eyes through the splashing. "Fuck!" I yelled, in a painfully hoarse voice. With my head tilted upward, I hoped the echoes would be heard in his fifth-floor apartment.

Five minutes later, as someone finally exited the building, I lunged for the door, pushing its heavy metal springs wide enough for me to slip inside before it slammed and locked behind me.

Heading to the elevator, I pounded the up button like a boxer bashing an opponent's face. Radically pissed thoughts screamed through my mind.

Where is this man? Why isn't he around? If he isn't home, why not let me know he was leaving? What the fuck?

The elevator crept up to the first level, the door squeaked open, and I stepped on and pressed the button for the fifth floor. Apartment 5F was a place I'd become accustomed to visiting. The building's elevators smelled like pee. Hallways rusty and dusty. The occasional brown rodent with wings crawling among corner crevices. Sean was only paying six hundred a month for a reason. I knocked on his door, hearing Lil' Kim kill her verse on "It's All About the Benjamins," blasting from the speakers. Still no answer. I knocked again. Banging, kicking, but still there was no answer. Out of breath from overexertion, I began coughing uncontrollably, a dry cackle stripping my throat of moisture. Leaning up against the wall, I slid to the floor, staring at my cell phone, waiting for anything. Something. A word of where this man was. Tears blurred my eyes.

Suddenly, the door to his apartment opened and a girl walked out. She was tall and thin, like a model, resembling an Ethiopian, with swarthy features. Her hair was in a bun, wrapped with an African scarf. She wore black sweatpants, a hoodie, and construction boots like mine. Walking out, she carried a bowl filled with something powdery.

"Thanks, neighbor. Now I can finish making my cake," she said, laughing. "You are so silly."

"Well, I hope I get some when you're finished, since"—he coughed a fake cough—"I am helping make it courtesy of that sugar there."

"Yes, you can have some when I'm done," she said, shaking the bowl and giggling. "I might be back to get some eggs. Ain't goin' nowhere in this weather."

"You can come back whenever you want, chef girl."

She laughed and turned to leave when she saw me. "Oh!" the bitch said, smiling. "Hey!"

"Hey," I answered dryly, slowly standing. My overnight bag had a huge wet spot in the bottom. Sean poked his head out the door.

"Oh, hey." He raised his eyebrows at his neighbor, smirked, and closed the door behind me. "I didn't know you were still coming."

"You didn't hear me knocking at the door?"

"No."

"Or buzzing downstairs."

"Nah, that's broke."

"Since when?"

"Since the other day."

"Since the other day when?"

"Since before you were mad at me and decided you didn't want to talk anymore."

I rolled my eyes and took off my coat. Opened the closet door, grabbed a hanger, hung it up, and turned the TV on, purposely not taking off my boots, tracking dirty, wet prints onto the floor.

"So which neighbor is that?" I sat down, resting my head on the couch, letting my feet slide across the wood.

"Oh, that's Monica," he said. "Um… you're making black puddles in my place. Can you take those big-ass boots off, please?"

"Excuse you," I said, looking up at him, before bending over to unlace my Timbs. "Anyway, as I was saying, she's pretty."

"Yeah, I know," he said, smiling. "She's Ethiopian and Asian."

"She's making a cake for you?"

"Nah, for some dude she's dating. He's sick or something. But dude is gay as hell. I told her."

"Well, at least she's making something for the sick person in her life," I said, blowing my nose. "I can't get a can of soup."

"What, is that a hint?"

"I don't give hints," I said, throwing my left boot toward the front door. "You know what I mean. You're a man of words, are you not?"

"Listen, Meena, you know I'm on deadline, I'm busy. But if you want me to make you something real quick, I will. What you want, soup?"

"No, I want you to do something for me without having to be asked."

"Yo, did you come over here to beef with me?"

"No, I came over for some TLC, but stood out in the rain for thirty minutes. Then outside your door for another thirty." I coughed, yanking off my right boot and throwing it toward the left. "You knew I was coming, but didn't act like it. I feel like shit. I trek over here and—"

"I don't know why you even came over here being sick." He plopped down into his computer chair and started typing something. "I gotta finish this story. I got juice in the fridge, you can lie in my bed, watch TV or something. You look and sound sick, so you need to just calm down. You must be on your period or something."

I stared at him for a long minute. Face turned up. Nose runny. Throat sore. I was so sick of his selfish ass. Not looking after me. Not taking care of me. Not giving to *me*. He typed on that damned laptop with the delicacy of a baby. But treated me like an old whore he'd slapped around with a pussy beater. I got up, stomped into my boots without tying them, and said, "I'm going home."

"A'ight," he answered, not even looking at me. "Peace."

Asshole motherfucker.

Last thing I heard was the door slamming behind me. The sound of its bang was like a bullet to the head, killing my old consciousness, making way for the birth of a new one. The epiphany was clear: I was done.

27

Ladies know the moment when we're finished. No need to look back. No hard feelings. Easy like a flip of the switch. You move on. Just like that. Lauryn Hill got me through it all. Her new album, *The Miseducation of Lauryn Hill*, blasted at the office and through my apartment, preaching wisdom reminders of self-love and healing. I continually pressed replay, listening to her single "Everything Is Everything" over and over, like a broken record. Strong empowerment beats banged uplifting emotional reminders of the path we're all destined to walk and the change that comes with each season.

Meredith told me it takes half the time you're with someone to get over them. And she was right. Eventually the pain faded. The pain of withdrawal and the rage of anger became easier with every week that passed by. The sluggish months of winter flipped by into the rebirth of spring. Then summer. Fall. Winter. And another birthday. Number twenty-seven. Same pink Post-it shit. Same e-mails, same memos, same parties, same meetings. After two years on staff, the excitement of *Buzz* became a bore. The only color came when Sean avoided me at industry events. I stared through him like he was a ghost, an unrecognizable peon. With the certainty a woman has when she's fully fed up. Fuck him. He was gone. I was over it. Yet still unhappy. Still bored, single, and resentful, trudging to work late, watching the clock until I could leave. I hated my seven o'clock alarm. I hated the nagging tightness in my tummy. And I hated the monotony of my life. I was tired of waking up, sun shining through mahogany shutters, butterflies fluttering to the beautiful, breezy blessing of another day, robins chirping. And there I was, instead of thanking the Lord, moaning an atheistic, ritualistic tune of self-deprecation that ended with me pulling the covers over my head and screaming, "*Fuck!*"

To escape reality and find some sort of spirituality, I read a book Denise had given me for my recent birthday: *The Artist's Way: A Spiritual Path to Higher Creativity*, by Julia Cameron. With daily tasks like journaling, I slowly began to remember my creative self. My love of writing. My love of freedom. My realization that I hated being an assistant, answering phones, filing, organizing, keeping everyone and everything together but my own damn life. My messy-ass apartment. Papers galore. Dirty dishes. Baskets of unwashed laundry. Because I was always working, out partying, avoiding the loneliness of home even though I'd outgrown the job I had once loved. Three months later, by the end of the book's twelve-week program, I celebrated Memorial Day by giving *Buzz* my two weeks' notice.

"You're quitting to write?" Denise's face was sad yet bright, smiling. "I knew I wouldn't keep you as an assistant for long. You're too amazing."

"Yeah, it's time to get this book out of my head," I said, standing tall, long legs shoulder-length apart, exuding Amazon-woman confidence. "I can do some freelancing on the side to add on to what I've saved. But I'm ready."

"Well, I know you're friends with all of the editors at those *other* magazines," she said, rolling her eyes, flipping through the Rolodex. "But I've got some agent friends to connect you with. You know *Buzz* has your back. So make us proud."

That was inevitable. But this was about me.

My professional life was always on point. Writing assignments rolled in. The economy in 2000 boomed, magazines paid their dollar-per-word stories on time. And I regularly wrote fifteen-hundred to three-thousand-word features monthly, added that to the checks I racked up from smaller-profile pieces for other publications, and afforded to consistently stay at least three months ahead of myself. Great for someone in her late twenties. I thought I was balling.

The problems were personal. Sleeping with men I didn't like. Using them for sex. Their eyes were soft, googley in love. And mine were icy, stiff, and numb. I was emotionless. I'd fuck and ask them politely to leave. They'd pout as I couldn't wait for them to get out. But when they were gone, I was lonely. Sad. Craving for more. Habitually staying busy in a state of emotional unavailability to avoid feeling the painful void of not having love from a man in my life.

"So you pull them close and push them away," Meredith said, sitting on my couch-staring at me. We sipped our red wine with Jill Scott's debut album *Who Is Jill Scott?* playing in the background. "You're like a guy."

"But I don't get it. I want them around. Till they start calling or texting too much. Then I need them to go. And when they leave, I want them back," I said shaking my head. "I got issues."

"Yes, you do."

I did a double take as Meredith began to crack up.

"Listen, it's abandonment shit. Fear. Scared of being hurt. Even though you want them close. You get all weird, anxious, and act out when they do. It's normal for someone like you. I mean, you didn't have your father, your mother has her issues, all that distrust and emotional baggage was passed down to you. You've been hurt. But you can heal, Meena. All wounds heal. You need to just take a break to focus and fall in love with you."

"What do you mean? No guys?"

"No men," she said, with a blank stare. "No sex?"

"Use a dildo. Give yourself some love."

"Whoa..." I said. My words trailed off into a state of wondering what it might be like not to have sex for an extended period of time. Celibacy just didn't seem normal. I didn't understand women who hadn't had sex in months or years. It was incomprehensible with all these fine men walking around. As ladies, we had our pick. It was easy to get dick in our lives. But without it, would I still be able to write? Would the lack of sex creatively block me? Would a battery operated dildo be enough?

After a few weeks of nervously contemplating Meredith's challenge, I was ready with a plan. The first step involved taking a break from dating altogether.

Step #1: Turn on the man blinders. (Man blinder (n): an emotional wall that ignores the sight of and interest in men.) To enable this tactic, I had to deafen the sound of the boy beeper, an internal alarm mechanism that triggers when a male is near.

Beep. Beep.

That's what I'd hear when I walked down the street and a handsome man floated by. The beeper would blare like a missile launcher. Like a submarine identifier. *Beep. Beep.* I'd feel my neck beginning its uncontrollable turn, like a magnet attracted, a positive charge meshing with the negative. Like Pavlov's dog hearing the bell. When I saw a man, I had to look. Had to turn. Had to have it.

Beep. Beep.

I was conscious of this. With the man blinders on, I learned to slowly resist my heavy, hardheaded noggin turn. Each day it became easier to fight the natural tendency to glance toward testosterone. I was in another galaxy with this tactic, like Captain Kirk fighting Borg mind power. I spoke in staccato as I fought the need for sex and a man. "I. Can. Resist."

After four weeks of this excruciating struggle, the beep became a chirp. In eight weeks, the chirp turned to a faint whisper, like a fire alarm battery that had died. The urge to gawk and slobber internally over dick was gone. I had trained myself to walk the disinterested posture—eyes forward, head up, back straight. Like a soldier focused on the mission at hand. Like an aggressive Lesbian disinterested in men. My "man-dar," as I liked to call it, had been trained to remain off. I craved respite from the physical, mental, and emotional yearning for a man. And I'd thought I'd finally gotten it.

All was good for eight months. Until my dry, celibate period had my clitoris throbbing and reaching toward any handsome man who gave me the eye. Then I ran into Carl Murphy.

I remembered him from high school as the socially awkward nerd sitting alone with a comic book at lunch. He ran one season of track before moving out of town when his dad died. Flash-forward to the present; he was a six-foot, two-hundred-pound chocolate candy bar. But he was coated in that same syrup of insecure, annoying, high school nervousness I remembered as he tried to continually find ways to compliment me.

"So what do I need to do to be like you?" He said this while following me out of Penn Station, after a chance meeting on the train.

"I don't know," I said, not looking at him, instead pointing at the MTA machine, trying to buy a MetroCard so I could go home and smoke my weed. "Just do the work."

"Well," his voice shook while he simultaneously smiled in awe.

"Are you a day writer or night writer?"

"I'm a writer. A writer writes," I snapped, impatiently checking my watch, staring down the empty train track. "Although I find myself working mostly at night."

"How long do you stay up?"

"Man, you ask a lot of questions."

"Does that bother you?"

"I don't know, are you CIA or something?"

"Maybe."

We looked at each other and laughed.

Something about him raised a familiar feeling. Something about his insecurity screamed for him to be taken advantage of. Hands locked above the head, me on top holding him down, injecting his penis into me with long, slow strokes and short, quick thrusts of my always juicy, rough-riding pussy. Licking his face. Kissing his body. Climbing up to straddle his mouth. I could turn him out easy and not call again for months. Till I wanted some more. *If* I wanted some more.

As we sat on the C train, I salivated over the muscles protruding from the sleeves of his fitted black T-shirt. I could see a book poking from his bag. *Soledad Brother: The Prison Letters of George Jackson.* He was smart. Conscious. Just what I liked. And his big feet meant…

"Meena Butler," he said, staring me up and down. Catching my daydream gaze.

"I believe that's my name."

"Oh!" he said, laughing. "Still sarcastic. And you look the same as high school. Do you age?"

"Eh, I guess. What's up? You studying to be a black revolutionary?" I pointed to the book in his bag.

"I'm actually in a master's program at NYU. African American studies." He nodded at the book sticking out of my purse. "You trying to find yourself?"

"I mean… I guess." I laughed uncomfortably, shoving Iyanla Vanzant's *In the Meantime* deeper into my bag. "Shut up. So what are you up to? Where are you headed?"

The question was leading. I only wanted to know whether he was traveling my way so I could invite him over, have a drink, smoke a blunt, and maybe get him to lick me.

"Oh, nowhere. I'm just gonna ride the train and read a bit." My face turned from seduction to confusion.

"Yeah," he said, slouching in his seat. "I can't focus at home because my girl and I are having some issues, arguing all the time. So I come on the train and just read."

"What's up with that?" I asked. Half wanting to know, half not hearing his response because as he began I phased out. Turned down the volume. His mouth moved in my silence, explaining every detail of his issues with his girlfriend. She says he's too busy. He's trying to get his degree. Blah, blah, blah, another emotionally unavailable man, stuck in the past, complaining about his ex or some girl breaking his heart.

"Your number still the same?"

I didn't answer. Caught in my thoughts about talking to another wrong man, yet again.

"Meena…"

"Huh? What?" I said, jumping out of my daze. "Yeah…"

"So you have the same number. From when I ran into you last time. That was like, what, two years ago?"

"Oh, yeah. Same number. Not changing."

"Okay, I'll call you."

———

And he did. We spoke once. But after another debrief of his girl-friend issues, the rest of his calls I let go to voice mail. Eventually they went away. That and my overactive libido. And thank God. You attract what you are. I was aggravated by the reality and my attraction to him; it all reminded me of one thing: there was more work to do.

Step #2: therapy.

It's something looked down upon in the black community, a sign of weakness. Even though we are among the ones who truly need it to heal from hundreds of years of post-traumatic stress dis-order, from the beatings of forced servitude, from systematic Jim Crow laws that separated us, kept us down economically, and sabo-taged our confidence, making us feel less than because of skin color, hopeless because of a crabs-in-a-barrel mentality. And distrustful of our men who were regularly taken from us, killed in front of us, and forced into leaving families led by women who built up anger and resentment toward the males who couldn't support them. All of this history weighs on the present. The inability to trust, love, and be vulnerable with our men. Learned from watching mothers. Passed down to unsuspecting daughters. I needed to figure out how to stop repeating my mother's relationship mistakes, which manifested in my staying too busy to sit still. Too scared to feel, swallow the truth, and deal. Like many perpetually single women, too distracted by work and church and this and that to realize our habit of choosing those who reflect our injured selves: emotionally unavailable men. Prone to eventually leaving us, further injuring the abandoned girl in us.

Although my mother seemed to be seeking self-healing herself. When I visited her one communion Sunday in November, she was dressed in a sharp yellow suit with an off-white purse, pearls, and heels to match; she was glowing. Humming. Stirring the greens on the stove as I grated cheddar cheese.

"So I've been reading Iyanla Vanzant," I said. "*In the Meantime*. It's really amazing. It's about—"

"Finding yourself and the love you want," Mom said, finishing my sentence. "I like her. Some of the ladies in the women's ministry were talking about it."

"Really?"

"Oh yeah. I joined a few weeks ago," she said, checking the roasted chicken in the oven. "We read books, pray, meditate, and just talk. Last week they brought in this minister to speak who's also a psychologist. And I met with her the other day. Actually felt good to talk to somebody who understands and doesn't judge. I mean, I don't know if it'll work. But, we'll see…"

Her words drifted off into a hum. She seemed happy. Felt lighter. And as she stood at the stove checking the Sunday meal, I squinted my lids and side-eyed her. Who was this woman? Who was this grinning imposter in the kitchen skipping around about therapy? Dropping her baggage and letting "it" go and working through the mental mud that keeps us backed up?

"Is Larry coming?" He had to be. This attitude of hers had him all over it.

"Larry? Please. We're not speaking anymore."

"Wow," I said in disbelief. "How long ago did this happen?"

"Since the beginning of the year. I didn't want to bring the New Year in again with a jerk."

A month later, after Christmas Eve service, we sat at brunch in a room filled with multiple tables, seated across from a buffet spread of assorted salads, bacon, sausage, eggs, biscuits, and cooks flipping fancy omelets and fluffy pancakes. Another cut thin slices of turkey and ham. My mother happily ate. And again, she was smiling. Bouncing almost. "I went to get a massage the other day, and a mani-pedi, and then I took myself to lunch. I deserve it. An early Christmas present to myself. I work hard. Dr., I mean, Reverend Dennis always says that." She smiled, digging into scrambled eggs, discussing her newfound self-love. Reverend Dr. Dennis had become a regular part of the conversations lately, as Mom called me more than she ever had, weekly, to check on how I was doing. When I returned the question, she'd always end up talking about her therapist with a sense of upbeat thankfulness. "Meena, I know I haven't always made the best decisions in the past," she said out of the blue. "I know I haven't been the best mom I could be. I really was very unhappy. Very depressed. Selfish. Hurt. Caught up in my own drama. And I'm sorry. That wasn't your fault. That was mine. I'm going to be a better mom to you. I promise. I love you."

I didn't know what to say. Just a grin. Side-eye waiting for the TV camera to jump out. All I could muster up was an awkward "I love you, too."

At the beginning of January, I called a list of therapists in my area accepting new patients. I was still on COBRA, paying way too much for health insurance, and decided to use it while I could afford to. But a month later, as the February snow slipped into blizzard mode and my 28th birthday passed, multiple resched-uled appointments and fear-driven cancellations characterized my half-ass attempt to seek help. It wasn't until after still seeing my mother floating high with smiles from her own counseling treat-ment, that I finally found the courage to trek to an office in down-town Brooklyn. I took an elevator up to the eleventh floor, to sit on a leather couch and wait to be seen.

"So what's going on?"

Not knowing what to say, I answered this question with a blank stare at a polyester pink blouse buttoned up to the neck. Tiny red polka dots spotted the shirt, tucked into rose-colored linen pants that flared down to flat black shoes. Her hair was shoulder-length, a broccoli-styled bushel of brown that accented age spots and crev-ices in her skin. Dark bags underlined the wiggly red lines streaking through her eyeballs. Dr. Weisman was my new therapist. Referred by Denise, who'd been going to her for months. When I hinted toward wanting to see someone, she forwarded me the e-mail with the contact information. Meredith, now two years deep into get-ting her PhD in psychology, looked Dr. Weisman up and found a five-star rating and glowing résumé filled with authored books and countless clinical research studies.

"So what's going on?" That question lingered. I knew what to say, but not where to begin. When I didn't immediately answer Dr. Weisman's question, she sat there silently, half smiling, waiting in her brown leather chair, in a tiny white office decorated with plaques certifying a medical degree in psychology from Stanford University. It was weird. Because the more I searched for the right words, the more things built up in my mind. *Do I begin with my father? My mother? The curse? The men? My work?* So many topics, issues, baggage, I was ashamed to begin.

"So you're a writer?" Dr. Weisman asked, saving me. "You mentioned that during our phone consultation. That must be fun."

"Well, yeah. I guess," I said, looking down at the rug with dark almond circles. "I've been getting a lot of freelance work. It's nothing big. Just little assignments. But it's something."

She was quiet again. Staring, transmitting psychic messages, urging me to fill the silence with words.

"I just want to focus," I said, looking around for my phone, leaving it glimmering at the bottom of my purse. "But my ex keeps texting me recently. Mercury or Venus must be in retrograde. And I feel like I'm going to make a mistake and reply."

"Oh, Mercury in retrograde. My computer always breaks," she answered. I was so relieved she understood. "What was his name again?"

"Sean."

She began scribbling. I continued sharing.

"He was a cheater. Always working. Only caring about himself. I was sick in the hospital and home for weeks and he never came to see me." I felt the anger bubbling as the words busted through my lips. "He almost gave me an STD. Gonorrhea. He had a full-blown case, but the doctors said I didn't, which tells me he was cheating. So fuck him. I finally broke up six months too late. Then I went back like an idiot. And I thought I was over him. But holiday time makes it hard. And he always texts me around the holidays and my birthday, which was a few weeks ago. I mean, I don't get it. It was over a year ago. I want him to go away. But I'm good."

"Congratulations," she said, nodding. Her face serious. Eyes squinting. Jotting something in a notebook. "I bet that took a lot of courage."

"Yeah. I always break up," I said, staring at a pigeon flying off the windowsill. "But it takes me so long. Like I do it after being emotionally abused forever. I wish I could see the signs early and leave before my feelings get caught up. But it's hard to let go."

"Or not pick them at all, right?" I paused before nodding my head in agreement. Tears about to come up. She assessed me for a long minute before saying, "Tell me about your father."

And it all came out. That crap lodged in my throat threw phlegm-filled issues into the world. The abuse, the abandonment, the search that always took place the same time yearly, around June, when advertisements for Father's Day began. It started with an internal quest, digging through feelings of fear, resentment, and anger. And then it morphed into maturity and sympathy, understanding that a relationship's demise took two. Last year, I'd actually e-mailed my mother looking for info on his whereabouts. And after a day or two, she responded with a subject line that made me shudder: INFO ON YOUR FATHER.

I stared at it for a week without opening it, wondering what that e-mail might say. *Does she know where he is? Does she have a phone number? Is she mad that I'm looking for him?* I hesitantly dragged the cursor, clicked, and read:

> *Your father was 5'6". He was in the army and went to school for a little while but later dropped out. He has a sister, Nancy, and mother, Gabrielle, who live in Philadelphia. He's from California, and played trumpet. He seemed to grow sad when thinking of his days in Cali. This is all I can remember about him. And I didn't think I'd remember this much. It's all coming back to me as I write this. I'm sorry I didn't tell you this earlier. But I had to leave your father for my own sanity and safety. I never tried to keep you away from him.*

I sat in Barnes & Noble reading this e-mail, staring out the window at a couple holding hands under the table. A small, blond baby girl walked over to grab my leg. Seconds later, her male twin, about thirty years older, scooped her up high, hoisting her tiny body around his shoulders. I smiled. Half loving the Hallmark moment, half masking the fear I felt over finding Dad. It plagued my life, prohibiting trust, enabling debilitating cycles of dysfunctional love. Not having a father made me insecure, lacking faith in men, picking the wrong ones, always wondering about the negative end and evil possibilities of love. The feeling of insecurity only lessened when I was inebriated or high, diminishing the fear of repeating past mistakes. It was a terrifying feeling that made me wonder whether I was forever destined to follow in the curse, the painfully accepted path of a daughter born to a family of fatherless, manless women.

Some days I'd sit, imagining the future, hoping to manifest a father-daughter meeting in a diner. We'd talk and laugh for hours. He'd share stories and tips on how to find a man and keep one. He'd walk me to his house, open the door, and a slew of family would fall out the door, dressed in their Sunday best. At dinner's end, my father and I would head back to the diner for coffee, discussing the past: his, mine, my mother's.

I've always heard Mom's side—about what happened with their relationship and why she called off the engagement. But in my dream sequence, Dad would divulge all the missing details. We'd cry over the years lost. Hold each other, hug and share stories about our physical similarities. Dry skin. Pimples on the back. Horrible seasonal allergies. And then we'd part with a renewed bond, one that saw us spending holiday dinners, weddings, and reunions together. This was my dream. But looking at that e-mail on the computer screen, the key to my past, to my destiny, to me, shook my mind into unmovable fear. I printed it out, filing evidence away atop disheveled papers I'd hidden behind a corner couch.

As I became emotionally naked for Dr. Weisman, the dime bag of weed in my pocket burned a hole in my denim shorts. I fidgeted on her love seat, anxious to roll a fat cigar full of marijuana so I could forget the tension and pain I was being forced to face.

She scribbled something in her notebook.

"Well, we're going to have to stop now," she said, glancing up at the clock. "Same time next week?"

My inner response confused me. Instead of feeling relief, grabbing my bag and running, I wanted to beg for ten more minutes.

I wanted to say more. I wanted to open up before the opportunity closed up. I wanted to deal and heal that day, that moment.

I whined on the inside. *Pleeease?*

But instead I said "Okay," dejected and flat, like a straight line on a heart monitor. I got up, wanting to reach out and grab her tight. I felt an urge to thank her for the empathic power that magnetically pulled painful hidden truths from my soul. But the emotionally unavailable side took over. The side that took pride in showing little emotion. The side that opened up just enough but never fully enough. The side that held my head high and stoic, staying strong, tucking vulnerability under the skin, drowning it in the blood that circulated through my body. I didn't trust her yet. I couldn't show her me. Not yet. So I simply said "Thank you," shaking her hand hard, nodding with approval, before turning to leave with a smile. I couldn't wait to see Dr. Weisman next week.

Later that evening...

"Hey."
"Hey."
"You home?"
"Yeah."
"You want some company?"
"Yeah."
"I'm on my way."

After I came, riding on top, screaming orgasmic pleasure like someone who hadn't had sex in months, I slid off Sean and lay next to him, staring up at the ceiling, having a conversation with God. *Why am I here? Why did I text him? What am I thinking? What the fuck? And it wasn't even that good. He couldn't even keep it up.*

Leave.

That was the only answer I got from God. So I rolled out of the bed, slipped on my panties, pants, hoodie, and boots.

"You leaving?"

"Um… yeah," I said, not looking at him. "I'm on deadline, I need to write."

"Damn. I suddenly feel used," he said, a smirk on his asshole face. "Well, it was good to see you. That was fun."

He sat up in the bed to stare at me as I got dressed. I gave him a fake smile and walked out the door. Ignored all of his calls and texts that eventually drifted away after a few weeks. Maybe that was the get-back and closure I needed. Maybe I just wanted to have sex. Maybe I was actually like Mom in not wanting to spend another year with a jerk.

28

Six months later...

"I WENT ON ANOTHER DATE LAST NIGHT."

"Did you?" Dr. Weisman said, pulling out her notepad, clicking the pen, and writing something down to mark what had become a monumental rare moment. "Was this someone you met online?"

"Uh... yeah."

"You sound embarrassed."

"I mean, I kind of want to meet someone the old-fashioned way. Not looking. When you look you don't find."

"And you also manifest what you believe. Words are power. So if you think this about looking, then why are you online?"

The truth was that I was still fighting the lonely feelings of wanting company, conversation, and the touch of a man. During the quiet moments alone when work slowed and I didn't have to transcribe or write, the empty feeling of being still made me want to stay busy. But I tried to fight it. I'd witnessed so many women in my family and professional circle do this. But it was only through therapy, meditation, and some of the self-help books I'd become obsessed with reading that I realized this and tried to do something different. From *The Road Less Traveled* by M. Scott Peck, and Gary Zukav's *Seat of the Soul*, to *Conversations with God* by

Neale Donald Walsch, I found myself in a spiritual zone of search-ing for something. Myself. Love. Happiness. The power to mani-fest, which I was dying to believe thanks to reading every Iyanla Vanzant book of affirmations I could find. I tried to sit still and feel. But the loneliness. The pain. The anger and insecurity were too much to feel, I couldn't take the tears. Didn't want to feel the anger making me reach for the weed with an addictive need to flee. The horny throb in my vagina made me eventually decide, or somehow convince myself, that after months of therapy, no dating, or real dick-to-clitoris orgasmic stimulation, I'd punished myself long enough. It was time to break down the man-dar walls, take a risk, and let one in.

So I headed to the Internet.

Write a few words about yourself.

Me? Well, I'm a witty, well read, eloquent, down-to-earth Jersey girl. I enjoy red wine, seafood, movies, CNN, HBO on Sundays. Definitely a no-chaser sort of person.
Delete. Version 2:

I'm about fun on the weekends. A homebody writer who enjoys an occasional glass of red wine and intellectual company.
Delete.

I just want a man. I deserve to have a healthy relationship. I'm beautiful, honest, hardworking, positive, and optimistic, with loads of talent, no kids, my own money, and lots of love to give.
Delete.

The mini bio was difficult to write for an online dating site. The only reason I'd decided to get on match.com was because of Meredith.

"Yeah, he's a doctor, a pharmacist," she said, as she parallel parked. "Just bought his mom a house and he's buying himself one, too."

"So, he lives alone?"

"No, he has a roommate." She paused after mentioning this to smear on lipstick, primping and prepping to walk into a party at the 40/40 Club. "He's saving up for his own place."

"So he bought his mom a house," I said slowly, registering what was just said. "But he doesn't have one of his own?"

"Yeah," she answered, looking at me, before patting her lips with a tissue. "I know it sounds weird, Meena. But that's what he said."

"You believe him?"

"Well, why not?"

Meredith was naive when it came to the opposite sex, ingraining words, wishes, and promises into binding, unfaltering truth. Believing in blind faith was something I admired to a point of exception when it came to most men. Trust toward testosterone needed to be earned, not given. But ironically, Meredith had never experienced the pain of having a guy cheat on her and had always maintained long relationships. The repercussions of picking properly. The training of a girl with a healthy mom and dad in her life. Months after her last breakup, she'd managed to become friends with her ex, nurturing a new, healthy, platonic path. I rarely spoke to my exes, full of thoughts that turned up my lip like the smell of moldy trash. Over our nearly sixteen-year friendship, the main difference between Meredith and me was that until recently, I'd looked for lies from the opposite sex, instead of living like her and expecting nothing but the truth. She went in with few expectations other than enjoying the moment. Excited to see where things would go. Open to where they might. Acceptant of where they landed. I always had an agenda. But I wanted to be like Meredith. It was just so hard.

"So yeah, girl, you gotta try match.com," she said, standing outside the car, pulling down her skirt. "It makes the search for a man so much easier. You can cancel out a lot of crap without wasting your time or an outfit on a whack date."

"I don't know, I don't like crazy people," I said, watching a homeless man wrapped in a tattered brown blanket limp by, talking to himself. "Online dating seems—and no disrespect to you—but it seems desperate."

"You can meet someone crazy in the street."

"Yeah, but I just want something natural. Not computer generated." I let out a deep sigh and continued. "I want something old-fashioned, like bumping into a man on the sidewalk, looking up, and having that magnetic attraction where time slows and you know in that moment, at that place and time, that God has sent you something, a once-in-a-lifetime find. A love, an energy so strong and magnetic that it defies odds and space, shifting thoughts and patterns, ideas and expressions into a kind of collage of hearts and question marks that make you question your fears, insecurities, life, the who, what, where, when, why, and how—"

"Um…" Meredith said, cutting me off, "not to interrupt your monologue, but just a quick reality check. It doesn't really happen like that in real life. I mean, I'm sure there are cases. But honestly, it's those caught up in thinking they're cursed who imagine that. Which is why so many women are alone. Buying into the fantasy. The fantasy is the curse. I ran into a couple of classmates the other day, and they were man bashing and talking about being cursed. Beautiful ladies. Single. And both wanted to meet love like you. Like some Disney princess fantasy. You can control how it happens. Just be open to the fact that it will and you might not know when or how."

The words stung like a scorpion. I hadn't mentioned the curse, at least not outside of therapy, in months. And I preferred not to give power to something that had affected my family so negatively.

But it was always there, lingering, ready to make an appearance and soak me with insecurity.

"That was harsh," I said, feeling caught off guard by her blunt words.

"Notice I said 'thinking' they're cursed," she said. "Listen, Meena, I don't think you are cursed. But you think you are. You are what you think. And the emotional barriers you put up by doubting that men are telling the truth when you don't even know them make you unavailable and automatically feed into that so-called bullshit curse of yours. I give people the benefit of the doubt. I don't automatically distrust what they're saying, until they show me why they're untrustworthy. And it'll be not because my dad abandoned me or some ex broke my heart. It will be because *they* hurt me. No one else."

Thanks to Meredith's lecture, I sat sulking at the bar that night, surrounded by men who were too old and women who were too big. Young boys with fake watches who wanted to be ballers. And girls in cheap, tight dresses looking for them. I sipped a screwdriver made with too much vodka, looking around at snakes in a smoky mirage, wondering: *Where is my soul mate? When is he coming? When will I notice him?*

"I know I'm venting, Lord," I said to myself, pushing aside an empty glass to make way for a new one. I closed my eyes. "I'm thankful for the path. Just please show me the way. Show me how to enjoy the moment. Show me how to stay in the moment."

Meredith came over, pulling my hand. I followed her to the dance floor. And when the DJ dropped an old-school eighties segment we busted all of our middle-school moves on the dance floor. The running man, the Wop, the Kid 'N Play. We sweated profusely and cracked up like goofy kids the entire time.

After leaving the club at three in the morning, I drove Meredith back to my apartment and watched her stumble up the stairs in her platform heels, fall on my couch, and pass out, muttering something about "He was cute, he's the one… I need to go study."

After she headed back to Jersey the next day, first thing I did was turn on the computer. "Okay, match.com. Let's see what magic you got," I said as I created the login identification using my middle name, last initial, month and day of birth: FeyB22. I added a picture, zoomed in to reveal only my eyes. Muslim men fell in love with women who only showed their eyes. Something about that was romantic to me, taking away the pressure to be judged by my body. If the soul could be seen through the eyes, then that's all I wanted to reveal. When I logged onto the site, pictures of men popped up. Colorful headshots, smiles, some with kids, others with dogs, most with serious faces, a few purposely looking stupid.

Ken28: Direct. Funny. Likes to drink. Lawyer. Goes to movies. Eats well. Travels a lot. Better to meet in person.

WaitingForTheOne31: I find myself spending Friday nights alone, watching romantic movies and pondering in places where I ask God, "When will I find the one?" I'm a good Christian man who believes in traditional Christian values. Looking for a lady to settle down with and make my, no, our, dreams come true.

GScan20: Brooklyn born and raised. Italian Stallion, that's right. Poet by day and night. I cook, clean, love a great book at night. Mama taught me right. On here in a rather last-ditch attempt to find my lady right. I just wanna take you out for a bite. See if we vibe and can talk through the night. Will you click my page and like?

And I did. The corny poem made me laugh. I loved a Brooklyn boy, a book reader, and a guy who wanted to take me out to eat. Plus his picture, a close-up with a goatee and light eyes and a New York Rangers hat tilted to the side, was rather cute. After speaking on the phone a few times, and a couple of dinner dates, I decided to head to a jazz show with George.

"So… I enjoyed the night," he said, smiling. Sitting in his black Toyota in front of my apartment, he smiled a toothy grin. "This is our third date, ya know?"

"Oh, yeah. I didn't even realize that." I did. I lied. But didn't want to point it out.

He moved closer. His seat belt stretched across his shoulder.

"So… I really like you. I think we have a connection and I haven't had that in a long time."

I knew George wanted to kiss. And I may have kissed him back. But his breath smelled like onions fresh from the fried loaf we'd ordered at dinner. I'd popped a peppermint into my mouth an hour prior. But when I offered one to him?

"Nah, I choked on one of those things as a kid," he'd said, shaking his head. "I'm still traumatized."

Should I have said "Your breath stinks"? Should I have offered a mint again, and hoped he got the hint?

As he stretched closer, I moved back. Thinking of what to say. "Okay… well, I gotta go write," was all I could think of. "I got a deadline. But this was nice." Keeping an eye on him, struggling to unhook my seat belt, I clicked it open and reached for the door handle. George pounced on my lips. Swallowed. Slobbered. Tongue all over. His entire onion face of sloppy spit ate my mouth alive. I finally found the knob and opened the door. The click of the handle moved him back to the driver's side. My face was twisted into a crooked, mushed mouth of disgust.

"Okay, well, good night," I said, trying to feign my best fake smile. Trying not to show that I never planned on calling him again.

When I shared the story with Dr. Weisman, she laughed. Louder than I'd ever heard her before. She'd always been so prim and proper, emotionless and direct, and now she was coming out of her shell. Cracking up.

"That was a colorful story," she said, smiling. "Onions, ya say?"

"Onions. It was the most gross thing."

She laughed again.

I smiled at the silliness. And beamed when she ended the session with "I'm glad you're starting to date again, Meena. I think it's good for you. I'm glad you're being brave."

As usual, I couldn't wait till next week's session.

29

MY DILDO AND I had become best friends. Mr. Do was his name. First name, Dil. He had ten levels of vibration and was shaped like a thick, nine-inch dick with the feel of Silly Putty. He had the ability to turn and morph into numerous positions with a circular suction cup at the end that I could use to stick it to any surface and ride it like a cowboy friend. And I did. For many months after, my first orgasm was so loud I moaned and groaned, my echoing screams bouncing off brownstones outside.

But the more I used it, the more I had to use my creativity. Coming up with unique ways to stretch my legs wide, on a pillow, over my head, wide like a gymnast. I began timing orgasm attempts to see how fast I could make myself come and scream to beat my best time of seven minutes. But after months of using a dildo that I bought after my embarrassing hookup with Sean, the August hot sun collided with the approaching end of fun that made me horny for something real. A real man, a real boner, a real someone I could grind and ride.

So I called Terry. Although I wasn't sure whether I truly wanted to sleep with him, I was willing to explore the possibility. A local Brooklyn MC who went by the name of Terror One, he'd been calling and begging to take me out, off and on for years, after we'd met outside a *Buzz* party. Each time he asked, I'd always say no. Entertaining his conversation, flattered by the attention, but more concerned with my reputation as a journalist. I had one unbreakable rule: Never sleep with rappers. Never be like so many other female writers who'd moistened sheets by blurring the line between groupie and media professional. Never kill the delicate reputation I'd spent time in the business building. But Terry kept begging, wooing, texting little blurbs that were romantically driven and lightly written, bouncing from cell phone screens into my head and slowly tapping at my heart. Although I still wasn't fully convinced, the next time he called I agreed to meet him one late afternoon for a movie and dinner. He ruined it with one question:

"So you wanna see my penis?"

"Do I wanna see your what?"

"My penis. It's small…"

When this conversation occurred, we were sitting at the twenty-four-hour diner on Thirty-fourth and Eighth, down the block from the local theater. I sipped my cheap house wine while flipping through the oversize menu. Appreciative of the length, I was able to use its gigantic size to hide my face from his horny, adoring glances and anyone who might notice that I was on a date with (gasp) *a rapper* (double gasp).

"You want to see it?" George stretched wide the elastic waist of his basketball pants and looked down. "Well, I think it's small. Look…"

"No, I don't wanna see your penis," I replied, face twisted in disgust. "What kind of question is that?"

"Well, why not?"

"'Cause… I don't," I said, suddenly remembering the clear boundary words Dr. Weisman had taught me. "And I'm not interested in sex with anyone outside of an exclusive relationship."

"But it's small," he replied dismissively. "I just want you to see it."

"Excuse me, did you want a large or small?" a slim brunette waitress with a nose ring asked. She seemed to pop up out of nowhere, holding my cranberry juice and his cold milk.

"I'm sorry," she said, glancing at me. "I believe you said small, but I couldn't remember."

"Actually, I ordered a large," I replied, glancing at Terry before refocusing on the waitress. "But I'm thirsty, so I'll take what you got." She placed the cups on the table. Terry smiled, picking up his milk and using his finger to stir the ice.

"Ill," I said, wincing. "Why are you drinking milk?"

"'Cause milk does ya body good."

"That's an overused cliché," I said, sucking my teeth. "Milk was a bad choice."

"Well," he said, taking a long gulp. "I need to grow."

"Grow into what?"

"A *big* boy…"

"Here's your large, ma'am," the waitress intervened, placing a tall glass of cranberry juice in front of me. "You should have what you want."

Terry and I looked at each other and began cracking up. The waitress, stunned, walked away confused.

The truth is that he and I had fun together, laughing in easy ways that made me forget he was an MC. That is, until he'd bring up sex. Or begin rhyming about shooting someone and "bitches in the studio." I remember the day he spontaneously grabbed my arm on an empty sidewalk, spun me around, and kissed my mouth as if a slobbery glob of wet jelly was smothered on his lips. It tasted like whiskey and Pepsi mixed with cigarettes and weed.

I stared at him in shock after the kiss, before pushing him away and screaming, "What the fuck!" I looked around frantically, making sure we hadn't been busted, before stomping down the block to hop on the train.

Fast-forward three weeks later, date number two, where I stared at him from across a restaurant table. Disappointed that his idiotic words had turned off my horny plans for him. Bored, ready to leave, I watched across the restaurant as some idiot manhandled a woman and, like a cop, dragged her by the upper arm out of the diner.

"You ever hit a girl before?" I asked, anticipating even the most minor reaction.

"Yeah, once or twice," he answered nonchalantly, twisting his hair. "You know her?"

"Do I know her?"

"No, I meant to phrase that as a declaration. 'You know her.' Joya. Joya Kelly."

A model turned actress, Joya had a role on one of the biggest TV dramas on NBC.

"That was your girlfriend?"

"She was my fiancée."

"You hit her?"

"She hit me first."

"Must've been a reason."

"She thought I was cheating."

"Were you?"

"Yeah, but she didn't know. She was just on some 'I had a dream' shit. Moody as fuck, on her cycle." He sipped his milk. "We used to fight and hit each other all the time."

My stomach flipped in a gassy, crampy limp, like the second achy day of menstruation.

"Why's your face look like that?" he asked, wincing at me. "Oh," I said, getting up to leave. "I don't feel well."

"We'll take a doggie bag," he said to the waitress, standing and grabbing my coat. "Let her pack ya food, and I'll get you a cab."

"Nah, I'm good." I began digging in my bag, looking for something, anything, a tissue. A nervous move to avoid looking at Terry. "I'ma just go."

"You a'ight?"

"No, my stomach hurts. I told you." I pushed down the uncontrollable aggravation mounting in my chest. "I gotta go. Maybe it was the food."

I took a deep breath.

"Yeah, um." I couldn't figure out what to say. "Well… thanks for dinner."

"But we didn't eat," he said loudly.

I speed-walked out the door and headed to the C train.

Never took any of Terry's calls again. Deleted his texts. Saved his name in my phone as "The Abuser." And that fall, when his song "She Left" hit no. 1 on the radio, with familiar lyrics like "She said goodbye / Without looking in the eye / When I told her the truth / About a time in my youth."

I initially wanted to call and say "Congratulations!" Tell him how flattered I was that he wrote a song about us, but I didn't because the truth was that I shouldn't have gone out with him to begin with. Breaking my own rules of journalism ethics. Embarrassed to even be seen with the man. And besides, if he abused her, he'd do it to me. Mental note: Stay in therapy.

30

AFTER TEN MONTHS IN THERAPY, with holiday time approaching again, it became less weird to endure Dr. Weisman's long pauses. The sessions allotted by my insurance were running out. I became expectant of her nuances. She'd wait, twisting her pink breast-cancer-awareness pen between wrinkly, skinny fingers, forcing me to speak. She'd strangely stare at me expressionlessly, paid to be patient with her clients by not blinking, but instead peering inside our brains. I'd uncomfortably attempt to look anywhere, out the window, at a tree, at something. Just not into her Medusa-like hypnotic eyes, trying to pull secrets from my soul and break them into tiny psychoanalytical pebbles.

"How's work?"

"Amazing," I said, relieved she'd broken the tension. "I found an agent who's shopping my book. She says the feedback is good. And I just got offered an editor's position with a new magazine start-up."

"Congratulations," she said, nodding with approval, jotting down notes. "How's dating been going?"

"Dating myself or men?"

"Both."

I'd made a fun habit of taking myself out weekly. Movies, restaurants, video arcades, museums; if it was something I wanted to do with a man, I did it by myself. If it was something I wanted a man to buy me, I bought it myself. Flowers. Brunch. Sexy panties. The love song I sang to myself harmonized with the golden suggestions of advice I followed from Dr. Weisman. "Date yourself before and while you date others. How can you want someone to do something for you if you haven't done it for yourself?" Amen.

I took her advice to another level, jogging several times a week, reminiscing of my high school winter track days. I took yoga, found karate classes, meditated, journaled daily, and worked overtime to take care of me. Taking hours, every day, for me. Cleaning my apartment, trashing the clutter, making room in my closet for love, giving away clothes I hadn't worn in a year, even taking moments throughout the day to resist the urge to move and instead sit in silence. Feeling the pain. Daring to cry or seethe in anger, or shiver with insecurity or simply crack up at my own silly self. I felt it all. My insides glowed from self-love. And for the first time I actually liked me. Thanks to the mirror I spoke to daily, I knew I was beautiful without needing to be told. I knew I was confident and courageous and could handle anything that came my way. I even made a point of talking to my mother more often. Fighting to finally forgive her. Releasing the resentment I'd held since childhood. It wasn't all gone. I still cautiously needed my space. But seeing her growth made me try. She was the healthiest I'd ever known her to be, always talking about her own therapy sessions. And I was happy, praying, and wishing her well. I was healing and becoming more clear than I'd been in my entire life.

"I haven't slept with anyone. I mean, thank God for dildos. Because I'm not even that interested. I mean I am, but it's not a priority," I said, laughing. "I've averaged maybe a date or two per month."

"And this is all from people you met online?"

"Just one or two. Here and there. One I met on the train. One at a get-together. Another online. I've got this new plan to just make friends. Actually be friends. No sex for a few months. Maybe not at all. Just really getting to know people before I decide to date. Meredith recommended it. Pre-dating. So I guess I'm not really dating yet. I'm just hanging out."

"I think that's a healthy thing to do," she said, smiling.

"Yeah, and if it doesn't work out for dating, at least I made a new friend. No expectations. Just friendly intentions."

"Sounds like a good plan. Anyone panning out?"

"There's one I like. He's nice, but weird."

"How?"

"Just…" My words drifted off as I looked into her pupils. "I don't know. He's different…"

"Why is that weird?"

I diverted her lingering, perplexed glare, fidgeting in my chair, thinking about Chad and how we'd met.

I'd periodically skim the online dating ads just to crack up. It was like a relationship commercial online where you're given fifty words to express yourself in the most poetic way. I clicked through the pages, surfing the love web, seeing whether anyone fit my account specifications: men 28–40, within a thirty-mile radius.

Skimming through my inbox, I noticed how mostly white guys hit me up. But color didn't matter to me. My soul mate could be any race. I was open to the possibilities. Smiling at their flirty e-mails, I came upon one brother who looked eerily familiar. He smiled in his photo, bright and shiny with a Yankee cap fitted atop his head. He was bald, with a full mustache and beard covering his smooth, brown face, dotted with round glasses that made for a British, academic look. He smiled brightly in a happy way that reminded me of a kid on Christmas Day.

ChadM28: New to this online dating thing, but figured I'd give it a try. I'm a nonprofit fundraising director living in NYC. I prefer a good book, dramatic movie, and great food with stimulating conversation. I couldn't come up with an alias for my profile, so I decided to use my name.

I think it's best to begin from a point of honesty. So I encourage you to reach out to me if you're looking for long-term dating and an activity partner.

Above his picture, in the right-hand corner, it read, "Rate this photo." I clicked on four stars out of five, leaving one off simply because I didn't know him. The next morning, I checked my phone and saw an e-mail message from ChadM.

Hello. You rated me 4 stars. I rated you 4. We have 92% in common. I think we should definitely have a conversation. What do you think? I'll begin...

And he went on to wittily write about his life—how he'd been single for a year and a half. How he worked for a nonprofit and wrote a novel on the side. How online dating was a last resort before he thought about retiring to a Buddhist monastery (sike).

I laughed out loud, impressed that he managed to write an entire paragraph without a typo, full of color and context, concise and grammatically correct. My reply led to a two-week e-mail exchange before we graduated to the next step: The Phone Call.

31

WE'D SCHEDULED A TIME to talk: Friday, nine o'clock. I'd call him.

He'd written me an e-mail: *Ok, hit me up when you're ready. I'm excited!*

Friday was perfect since my normal, end-of-week routine was to sit around with my feet up. So when nine came, I dialed. But it went straight to voice mail.

"You know the deal," the recording said. "Leave a message."

The prompt was so short that I didn't have time to think of what I wanted to say.

"Hi, this is Fey?" My voice was crackly. Literally like static on a cell phone, barely comprehensible, uneasy, like a pubescent child who adds question marks to the end of each sentence. "Um, from match.com? So... I'm calling at nine like I said I would? Um, okay, well, you can call me. Um, okay. Bye."

Stupid. I sounded like an idiot, bumbling and tripping over words like feet struggling for room to walk inside a mouth. In the midst of being angry at myself, I was upset at him for not answering. For putting me through the agony of having to leave what I saw as recorded blackmail. I mean, why make a phone date only to flake out?

There I was with the questions again. Marks of insecurity set in. Moments of the less-evolved, puppy part of me licking old wounds while crying in protest, pained to the core. I pulled out my journal and used a technique from the book Dr. Weisman suggested: *The Journey from Heartbreak to Connection*, by Susan Anderson. She specialized in healing those who'd been abandoned by parents, lovers, friends. I'd become more conscious of my sexual urges after reading her explanation of how abandonment survivors tend to use sex as a means of control. As a way to soothe the pain and provide protection, the urge to have sex is like a baby's urge to grab a blanket or teddy bear in response to the fear of being hurt or abandoned. It's a means of wanting safety and power and control over the anxieties of being left. After reading about this, I understood why I slept with Sean that last time. And although I hadn't had sex with Chad, yet, the fear of being rejected produced an unbearable tension in my chest.

So I worked on Anderson's suggested exercise called "Inner Child." It consisted of talking to the childlike self, the scared little girl who'd been neglected and abandoned. I called her "Lil." She was protected by "Big," my mature, assertive, grown-up, nurturing, protective, and logical side. By paying attention and giving voice to fears, the likelihood of manifesting them in toxic ways diminishes and gives way to a potent inner dialogue between the self-assured and less confident parts of the mind.

Lil: Where is he? Why is he not answering? He's dissin'. He knew we were supposed to talk and he's ignoring me.

Big: Well, how do you know he's not in the bathroom?

Lil: No, he could've waited or taken the phone with him.

Big: You want him to use the bathroom and talk on the phone? Wouldn't that be rude and gross?

Lil: I mean, yeah, I guess. But…

Big: But what?

Lil: I just want to talk to him.

Big: And you will. Just be patient. Let him call you. Isn't faith important?

Lil: Yeah.

Big: Why is faith important?

Lil: 'Cause God blesses those who believe. Leap and the net will appear.

Big: Right. I want you to try hard to remember that. I know it's difficult. But you can't scare yourself away before you've even tried. Because things aren't going as you've planned. God laughs at plans. So you have to go with the flow and believe that no matter what happens, you will get what's best for you. Everything happens for a good reason. Right?

Lil: Yeah. I just get so scared. What if he doesn't call?

Big: If he doesn't call, that's God blessing and protecting you from someone who doesn't deserve you. Someone doing you a favor. It might hurt. But you will get over it and someone better will come. You are a big, brave girl. You respect yourself. You don't chase love. Someone who wants to get to know you will call you and show you. Someone nice will give you love. Do you believe that?

Lil: (sigh) Yes. OK. I will be brave. And if he doesn't call, forget him. He's a jerk. And if he does? Well, we'll see.

Big: Good girl. Either way you'll be fine. Still beautiful. Still wonderful. Still worthy of love. And I will protect you. Always have, always will. Just give me a chance, okay?

Lil: Okay.

Big: I love you, Lil, forever and ever.

Lil: I love you, too.

The phone rang. It was nine twenty.

"Hello, may I speak to Fey?"

"Speaking."

"Hey, this is Chad."

"Oh," I tried to say in my most nonchalant voice. "Hey."

"Yeah, sorry for being late. I came home from work and my dog had shit in the hallway of my building. So embarrassing. My landlord was there showing an apartment. She stank up my entire hallway. And when I bent over to clean it, my phone fell on the floor, centimeters from the poop, the battery popped out, millimeters away, it was a mess. So I was mopping the floor, picking up crap, and fixing the phone at the time you called. I'm sorry for not answering. Is Mercury in retrograde? I mean, I've been looking forward to this talk all day, and as soon as I rush home and get myself together, things go haywire. It's not my style to be late for a first date. 'Cause I know first impressions mean everything. Not to use a cliché, but they really are lasting."

"Did that feel better?" I asked, with a huge smile on my face. "Can you breathe now?"

"Yes," he said, coughing. "I just needed to get that off my chest. I'm all discombobulated. Today was a long day."

"Discombobulated? Do you normally use that word?"

"No, but it just came out. I think I'm nervous. Trying to sound smart."

We both laughed and moved on to meshed ideas and internal vibes. Sharing our days, pasts, and hopeful futures. Nodding and acknowledging supportive agreements that felt like warm blankets across our backs. Safe. Consoling. It felt right talking for two hours, touching on topics from politics to entertainment, sports, food, family, and friends. He told me about his monogamy-prone love life, full of wrong turns and erroneous choices. He shared stories of his father being killed in a fight when he was fourteen. And his mother, wanting to have a grandchild before she dies, to carry on the family's genes and name. He confessed his drama of writing, taking a decade to finish his novel by night, while going to grad school and working as a nonprofit communications director. Two hours seemed like thirty minutes, as we talked and ignored the sweat sucking the phone to our skulls, melting wax and smearing makeup into my ear canal. Messy, yet amazing.

"Your eyes are beautiful, by the way," he said. "That's why I e-mailed you. I mean, I really liked what you wrote online. It was poetic. But what stood out is that you didn't feel the need to use a sexy profile picture. Just your eyes. I like them. They're honest. Sensitive. Caring. Really pretty."

He called again a few days later. A few days after that.

"So you think this is strange?" Dr. Weisman asked. Her head tilted to the side. Pen in hand, ready to take notes. "His calling you regularly bothers you?"

"I mean, I just guess I'm not used to it."

"He sounds attentive to me. Sounds like he likes you."

"I mean, is that normal? The frequency of calling?"

"If a man likes you and is interested, he will call you."

"So why do I feel like I want to dodge his calls sometimes? Like he's bothering me. One time I purposely let it go to voice mail. And then I called him back, not wanting to play games. I mean, I like talking to him. But then I get scared. Like it's going to go downhill at any moment."

Dr. Weisman nodded. "You're an abandoned child. An abused child. Many typically push away those who give them healthy attention, while chasing the ones who hurt and abandon them. It's an addiction in a way. You often attract lovers with your same emotional issues. Where the abandonment feels normal, familiar, pushing all the buttons of attraction, pointing to toxic love. Making you feel like pain and rejection is what love is. Because that's how you grew up. That's what you got from your parents and those who were supposed to support, nurture, and love you unconditionally. But because they didn't, attention from someone who actually shows healthy availability is new and unfamiliar. It often makes someone abandoned feel distrustful or turned off. Fearful. They subconsciously question why someone would want to pay attention to them. They push it away or sabotage it."

"Wow," I said as Dr. Weisman stood to open the blinds, noting the end of the session. "That's interesting. The human mind is amazing." The glare of the sun made me stretch my lids wide, waking me up to common sense. Sitting forward on the edge of the couch, back straight and alert. "And I'm a good person, dammit. I deserve love."

"Yes, you are," she said, smiling. "Yes, you do. And you'll have it. Healing takes time. But you can heal. You will. And you are."

"I've never heard anyone say that before. I mean, except Meredith." I sat with my hands under my thighs. "I've always felt like I'd have abandonment issues forever. Always dealing with my mommy shit, my daddy shit, my family-curse shit."

"All wounds heal if you have the courage to take care of them properly," she said, smiling. "And yours will, too."

32

"You're intelligent, beautiful, talented. Why are you single?"

I paused before answering Chad's question. Concerned about inquiries that might make him formulate judgments that, whether right or wrong, made me cringe with apprehension at revealing the baggage of a curse I was born to hold for life.

"I'm embarrassed to say," I whispered, happy he couldn't see the blush of insecurity rising in my cheeks. "It's... weird."

"Listen, I'm a serial monogamist. I'm in love with being in love," he said. "But because of this habit, I realize I've rushed and gotten into a number of questionable relationships that I knew from week one I shouldn't have pursued because I've been afraid to be alone."

"Wow, I don't think I've ever heard a guy say that."

"Yeah, well, I'm not typical," he said, laughing. "And I'm not gay. Although I am in touch with my inner self."

That statement was another first.

"Fey, I would go on first dates hearing my mother's voice whining about wanting to be the old lady in the shoe with a bunch of grandkids. And I knew after a couple of conversations that this woman I was spending money on for dinner wasn't the one. But I'd see my mother's face crying when my older brother was shot dead before twenty-five. Since then, she always finds a way to nag me about how I'm 'the last resort' to carry on the family name. After thirty years, and a good therapist, I finally believe what I've been telling her my entire life. The right woman will come when the time is right—when I'm happy, stable, and ready. All of which I am now. I'm starting this new New Year right. But it takes time to move past those blocks we have ingrained in us, because of our families. So I get it, Fey."

I let his words soak in. "Well, apparently I'm still single because…" The words drifted as I stalled. "I'm… apparently I'm cursed."

"That's interesting…" Chad said, his sentence trailing off into intrigue. "What kind of curse?"

"Well, the story goes that my great-great-grandmother slept with a pastor, and the pastor's wife put a curse on her and all of the women of the Mitchell family to be alone and without a man forever. Destined to never be married."

"But your last name is Butler."

"Yeah, but I'm from the Mitchell family."

"True, but you don't have the surname. You're a Butler. I've heard of this curse before," he said. "My family is Creole. My great-grandfather used to always talk about voodoo, spirits, and creepy shit."

"Okay, so tell me what this thing is." I was eager, standing in the middle of my bedroom, motionless, mushing the phone into my head, wishing I could jump through the receiver and see Chad in person to explain what's haunted me for years.

"Apparently my great-great-great-grandmother Mercy Decroix was a hateful bitch. She stopped going to church and got into spells after her husband cheated with her sister, Hope. Word is, on her deathbed, Mercy testified, accepted God, and admitted to all the bad curses she'd done, including the one she placed on Hope, preventing her from ever getting married. The way the sister was able to break the curse was to give her children a different last name from her own."

"Wait, so the man curse is in your family, too?"

"Apparently it was, because there are no more Decroixs in the family. Mercy didn't realize that when she placed her curse, she hexed the entire family's name as well as her own. So the only child Hope had out of wedlock, a daughter, was given the father's surname. That daughter married a Murphy and gave birth to my great-grandfather, who told me this story."

A long silence followed on my end as I exhaled the weight of a false truth passed through generations, heaving in my soul, suffocating my security, pressuring my mind with frustrating fears of a lifetime spent alone—one devoid of healthy love, rife with drama, dysfunction, and pain, all with the man curse at the root.

"Um… hello?" Chad asked, breaking my stunned silence. "Did I scare you?"

"No…" I said. "I've just been living with what I thought was a curse on me my entire life. And to hear what you said is surreal."

"Well, on the flip side, maybe there is a curse. The mind is powerful. If you tell yourself something long enough, you'll start to believe it. If it comes from a parent, the child believes it," he said. "If you believe a lie about yourself long enough, you manifest its reality. The minute it loses power is when you realize the truth, think something different, truly believe, say and accept it. Truth is love."

I was still silent. Quiet in awe. Mesmerized by truth. Loving what Chad had told me as I slowly flashed back to every time I'd heard word of "the curse" throughout my entire life. To every feeling that I didn't fully fit in with my family because I was a Butler and everyone else was a Mitchell. At that moment, I knew the truth. The epiphany. There was no damn curse. It was all in my head. And if there was one, like Chad's family believed, it was all on the Mitchell side. I was safe.

"So," he continued, "now that you know you're not cursed anymore, when can we meet? Are you free Sunday afternoon for brunch?"

"You don't want a picture of me?"

"Well, I've dated many women with beautiful bodies and ugly personalities. You have a beautiful personality, eyes, laugh. So you know what? I'll see the rest of you in person."

"That's risky."

"It is. But I have a good feeling about you. I like to go with my gut. So we'll see if I'm right on this one. I have nothing to lose," he said, before coughing. "Unless you rob me or something."

We met at an Italian restaurant on a side street near the Hudson River. The place evoked old-world Sicilian charm, with cobblestone streets and dimly lit corners holding old gentlemen with black blazers. Their legs crossed as they sipped red wine at two in the afternoon; Frank Sinatra played from the speakers, vibrating sounds that bounced from tables aglow with candles. Tiny flames gave light to old, wooden, two-person seating arrangements. Wobbling, the tables ached for the weight of customers to add charm.

When I stepped inside, I looked around for Chad. No sign, that was unless he was the old man sipping the wine, and I couldn't see that.

Lil, the critic, began chattering with unsure vulnerability inside my head. *Why is he not here? Is he coming? Is he late? That's not good. He's going to cancel.*

Big came to her defense: *He'll be here. Why wouldn't he? It's you. The queen.*

I pulled out my phone to send a text. *Hey Chad. I'm here.*

His reply seconds later: *Me too. Outside.*

I headed to the front door, stepped outside, and heard, "Oh! Meena Butler! Superstar in the flesh. Wow."

I looked up at the brother staring at me. He wore a black fedora and a brown blazer. I squinted my eyes to jog the memory. His familiar face softened as I remembered the name.

"Carl Murphy? Remember? I know I look different. I cut my dreads. I gained weight. I know, I'm working on that. And last night I shaved my beard. I mean, you never saw me with that, but

I did. Cleaned up a bit. But look at you!" He looked down at my dress. "You look beautiful. Like a model…"

"Last I saw you was a year and a half ago on the C train complaining about your girlfriend. You were hiding under a hood and behind a book." I laughed, staring at him up and down. He looked different. No longer the insecure, geeky kid from high school, hiding out in the library. He was beautiful. A bit overweight but still handsome, and way more confident than I remembered. The messy dreads he wore back then had hidden his face and soft, caring eyes. And he'd gotten his teeth fixed, straightening into a perfect Hollywood smile. "You were at NYU, right?"

"Got the master's. Working in the city now. Helping the people. You look nice. All fancy. Let's step inside. Don't want you to freeze."

He opened the door and winked at me. I blushed. "Oh, this is my date outfit."

"Funny." He laughed. "I've got my date outfit on, too. You like?" He posed and tipped his hat with a curl. His brown blazer with white collared shirt and matching brown pants exuded a Sunday-afternoon, post-church charm.

"Very sharp," I said. "Looks like you just came from church."

"Well, thank you, my dear. Because I did," he said, laughing. "I had to go pray that this date went well. And I was about to think she stood me up till I got a text from her. She should be coming out any minute. Use your journalistic instincts to tell me what kind of vibe you get, okay?"

I nodded.

"What have you been up to?" he continued. "Still writing masterpieces?"

"Trying, writing, living, being free, and now attempting to date. Pre-dating."

"Pre-dating?"

"You know, making friends and hanging out before you decide if you actually want to date someone?"

"That's dope. I'm using that from now on. I'm stealing that term. Pre-dating. Hell yeah," he said, glancing at the front door of the restaurant. "But it's funny, 'cause I actually am on a blind date today. Trying to start the year off right and get my personal life on track." He shook his head and giggled nervously. "Somebody I met online. Isn't that crazy?"

My body went numb. Dead.

"The interesting thing is, she seems cool. I mean, we have a lot in common and I can't wait to meet her. I hope she's not fat. But even if she is, it's cool. I'm kinda fat. So we can just jiggle stomachs together." He started laughing. "Nah, but her personality seems golden. I like it. And we stay on the phone for hours."

Carl talked. And I just looked at him. Unable to speak, squinting and imagining what he'd look like if he wore glasses and had a beard, until I gathered my wits and asked, "What's her name?"

"Fey," he said, glancing at the door again.

"That's my middle name. Meena Fey Butler. And I'm here to meet my blind date, Chad."

Carl stopped midsentence, staring wide-eyed in disbelief. His pupils were huge, face shifting from shock to amusement, back to amazement, and then into a warm smile.

"That's crazy, because Chad is my middle name. Carl Chad Murphy."

Moments moved at the rate of thick Southern molasses, sticking together, freezing frames.

We'd talked so much about my work, his nonprofit life saving the world, his mother, and our personal dreams and relationship issues that we never fully delved into where he went to high school.

We stared at each other as if we were fine porcelain sculptures. "This is weird!" he said, shattering the awkward hypnotic moment. "Oh shit!"

We both cracked up.

"Well, nice to meet you, Fey. I mean, um, Meena *Fey* Butler."

I smiled as he yanked me up, giving a huge bear hug that made me laugh out loud.

33

FOR THE FIRST FEW MONTHS we pre-dated. Flirting each moment. Teasing and cracking jokes the next. Talking nonstop. Hanging out like old friends. By Spring, we'd negotiated the next phase of official exclusive dating. Touching. Kissing. Eventually sexing. That last part was the most mature experience I'd ever had. We didn't just fall into bed after boozing over glasses of sangria. We discussed it in depth. What sex would mean, what we liked, what it might be like, what would happen after, the emotions that might come. We finally agreed and decided that when we did sleep together, we should be exclusive. And we were. For the first time, it wasn't the casual romp we'd both been accustomed to having. It was between a man and a woman putting all of their energy and focus into making it work with each other. I'd never felt so safe.

He grabbed me with a delicate yet firm force that pinned my arms over my head. Then he slowly kissed me, licked me, like a feather tickling every bit of me. His final move of the lips landed between my legs. Massaging me down with the length of his tongue. When he whispered in my ear as he pushed himself inside of me, he asked, "You like this, Meena?"

But I couldn't speak. I mumbled something inaudible. My eyes were closed. The room was spinning. And the intensity of the experience threw me into a space full of twinkling stars, bursting bright lights, and flashes of ecstasy that I'd never seen or felt on this Earth before. It was the best sex I'd ever had. And I knew right then I was falling in love.

Six months later, the problem became that the spell of unexpressed love began to creep in with its uncontrollable passions and high-strung emotions. The insecure baggage popped up to be unpacked.

"Do you always read people's cell phones?"

Carl typed a message. I casually leaned in, looking. He kept typing.

"I mean, I don't care if you read my cell phone."

"And I don't care that you read mine," he said, texting away. "But the difference is that you always look at mine. Like, I feel like I'm under investigation. Do you trust me?"

I let the question linger. Probably for a second too long before answering, "Yeah?"

I sounded like a ten-year-old in a twenty-nine-year-old body. Adding a question mark to the end of my sentence, full of uncertainty and shame.

"What's that?" he asked, putting down his phone. "Are you not sure?"

"No, I'm sure. I just… I mean, I don't know why I said it like that. Do you not want me to look at your phone? Fine. I won't look at it anymore. I mean, I don't have anything to hide."

"I don't care that you look at my phone. I have nothing to hide. As long as you're not doing that sneaky snooping shit."

I found the most interesting piece of lint creeping along the floor, feeling like a guilty spy.

"But it just seems like you tend to make an effort to watch," he continued. "Not like we're sitting next to each other and typing. But like you walk over to me. Or you might say something sarcastic."

"I do not."

"You do. You did it last week. You went, 'Who's that? Your boo?' You do it a lot. And I typically never say anything. But since we're having the conversation, I feel the need to bring it up. If we don't have trust, we have nothing. Have I given you a reason to not trust me?"

"No."

"Do you think I'm going to hurt you?"

"N-no," I stuttered. "I-I don't think so."

"See, you paused. What's up with that?"

I didn't know. I didn't know how to answer or break the tension or change the vibe of the room. So I walked over to him, sat on his lap, kissed him, and began unbuckling his pants.

"No." He gently moved my hand to the side. "I'm not feeling that tonight. We can have sex *after* we deal with this."

I sat there in awe. Mouth damn near open. No one had ever resisted my advances. Carl had never denied me. He waited for me to say something. And I just sat there. Embarrassed. In shock. Mouth frozen in dumbness.

Standing to fix his pants, he grabbed his coat. "I'll call you when I get back from the conference." He leaned over and kissed me on the lips. "I just want you to trust me, Meena. I need you to trust."

Still silence from me. I honestly didn't know what to say or how to say it.

He looked me in the eye for a long, uncomfortable stretch, then left.

When I heard his car pull away, I could move again. Fear ran through my fingers and I dialed Meredith.

No answer. She had her new dentist man, was all happy in love, and catching her at night was difficult some days. So I pulled out my journal. With tears in my eyes I began to write.

Lil: I'm fucking up. What's wrong with me? He's going to break up with me.

Big: You don't know that. People don't break up with you for making one mistake.

Lil: But he thinks I don't trust him.

Big: Well, do you?

Lil: I want to.

Big: Has he done anything for you to not trust him?

Lil: No. But so many guys have cheated on me and hurt me.

Big: He is not so many guys, Meena. He's Carl. Remember? Geeky dude reading the thick comic books with the corny lines who always complimented you in high school. Remember?

Lil: Yeah. But he's not the same guy.

Big: And he's not your father. He's not Sean or Dexter, Michael Tubman or Emmanuel, or any of the other idiots that hurt you. He's Carl. He's a good guy. He's done nothing to hurt you.

Lil: I know. I think I love him. And I'm scared. I'll never admit that to another man. I don't want to be hurt.

Big: You might want to talk to somebody about this. You haven't been to Dr. Weisman in months.

Lil: I'm all better now. I have a boyfriend.

Big: Just because you have a relationship doesn't mean you're healed. There are plenty of people in pain who are in relationships. It's OK to talk to someone. Brush up on what you learned and may have forgotten.

Lil: But I was in therapy a year. I should be better by now.

Big: I know you want to heal on your time. On your clock. Control it all. But be gentle with yourself, Lil. It takes time. And if you're patient, you will heal. And that's not to say old issues won't pop back up. They might. You just have to recognize them and deal. Listen, you didn't wound yourself. But now that you know where it comes from, it is your responsibility to heal it. Now that you know the root of the issues, you can't blame anyone for where you are today or what happens in your life. You're all grown up. It's all up to you. And you can do it.

Lil: (sigh) I know. It's so hard.

Big: Sometimes it is. But it gets easier with time. You can't bail because it gets tough. You have to stay committed and stick in there. You wanted a relationship with a nice guy. Here it is. Now do the work to make it work. That might mean looking at yourself. And I'm so proud of you for all the work you've done toward healing. I know you're brave enough to do more and finish it.

Lil: I'm brave.

Big: I know you are. Are you brave enough to call Dr. Weisman tomorrow?

Lil: Yeah.

Big: Good job. I love you. I am so proud of you for taking the steps to be better and do better.

Lil: I love you, too.

The next morning I called Dr. Weisman. Although she was heading out of town on a two-week vacation, she took the time to counsel me over the phone.

"Have you communicated to him why you might feel like this? This distrust?"

"Well…" The words trailed off into embarrassment. "He knows about my past a bit."

"Tell him how you feel. Your fears are normal. You are an abandonment survivor. Tell him what you've learned."

"I think I love him." Hearing myself say that out loud—it was as if an anchor was pulled up out of my heart and through my mouth. I suddenly felt lighter. "I told Meredith that. But I don't want to tell him. I don't want to scare him away."

"Love shouldn't scare someone who truly cares about you away."

"But it scared the shit out of me."

"That's understandable. You've been through a lot of pain," she said softly. "It's the authentic you he cares about. Expressing your feelings in a caring way, being honest about what you feel, even what you're not sure you feel, is healthy. It's called being vulnerable."

"It's called being a damn punk," I said, sucking my teeth. "I am so scared."

"Being vulnerable is a brave thing to do. And you might be surprised by what he says in response. Treat him the way you want him to treat you. Stay conscious. And when those little inner-child feelings come up, have that inner dialogue so she doesn't act out. Daily. You have to do this daily, Meena. Snooping and spying is acting out. Fear. Would you want him to do that to you?"

"No." I was like a kid answering. The embarrassment of knowing the truth and still acting like a child. Dr. Weisman called me out without actually doing so. She pointed it out via questioning.

"Do you think you can be honest with him? Tell him what you're scared of?"

I was quiet. Silent for a long minute in considering the repercussions of being vulnerable. Of actually showing someone the flaw I had in being scared of rejection. Abandonment. Of not being able to deal with not being loved back. I didn't want to push him away. But the fear made me do it. And I hated it. I needed to face it. But how? "I can try," I finally said. "Maybe I'll write it out first or something."

"That's okay. Or you can just speak from the heart. Whatever makes you feel comfortable. Let's set up an appointment for when I get back. I want to see you in two weeks. Okay? You'll get through this."

I hadn't spoken to Carl in a week. He was off in Arizona at a leadership-building conference and I was back in Brooklyn, shaken. Nervous. Staying in the moment the best I could not to dwell on my fears of an impending breakup. I'd texted him a couple of times. He took hours to reply. And when he did, they were short. Cold.

Yes. No. Cool. Busy.

I hated that. I hated texting. So I stopped what felt like that familiar old habit of chasing creeping back.

"Just give him some space, girl," Meredith said one night. We sat at a sports bar, eating nachos, sipping margaritas, and watching the Knicks game. "Fall back. You know they always come back."

"But what if he breaks up with me?"

"Then it's not meant to be. It's his loss. And if he breaks up with you over one thing, then he wasn't really feeling you to begin with. There are other fish in the sea, girl." She smiled at the cutie behind the bar. "Trust."

The Knicks were down by forty, mopping up the court with the same losing spirit I dragged off the stool to the ladies' room. Digging for my lipstick, I spotted my cell phone light flickering from the bottom of my purse. As I pulled it out, my smile stretched as I read my four favorite words of the week:

Missed call from Carl.

The minute I got home, coat still on, keys in hand, I dialed his number.

"Hey."

"Hey."

The silence lingered in that awkward, tense, one-word space for several seconds.

"So," he began, "I heard your whack team lost again."

"Listen, don't talk about my Knicks. They had a bad night."

"They're having a bad decade."

We laughed. We talked. I threw everything out on the table. My fears. My concerns. My apologies. My issues. "I'm scared. I'm terrified of messing up or being hurt," I said, dancing around sharing "those three words." He jumped in.

"I appreciate your honesty. I really appreciate you saying that, Meena. I mean, I'm scared too," he said. "And I had a chance to do a lot of thinking this past week. And I missed you. All of you. Your quirks, your idiosyncrasies, your sexy walk and talk, those eyes, just you. I still have a crush on you, ever since the first time I saw you walk and trip into the lunchroom freshman year in high school."

"When I fell and the milk splattered all over the principal," I said, "and everybody went, 'Ooooh'?"

"Exactly."

"That was the worst."

"That was funny. But the point I'm making is, I only want you, Meena. Always have. Always will. I'm not going anywhere. I love you."

The future. Thirty-six months, three weeks, one day, eighteen hours, and five minutes later...

I sat on a Jamaican shore, holding up a wineglass reflecting the setting sun. A waiter approached.

"Ma'am," he said with a patois accent, handing me a white square envelope. "This is for you."

Inside was a card that read:

We manifest our words and thoughts. Thinking is the fuel. Speaking is the spark. Soul mate love is the fire that blazes from faith. Our tendency toward fear, habitual mental blocks, and hurdles are the walls we place between our heads and hearts that manifest into existence. Let's continue to conjure up a spell so powerful that it continues to block all negativity that attempts to taint our love. Let's be brave, face and kill the curse of doubt together, beating it into non-existent oblivion. I will fight that and anything for you. I got you. By any means necessary. Because I love you forever, Mrs. Meena Fey Murphy.

So proud to be your new (your first and only and last) husband, Carl

My finger sparkled with a glistening rock emitting bright light beams of hope, possibility, faith, and love. Thank you, Lord.

ACKNOWLEDGMENTS

It takes a village to birth a book. Many thanks to those who read and loved it early on, like Courtney Patterson. You've been there for me unconditionally since high school. I am thankful and blessed to have your unwavering friendship.

Thank you and love to my family and especially my brother, Marc Carmichael, for the texts and phone calls to see if I made my page count.

To those who read *The Man Curse* in its early pre-edited drafts, like Stacy Gueraseva, thank you. I will never forget your professional novelist feedback and the emotions you expressed after reading it.

To Karen Hunter: You took a chance on me that led to manifesting a dream I've had since the fourth grade. Without you, there would be no book for the world to see. I'm eternally grateful. Thank you.

To Karen Hunter's book publishing class at Hunter College: you became my beta test group. Your feedback gave Meena and *The Man Curse* new life. And me a renewed confidence in my abilities as an author. I am truly appreciative for that experience. Thank you for the time.

To John Paine: A good editor is so hard to find. But you polished me up. Thank you for helping me shine. Thank you for the encouragement and confidence in my talent as a writer.

To those who say *The Man Curse* has changed their lives, please share it with those who need it. And to anyone who has shown or sent love and support: Thank you. Every single word, referral, interview, write-up, repost, retweet, comment, like, or positive thought has helped make this dream come true. I couldn't have done this without you. I will always be grateful. Thank you.

About the Author

Author, screenwriter, executive producer, and host of the podcast *Real Black News*—named in 2019 as one of the top 50 podcasts in the country—Raqiyah Mays launched her career at *VIBE* magazine as an executive assistant. From there, she reported on the intersection of social issues, hip-hop, film, and TV for outlets like The Associated Press, *Essence, Billboard, Black Enterprise, The Source, Complex, XXL*, and more.

Mays was later recruited to work for Sirius/XM, where she wrote and produced a daily show for the legendary DJ Grandmaster Flash. She also hosted weekends on the hip-hop station Hot 97, NYC's 107.5 WBLS, and the morning show on 98.7 Kiss FM.

Since its first release in 2015, *The Man Curse* was turned into an empowerment workshop at domestic violence shelters and adapted for the screen by Mays. She's written nationally and globally televised speeches for activists like Tamika Mallory, co-founder of Until Freedom. She also contributed a chapter to *Where Did Our Love Go: Love & Relationships in the African American Community*, an anthology written by African American Film Critics Association (AAFCA) President, Gil Robertson. She was reporter-at-large for *Unbelievable: The Life, Death, and Afterlife of The Notorious B.I.G* by showrunner and *Luke Cage* creator Cheo Hodari Coker. His book was adapted into his debut feature film,

Notorious. Mays was also featured in author Thembisa Mshaka's
Put Your Dreams First: Handle Your Entertainment Business.

The fashion brand The Limited selected Mays as one of its
dynamic female leaders featured in its nationwide "New Look
of Leadership" campaign. VH1 picked her for its iconic "Future
Leader of Black History" commercial series. In addition to win-
ning several awards, Mays has appeared on ABC, BET, TV One,
Fox, Fuse, and Fox News.